L'Épine's
The Legend of Croquemitaine,
and the Chivalric Times of Charlemagne

Mitaine and Oghris

L'Épine's
The Legend of Croquemitaine,
and the Chivalric Times of Charlemagne

Translated by
Tom Hood

Illustrated by
Gustave Doré

Coachwhip Publications
Landisville, Pennsylvania

L'Épine's The Legend of Croquemitaine
Copyright © 2009 Coachwhip Publications
From English translation, published 1877

ISBN 1-930585-72-1
ISBN-13 978-1-930585-72-0

Coachwhipbooks.com

PREFACE.

In translating M. L'Epine's charming legend, I have felt it my duty to adhere as closely as possible to the text. "Adaptations" and "versions," whether presented on the stage or set down in black and white, seem to claim for those, who give them in English, a greater share of the glory than I feel myself to deserve, in the slightest degree, in this instance. The delicacy with which the moral is interwoven in the narrative, without in the least injuring the true legendary tone of the adventures related, is as far beyond any improvement I could make, as it is above the usual clap-trap "tag" with which dramas and children's stories are ordinarily burdened.

I scarcely know to whom I should appeal as my readers, for the story I have delighted in rendering into English seems to me likely to afford pleasure in the perusal to older heads than those which I am sure would gather over the pages in the nursery. For there are a quiet humour and a delicate fancy running through the legend, amid all the exciting accounts of loves and wars, tourneys and battles, accidents and adventures, which do not lose interest because they are illustrated by the powerful pencil of Gustave Doré. That great artist's fancy supplies these introductory lines with a tail-piece, which aptly typifies the book. Its author has ably made the doings of knights and paladins point a useful moral as well as adorn an interesting tale, just as the artist makes the arms of the chivalric age serve to frighten the birds from the fields that supply our humble daily bread.

Book the First.
The Tourney at Fronsac, A.D. 769.

I. CHARLEMAGNE.

The story which I am about to relate happened (if it ever did happen) in the time of the famous Emperor Charlemagne. There is no necessity, in speaking of that remarkable epoch, to invent facts. The truth is so astounding that it will make you open your eyes quite wide enough. What marvellous doings of fairies, ogres, or demons, can compare with the deeds of Charlemagne? and what magic ring could be as potent as his sword?

But before I proceed further it will be as well to sketch for you, in a few lines, the portrait of this hero.

He was eight feet in height, according to the measurement of his own feet, which historians allege with fervour were of remarkable length. His eyes were large and piercing. When he was enraged you could almost have fancied they flashed fire. His face was broad and ruddy, his hair brown, and he wore a beard that was innocent of the barber's shears. Although he measured eight feet round the middle, his figure was well-proportioned. He devoured with ease at one repast a quarter of mutton, or a goose, or a ham, or a peacock. He was moderate in the matter of wine, which he used to take with water.

His strength was so enormous that it was mere child's play to him to straighten with his naked hands three horse-shoes at a time. He could lift at arm's length, on the palm of his hand, a knight in full armour; and he could cleave in twain, with one blow of his sword, a horseman in panoply of war—aye, and his horse into the bargain. This was mere sport to him, and often, with a charming complaisance which was peculiarly his own, he would take pleasure in thus giving those about him an ocular demonstration of his superhuman strength.

His anger was as terrible as the thunder, for it was as ready to burst forth and to strike.

With the compassion of a Titus, the sound judgment of a Solomon, the piety of a Joseph, the magnificence of a Sardanapalus, and the wisdom of an Æsop, he united two qualities more rare than all these put together: when he spoke he meant what he said, and when others spoke to him he took time for reflection, in order to make sure that he thoroughly understood their meaning.

He carves out a kingdom.

The dominion which his father bequeathed him did not suit the largeness of his views, so he carved out for himself a kingdom which was more in harmony with his gigantic instincts.

11

Born in 742, and raised to the throne in 768, he had in 770 already made conquest of Aquitaine and Lombardy. Four years after Germany was subjugated by him. He made fifty-three military expeditions, and he began the ninth century by having himself crowned Emperor of the West by Pope Leo the Third. He was a generous dispenser of crowns, and gave away principalities and duchies as freely as now-a-days we give away recorderships. He had two capitals in his dominions: the one was Rome, the other was Aix-la-Chapelle. He promulgated the code of laws known as Capitularies. He defended religion, spread the Gospel, encouraged the fine arts, and introduced into his cathedrals organs which he imported from Lombardy. Surrounded by mighty minds, whose efforts he stimulated, and whose labours he shared, he founded many schools and universities. He died in 814, after three-and-forty years of sovereign power—three-and-forty years of victories and wonders.

Really, my dear readers, if you are not satisfied with Charlemagne for a hero, you must be very difficult to please!

The inheritance divided.

II. Which the Author Congratulates Himself on Not Having to Read.

I should be extremely sorry to weary you, my dear readers; in fact, I should be wretched if you were to look on this volume as serious reading, and yet I am compelled to sum up in a few words the great events which agitated France at the time my story commences. However, put a bold face on it, and bolt this chapter without taking breath, as you would swallow any peculiarly nauseous draught.

After the death of Pepin the Short, in 768, his two sons, Carloman and Charlemagne, divided his kingdom. Carloman, who was the elder, took Burgundy, Provence, Septimania, and the chief part of Neustria. His coronation took place on the 9th October, 768, at Laon. Charlemagne had part of Neustria, Bavaria, and Thuringia. He was crowned at Soissons on the same day as Carloman. Aquitaine was also shared between the brothers. You are probably aware that Pepin the Short was the founder of the second line of French kings. The first line, that of the Merovingians, was not, however, extinct when he came to the throne, for the Dukes of Aquitaine were of Merovingian descent. They sprang from Caribert, King of Toulouse, the son of Clotaire the Second. Eudes, who shares with Charles Martel the glory of having conquered the Saracens in the sanguinary battle of Poitiers, in 732, was also of this family.

Hunald, the son of Eudes, had, at the time of Pepin's death, lived five-and-twenty years in the convent to which that monarch had consigned him. Now, the Merovingian Dukes of Aquitaine had a fierce hatred of the Carlovingian Kings of France,

Hunald quits the Monastery.

and accordingly, as soon as Hunald heard of the accession of Carloman and Charlemagne, he quitted the monastery, took up arms, and proclaimed the independence of Aquitaine.

They almost come to blows.

The two newly-crowned kings had reason to be alarmed at an outbreak like this, for, unless put down at the outset, it might arouse and encourage the pretensions of the descendants of Clovis with regard to Neustria. Charlemagne summoned a Parliament, to which he invited his brother. They both came to it, attended by their ecclesiastics and nobles, and war was decided upon.

The two kings crossed the Loire together; but Carloman, who, if one may judge from the chronicles of the period, was of an unamiable disposition, had such quarrels with his brother about the partition of their inheritance, that it was even feared they would come to blows. They therefore determined to part company. Carloman returned to Laon, and Charlemagne prosecuted the enterprise alone. He overran Aquitaine without meeting any resistance, as Charles Martel had done before him. Hunald, a fugitive, and hard pressed, found himself obliged to seek shelter with his nephew, Wolf, Duke of Gascony. Wolf! When was a name in a fairy tale bestowed with more propriety? This Wolf was most deservedly called so, as you will see. As soon as Charlemagne discovered where his enemy had found an asylum, he dispatched some of his foremost knights to the Duke of Gascony, commanding him to deliver up the

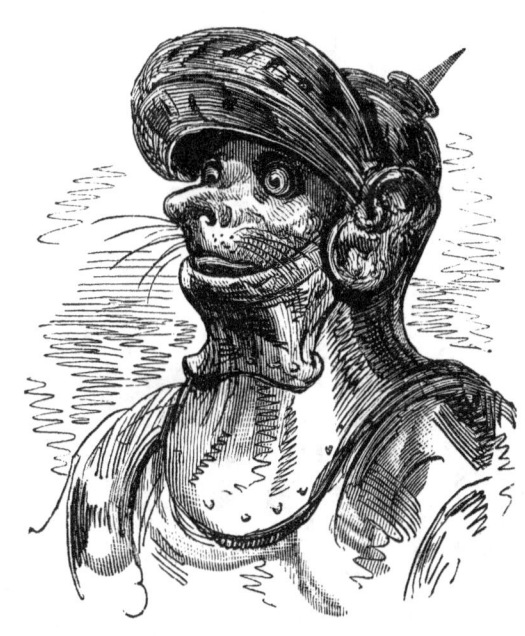

The Wolf of Gascony.

fugitive, and threatening, if he refused, to enter duchy and lay it waste.

In those days, my dear readers, travelling was not quite so expeditious as it is now; so Charlemagne, foreseeing he would have to wait some months, established his camp on the borders of the forest. In the next place, in order to put the time of his stay to profitable use, and to give employment to his troops, about five leagues from Bordeaux he had a strong fortress built, which was called Fronsac, or rather Fransiac, the castle of the Franks. The building of the castle was hardly completed when the ambassadors returned, accompanied by Wolf of Gascony, who did not in the least scruple to deliver up to Charlemagne, as a proof of his fealty, Hunald and his family, who had claimed shelter of him.

The insurrection having been thus deprived of its leader, Aquitaine submitted to Charlemagne.

15

The tents of the needy warriors.

III. CHARLEMAGNE'S CORTÈGE.

Charlemagne determined to celebrate the fortunate issue of his campaign. Jousts and tourneys were organised, and heralds were sent out far and wide; and before long knights began to pour in from the various provinces: some to show their courage and exercise their strength and skill, others in the hope of enriching themselves with the spoils of their vanquished adversaries.

The spot chosen for the tournament was an extent of velvet sward situated at the edge of a forest of oaks that were five hundred years old. A semi-circle of low hills formed a sort of amphitheatre, in the centre of which a vast area, reserved for the combatants, was surrounded with palisades. There were two entrances to the lists—one on the north, the other on the south—each wide enough to admit of the passage of six knights on horseback abreast. Two heralds and six pursuivants had charge of each of these entries. Small detachments were scattered about here and there to maintain order—no easy task, for the inhabitants of the surrounding country, with their wives, had assembled from all quarters alongside of the camp. On them it was difficult to impress a due observance of discipline, and the unmanageable came in for showers of blows that were not laid on less heavily because it was a conquered country.

On a level space not far from the northern gate were raised twelve gorgeous pavilions, reserved for the twelve principal French champions who held the lists. Pennons with their colours, and those of

The various branches of spectators.

their lady-loves, fluttering in the wind, waved in the sunlight like flying serpents. Each knight had his shield suspended before his tent, under the charge of a squire.

Further off, less costly tents served as lodgings for numerous warriors, who were drawn together either by friendship or want of means. This community formed a quaint sort of town, which had, as it were, suburbs consisting of stable-sheds, and huts of all sorts, occupied by armourers, farriers, surgeons, and artisans, whose presence on such occasions was indispensable. Merchants at these times were exempted from all tolls and taxes, and accordingly the Jews had come to sell Venetian trinkets and Oriental perfumes to the ladies; the Bretons brought their honey for sale, and the Provençals displayed their clear olive oil; and amid all these good things were to be seen, rambling about at random, jugglers, troubadours, minstrels, and all other classes of poor Bohemians, whose wits are sharp if their purses are scant. On the borders of the wood was erected a pavilion more magnificent than all the others—it was that of Charlemagne; it was of cloth of gold, with purple stripes, powdered with gold eagles, and it was so bright that one would have needed the eye of an eagle to support its lustre for an instant. All about it were knights, squires, lackeys, and pages, coming and going as thickly as bees in a hive around their queen. On either side of the royal tent, and all along the edge of the forest, were erected seats for the spectators of rank, who promised to be numerous. They flocked-in every hour in crowds, so delighted were they with spectacles of this description, and, above all, so desirous were they of beholding Charlemagne, whose name had already begun to resound through Europe. The royal box, more lofty than the others, and more richly decorated, was a little in front of the tent. Charlemagne had ordained that the Queen of Beauty should share this with him, in order that she might be surrounded by the most valiant knights and the most lovely ladies. The two retinues attended on her amid incessant peals of mirth and merriment.

Finally, my dear readers, to finish the picture, figure to yourselves, situated half-way between the lists and the forest, and surmounted by a huge iron cross, a Gothic chapel, in which, each morning, Turpin,

At last came the peers and barons, clad in their most splendid armour.

the good and gallant Bishop of Rheims, officiated as priest in the presence of the kneeling multitude.

At length the day of the tournament arrived. There had been many jousts before, but never had there been one of equal magnificence. From the earliest dawn the places were all occupied. Even the old trees were as thickly loaded with curious spectators as a plum-tree in August; and the good folks were right to crowd so, for had they lived their lives six times over, they would never have seen anything equal to the sight again. It was absolutely necessary for the soldiers to lay about with their pike-staves, in order to calm the eager ardour of the most enthusiastic; but nobody took any notice of thumps that, under any other circumstances, would have been received with an ill grace.

All of a sudden a flourish of trumpets made the air resound. A glittering advanced-guard entered the enclosure and took up their position, and then Charlemagne entered the arena at the head of a numerous escort of knights and nobles, and of ecclesiastics in rich vestments. Enthusiasm knew no bounds. "Montjoie! Montjoie!" resounded on every side. Charlemagne, who later in life affected the greatest simplicity in dress, had assumed for this great occasion the most brilliant attire. His shirt was of fine linen, its border enriched with gold embroidery. His tunic was of silk, plated with gold, and was covered with precious stones of surpassing brightness—emeralds, rubies, and topaz. His armlets and girdle were chased with the most exquisite art, and his alms-pouch, which hung at his side, was besprinkled with pearls and gems enough to dazzle a blind man. His brow was bound with a glittering diadem. His whole figure shone with an unaccustomed splendour, and he greatly surpassed in magnificence the grandest of his dukes, counts, or barons. His steed, covered with gold and rich trappings, seemed proud of the burthen it carried.

The Queen Himiltrude, a Frank by birth, advanced in the midst of her attendants. Her neck was tinged with a delicate rose, like that of a Roman matron in former ages. Her locks were bound about her temples with gold and purple bands; her robe was looped up with ruby clasps. Her coronet and her purple robes gave her an air of surpassing majesty. She was a worthy queen of Charlemagne. But if the queen surpassed all other women in nobleness of mien, Aude, the niece of Gerard of Vienne, and sister of Oliver the Brave, surpassed her as much by her beauty, her grace, and her attractiveness. She wore a light crown, embossed with jewels of all colours. Her hair was fair, falling naturally into becoming curls; her eyes were blue as the sea of the south; her complexion was pink, like the heart of a white rose; and her hands were marvellously small. As she passed Roland, she turned slightly pale. If she had been less lovely, I should have said more about her rich attire; but what is the use, since nobody notices it? The queen must have been very strong-minded, to retain so charming a lady of honour about her person. On seeing the beautiful Aude, every one said, "There, or I'll die for it, is the Queen of Beauty!"

Aude had near her her sister Mita, fair as herself, but slightly browned by the Spanish sun under which she had been brought up. Two black eyes, full lips, a finely-cut and regular nose, hair hanging down in heavy masses, entwined with long strings of threaded pearls and diamonds—there you have her portrait in a few words.

Her bodice was covered with small pearls; you might have called it a pearl corslet. Indeed, those who saw her pass, admiring her martial bearing and her rich breastplate, gave her the nickname of "the little knight in pearl."

After Aude and her sister came a bevy of beautiful young girls, but the people hardly cared to look at them.

At last came the peers and barons, clad in their most splendid armour. What a clash of gold, iron, and steel! How many swords that had won renown! Every one of these puissant arms was worth ten ordinary knights in the tourney-ground—in battle worth a thousand!

It is difficult to explain the agility displayed by these men under such a formidable weight of armour. An ox in these days could scarcely carry one of them. The helmet alone weighed a hundred and twenty-five pounds. They handled like playthings swords which we can hardly lift. "At the battle of Hastings," says Robert Wace, "Taillefer threw his up, and caught it as if it had been a light stick." The horses were as powerful as the men. Reared in the rich pastures of the Rhine borders or Bavaria, high-standing and big-chested, they often took

Last of all appeared Roland, Count of Mans and Knight of Blaives.

part in the contest, tearing with their splendid teeth the enemies of their masters. As soon as they were broken they were clad in iron, to protect them against javelins, spears, and swords.

Last of all appeared Roland, Count of Mans and Knight of Blaives, son of Duke Milo of Aiglant, and of Bertha, the sister of Charlemagne. You would have taken him for a statue of iron and marble. His right hand brandished a spear that in these days would serve for the mast of a frigate; his left reposed on his faithful sword Durandal. I know of no one to whom to compare him but the Archangel Michael. His air is at once terrible and tender: should one love him or fear him? He is of such a majestic, awe-inspiring presence, that one can hardly be astonished at any wonders he performs. He appears to belong to a race that is more than human, and you would hardly be surprised were he to drag a star from its sphere or seize a comet by the beard. He is of the same height as Charlemagne, but more imposing in figure and gait. His open countenance invites confidence and inspires respect. When Roland gives a man his hand, the lucky fellow, who is thus honoured as with a royal favour, feels, in the pride of having achieved such a distinction, a greater confidence in his own worth. Roland is mounted on Veillantif, the only horse in the world worthy of such a rider.

Close at hand is Oliver, Count of Genes, the brother of the beautiful Aude. He is hardly second to Roland in strength, in agility, and in appearance. At his side gleams Haute-Claire, and he is mounted on Ferrant d'Espagne, a steed that darts straight towards the foe like an arrow. Then follow Duke Oger, Richard of Normandy, Thibault of Rheims, Guy of Burgundy, Ogier the Dane, Duke Nairnes of Bavaria, Girard of Montdidier, Bernard, the uncle of Charlemagne; Miton of Rennes, the friend of Roland; William of Orange, with the short nose, whose name made evil-doers tremble (as you have trembled, little people, at the name of Bogey!); besides a thousand others, not forgetting Turpin, the good Archbishop of Rheims, so learned in the council-hall, so pious in the cathedral, so brave on the field of battle. Turpin was armed in warlike fashion; his rosary and his mace hung side by side; in the handle of the latter was enclosed a precious relic, a bone of St. Clet. He could not wield a sword, for his religion forbade him to shed blood; but it is a fact that his mace weighed a hundred and fifty pounds.

Near Charlemagne was to be seen Wolf, Duke of Gascony—Wolf, who sold his guest and his family—Wolf, who was without a rival in treachery, except Ganelon. Oh, how you will hate the pair of them, my friends, if you read my story to the end! Wolf was chiefly noticeable for

William with the short nose.

his armour, which was of browned steel, damasked with silver, and which he had purchased of the Saracens in Spain. He is more terrible in peace than in war, and his favourite weapon is the gallows. He was less feared by his enemies than by his subjects, and would sooner knock a man down with a blow of his fist than say, "Thank you." He was noted for his ingenuity in matters of torture, and has the credit of being the originator of the plan of tying wetted ropes round the temples of his prisoners to make their eyeballs start out of their sockets. It was he, too, who had them sewed up in freshly-stript bulls' hides, and exposed to the sun until the hides in shrinking broke their bones. But what is the most awful to tell is that no one had ever seen him in a rage. He was cruel in cold blood from inclination and appetite. The smell of blood delighted him more than frankincense or verbena. Charlemagne hardly spoke to him, and it was with difficulty that he could prevent his dislike of him from appearing.

Count Ganelon, of Mayence, was not quite so base a savage. At all events, his bravery was unquestionable; he could be a useful councillor, and if the envy with which Roland inspired him had not driven him to evil deeds, he might have been one of the foremost of Charlemagne's followers. A lover of solitude, a taciturn and even savage man, an irreligious unbeliever in all noble sentiments—such was Ganelon in moral disposition. Need I say he had no friends? In height he was hardly six feet and a half, and he wished all those who were taller than he was, even by the breadth of a line, were of his height. His eyes glared from beneath the shadow of his fiery locks, like those of a savage hound. He loved gold only to hoard it, and affected great poverty. You would have thought him one of Attila's Huns rather than one of the paladins of Charlemagne's court. Ganelon could not forgive Roland for having rendered him a service on several occasions. The superiority of Charlemagne's nephew drove him mad. This may, perhaps, surprise some of the younger of my readers, but it is too true that to evil minds gratitude is displeasing and troublesome. But I had better make you acquainted with the particular grievances of the Count of Mayence.

The good Bishop Turpin.

The wounded and the slain.

IV. How Ganelon, Count of Mayence, was Nearly Smoked in the Company of Two Hogs, and What Followed Thereafter.

Ganelon's castle was situated on the loftiest peak of the Hartz Mountains, the Blocksberg. There, in the midst of the Hercynian forest, which cannot be less than twenty-four leagues in length by ten in breadth, towered the eyrie of this vulture. One road, and only one, traversed this vast extent of forest, but Ganelon took care that it should always be in good repair; it was a courtesy which he felt was due from him to the travellers he despoiled.

The count had gathered round him a collection of the best assorted ruffians of every country; Saxons, Danes, Lombards, Jews, and Saracens, lent him a hand to forward the interests of the Evil One. One morning he called them all together, and said to them—

"I have pleasant news for you. We have the opportunity of playing a pretty trick on some Saxon traders. I have just been informed that a caravan, consisting of thirty mules, laden with treasure, and conveyed by a small escort, is about to cross the Hartz Mountains this morning, to attend the fair of St. Denis.

"I have conceived the design of protecting French commerce, and putting a stop to the opposition which is meditated against it. Under

Ganelon's Castle was situated on the loftiest peak of the Hartz Mountains.

the protection of our patron saints, the two thieves, we will make ourselves masters of this venture."

Ganelon and his rascals placed themselves in ambush along the border of the forest, and before long saw a thick cloud of dust rising along the road in the distance.

"Here," cried they, "beyond a doubt, are those we are waiting for. Let us save them three-quarters of their journey;" and they rushed forward, sword in hand. The two opposing storms of dust approached each other, and from the further came the cry, "Hi! what are you doing? You'll destroy the beasts!"

Ganelon and his men had charged into the midst of an army of porkers, driven by Westphalian swineherds.

The charge upon the swine.

The surprise of the assailants was so great that it allowed the swineherds time to form in a body and draw their knives; and those weapons were not to be sneered at, readers mine, for they were those which butchers use for quartering and cutting up carcases.

Ganelon remained for a moment undecided. That hesitation was fatal. The Jews and Saracens, to whom pork is a forbidden dish, did not think it worth while to press matters further. They accordingly retreated, taking with them several of their fellows, who thought their chief would retire into ambuscade again. But a Count of Mayence is not the man to despise bacon and sour-crout. So Ganelon, gazing over the ocean of lard which grunted at his feet, began to lick his lips, and think that here was a booty which was quite as well worth having as the other. But the swineherds knew with whom they had to deal, and, indeed, had come in such numbers solely because they expected an attack. They rushed on the count and his lances, and began to hamstring the horses. The horsemen were soon rolling in the dust among the hogs. Two of them, who showed an inclination to resist, were very properly run through on the spot, and mingled their lifeblood with that of two pigs that had been run down by the horses. The others were disarmed, and allowed to escape. As for Ganelon, they tied his hands tightly behind his back.

"Now then," said the head swineherd, "before they pluck up courage to come back in force, suppose we hang their leader?"

This idea appeared very agreeable to everybody except Ganelon, who uttered the most furious oaths. But they dragged him, armed as he was, under an oak, and then, having chosen a stout bough worthy of such fine fruit, they adjusted the cord round his neck. Then they brought the two slaughtered pigs—the only victims of the Count of Mayence—and having fitted each with a strong hempen cravat, suspended them one at each end of the bough, reserving the post of honour for the knight. These preparations concluded, Ganelon was dragged, bound hand and foot, to the place of execution. He writhed about in the madness of his rage, foaming at the mouth, calling on his companions in villany, and cursing them for their desertion. In vain did he struggle—a score of sturdy arms speedily hoisted him up between his two companions.

Ganelon's antics on the tight rope.

"Pull down his visor," said the head swineherd to the man who was on the bough adjusting the noose, "the monster is hideous enough at the best of times—what will he look like presently?"

Ganelon continued to struggle at the end of the cord, to the great delight of the spectators, who, though they found him tenacious of life, did not complain on that account.

Meanwhile, the count began to find that death was rather slow in coming. He had hanged too many not to know something about it, and in this instance it was so personally interesting to him that it could not fail to arrest his attention. "These knaves," said he to himself, "have made a sad bungle of the job. I ought to have been dead some time." And then it dawned on him that he was only suspended, not hanged. His executioners had put the noose round the gorget of his helmet.

"Oho!" said Ganelon to himself, "this is quite another affair, and all is not yet lost, possibly. Only, if I continue my gambols, I may, perhaps, give the hint to these idiots, and they might hang me again more carefully. I'll sham dead, and it's odd if the Evil One doesn't send some one to my aid. It would be very inconsiderate of him to let me die like this!"

Nevertheless, for one who wasn't dead, the count was uncommonly near death. The blood rushed to his head, and filled his eyes. He began to hear a dismal noise in his ears, like the tolling of a bell. His mouth grew dry, his lips were contracted, and presently his limbs gave one last convulsive struggle. Ganelon confessed to himself that all was over, and lost consciousness while faintly murmuring a final imprecation. The swineherds, encouraged by their success, and not wishing to leave the two hogs for the enemy, resolved to cook and eat them. They posted sentinels, collected their herds, and prepared to celebrate their victory with a feast.

"It strikes me," said the chief swineherd, "if we were to omit an opportunity of throwing a light on a point of interest to culinary science, we should regret it all our lives. A rare and remarkable opportunity offers itself to us now — we must not allow it to escape us. Are you not all equally anxious, with myself, to learn whether it takes longer to smoke a peer than a pig?"

The suggestion was a great success. They collected a heap of sticks and leaves under each of the three victims, and lighted it. And then, joining hands, they began to dance round, uttering wild shouts.

Roland, it so chanced, was returning this way from Saxony,

Roland to the rescue.

31

whither he had been sent by Charlemagne. He had, certes, in war laid many a man dead in his path, but he had never permitted a cruelty to be committed in his presence. His indignation was roused by these vile chantings, this demoniac dance, and all the hideous apparatus of torture. He was not long in deciding what course to pursue. He rode at the dancers, and dispersed them with the flat of his sword, not deigning to honour them by using against them the edge, which he reserved for foemen more worthy of him.

Then he made to the hanging man, and in order to cut the rope, had to keep Veillantif for a few seconds trampling on the embers in the midst of the flames. The Count of Mayence tumbled heavily into the middle of the fire. Roland dismounted, with one hearty kick sent him rolling some fifty paces, and then ran to assist him.

His first care was to relieve him of his helmet. When he recognised whose life he had saved, I must admit he made a grimace. The Count of Mans, the faultless mirror of chivalry, could feel no liking for such wretches, but he was not the less ready to aid them.

Ganelon re-opened his eyes. His succession of tumbles had done more to recover him than all

Ganelon's recovery.

the eau-de-cologne in the world would have done. When he saw his preserver, he heartily wished it had not been Roland.

"Are you hurt, count? What can I do to assist you?"

"I don't want your pity, Knight of Blaives. Why have you rescued me? I am not of a race or of a disposition likely to love those who place me under an obligation, and it would have been less bitter for me to die than to owe my life to you!"

"I forgive these words, Sir Ganelon. You have just undergone such a shock, that you have evidently not quite recovered your senses!"

Roland gives
Ganelon a lift.

At these words the Count of Mayence was seized with such a paroxysm of rage, that he found strength enough to try to avenge the insult. He flung himself on his preserver, and seized him by the throat.

"You'll make yourself ill again," said Roland, coolly freeing himself from the other's grasp. "You forget that you are not quite well yet. Allow me to administer a curative process which you ought to undergo."

With these words he caught his adversary by the scruff of the neck, dragged him beside his horse into the heart of the forest, tied his hands with the cord that had already served him as a halter, and bound him fast to a tree.

Ganelon foamed at the mouth, and bit his lips till the blood came. The fury in his eyes would have been terrible to any but Roland.

Ganelon fast bound.

"Now, count, calm yourself. You see I am anxious to cure you in spite of yourself. Nothing conduces to meditation like solitude. Now that you are alone, you will have time for reflection; and if you are a wise man, you will say to yourself, 'This Roland is a very good fellow not to break every bone in my body;' and, since you are a coward and a villain, you will possibly say, 'This Roland was a fool not to kill me outright.' You will finish by perceiving that

33

such a man as I can only despise one like you. Meditate, and if Heaven is kind, it will counsel you prudence. Anyhow, do not make an uproar, for fear your enemies should disturb your re-flections, which, in that case, very likely, might come to a termination at the end of a rope. I will call at your castle, and send some one to your assistance: as my royal uncle is awaiting me at Cologne, you must excuse my attending on you further. Don't forget, moreover, that I am, and

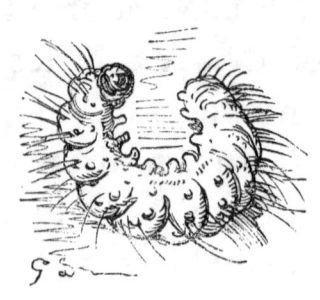

The innocent victim.

always shall be, ready to honour you with a thrust of my lance or blow of my sword, in spite of the disgust I should feel at having to cross swords with a highway robber!"

Ganelon's thoughts were so frightful that the human language is unable to express them. He hung down his head, and when he found himself alone he wept. His tears fell upon the grass; an innocent cater-pillar, wandering in search of food, mistook them for dewdrops, tasted them, and died of the poison.

Two hours after, the swineherds had disappeared, and Ganelon re-entered his castle. Eight hours after, all whom Ganelon believed to be acquainted with his mishap were dead.

Six months after, he was at the court of Charlemagne, seated at the same table as Roland. Pork was placed on the table, but the Count of Mayence refused it.

"You bear malice, count," said Roland; "that is wrong. Who knows? perhaps you are refusing an old brother in misfortune."

Ganelon turned livid, but he did not stir. After the feast was over Roland came to him.

Roland and Ganelon.

34

"Have you forgotten," he asked, the threats you uttered and the offer I made to you in your domain on the Hartz?"

"I never forget," said the Count of Mayence.

Here, then, was the prime cause of Ganelon's hatred of Roland.

V. Angoulaffre of the Brazen Teeth, Governor of Jerusalem.

While I have been wandering with you, my friends, on the Blocksberg, Charlemagne, followed by his brilliant retinue, has been making a tour of the list upon his prancing charger.

He had just regained the royal tent when a shout was heard from the crowd. All eyes were turned towards the Southern gate, whence proceed strains of wild music and strange cries. Charlemagne halted, and sent to inquire who ventured to disturb the ceremony. A squire rode off at full galop, and promptly returned to make the following report:—

"Sire, certain miscreant Saracens from Spain have come to challenge your peers in the name of King Marsillus, who holds his court at Saragossa. Their appearance is frightful. They come in procession, preceded by a band of unearthly music truly worthy of pagans, and demand admittance to your presence."

"Let them enter," said Charlemagne, motioning to the heralds who guarded the gate.

"See," he added, turning to his barons, "what a lucky chance is yours. You will be able to try your hands on the Spanish hounds in anticipation of the time when we shall pay them a visit at Saragossa — ay, and even at Granada, for we must compel then to be baptised for the glory of God and the safety of their souls."

"Have they lost all shame that they dare look a Christian in the face?" said Miton of Rennes, "Why, the earth has barely yet had time to drink up all the blood that was shed on the plains of Poitiers."

"No doubt they are bent upon a pilgrimage thither," remarked Turpin, "to pray for the repose of their sires—that is, if such miscreants have fathers, and do not spring fully grown and ready armed from the jaws of hell!"

"How could they blush?" said Aude, pointing to the first of the Saracens who had passed the barriers; "their complexion is of the colour of our horses' harness."

"Oh, the hideous brutes!" said Himiltrude, shutting her eyes. "It is impossible they can be men."

"Let none forget that these are our guests," said Charlemagne: "We must be courteous even to Pagans."

Curiosity was at its height. Every one rose to catch a glimpse of the emissaries of Marsillus; even the knights of Charlemagne's escort raised themselves in their stirrups to obtain a view of the strangers.

There entered first sixty horsemen, blacker than Satan. Their flattened noses, their huge ears decorated with large ear-rings, their thick lips, were for the spectators so many objects of ridicule. Their bare arms were loaded with bracelets from wrist to shoulder; their heads were protected by light casques, around which were wound turbans of white silk. All were clad in the richest stuffs, and vied with one another in appearance. Some were loudly beating kettle-drums; others were blowing with distended cheeks horns of extraordinary shape; others, again, were ringing hand-bells or striking triangles of steel; while from time to time there resounded the deep bellowing of ten bronze gongs, whose vibrations so vehemently shook the spectator as even to induce a desire to cough!

Immediately after these came a hundred knights, of noble aspect, clad in triple mail, so flexible and light that a girl of fifteen might wear it with ease, and yet so stout that it was proof against the thrust of a Saracen lance; as for the thrust of a French lance, we will see about that by and by. Their faces were protected by Saragossan helmets, and they were armed with the heavy spear of Valence; while their swords, although light, could cut through or hack away steel armour, so dexterous were they in wielding them.

Behind them marched twelve standard-bearers. Here the crescent and the horse-tail of the Moslem took the place of the red cross and the bannerets which led the Christians to combat

Last of all, ten horse-lengths from this vanguard, appeared the envoys of Marsillus, King of Portugal, Castile, Arragon, Leon, and

Valence. All who beheld them trembled, and ridicule gave place to alarm.

First rode Angoulaffre of the Brazen Teeth.

He was twelve cubits in height, and his face measured three feet across, his nose being nine inches long. His arms and legs were six feet long; his fingers were six inches and two lines. His inordinately large mouth was armed with sharp-pointed yellow tusks, and seemed less like human jaws than the portcullis of some rude stronghold. He was descended from Goliath, and assumed the title of Governor of Jerusalem. He had the strength of thirty men, and his mace was made of the trunk of an oak three hundred years old.*

This monster was attired in the hides of strange wild beasts, slain by himself on the peaks of Atlas, whither no other mortal had been able to penetrate.

His horse was without a match in the world, for it was up to his enormous weight. It gave a loud neigh

The Knight of the
Brazen Teeth.

---

* Some of the learned have alleged that Angoulaffre travelled in Italy, and that one evening, while at Pisa, being a little the worse for his potations, he leant against the well-known tower, which, unable to bear his weight, lost from that moment its centre of gravity. This is an error, which I am glad to have an opportunity of rectifying. The Leaning Tower, begun in the year 1174, was not finished until the middle of the fourteenth century.

38

on entering the list, and so alarmed all the other steeds that they reared, and in some instances unseated their riders—a disaster at which the Saracens burst into roars of laughter.

Himiltrude, in her terror, crossed herself, convinced that the new-comers would vanish in smoke before she could say "Amen!" But the Pagans continued to advance in good order.

"Hell must surely have gaped to-day!" said Mita.

"I do not know," said Oliver, "whether these miscreants have issued thence this morning, but I'm sure they will sleep there tonight!"

Charlemagne knitted his brows. Aude trembled for Roland, whose thoughts she could read in his face.

Hard by Angoulaffre of the Brazen Teeth rode Murad Henakyeh Meimoumovassi, son of Marsillus. He was styled "The Lord of the Lion." Why, I will relate to you.

Himiltrude horrified.

The Nubians exploring.

VI. MURAD'S THREE WHIMS.

Marsillus one day observed that his son's manner was more caressing than usual, so he took him on his knee and said—"What does my child want to-day? Generally he does not embrace me at all, but since the morning he has done so three times!"

"Sire," said Murad, leaning his little head on his father's shoulder, "I should like to have your yataghan that hangs at your side!"

The bold Murad.

"What! Have you broken all your toys, or are you tired of play that you ask me for such a formidable weapon?"

"I am seven years old," said Murad, drawing himself up; "I am no longer a child, and can carry arms. The sight of blood has no terror for me—nay! look"—and rapidly snatching the yataghan before the king had time to stop him, he gave himself a gash in the arm. Then, without flinching, he looked at his father, and said, "You see you can trust me with it!" The king staunched the blood and bound up the gash with his scarf. Then, embracing his son, he gave him the coveted weapon

The same evening Murad was seized with a second whim.

He had never been allowed to go out alone—what could be more delightful than to take a stroll abroad at night? He only knew the face of Nature by day, he wished to see her in her silent moments, in the hours of gloom and half-obscured moonlight. He had heard of the songs of night-birds, of the roar of the hungry lion; of those insects which, glittering among the leaves, turn every bush into a casket of diamonds; of the mysterious odours which earth yields to the flowers only in the solemn hours of darkness; but now he determined to see, to hear, and to learn all these for himself.

He retired to rest as usual, placed his yataghan under his pillow, and waited till all was quiet in the palace. Then he rose softly, dressed himself, and walked to the door of his apartments. There he found his governor sleeping across the threshold. He paused to reflect.

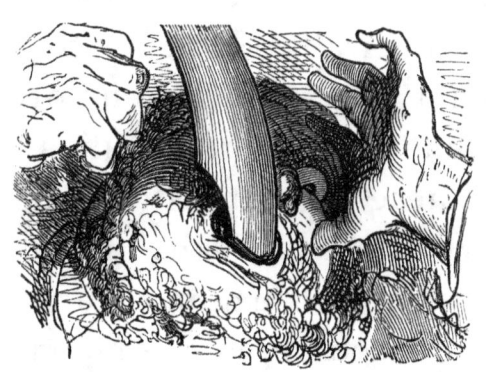

Murad's treatment
of his tutor.

"If I try to open this door, I shall rouse my guardian. If I wake him, will he grant my prayers? Certainly not. Will he yield to my threats? No; he will only laugh at them. If I disturb his slumbers, therefore, it will be to place him in a position of great difficulty, which I should exceedingly regret. It will be better, then, not to wake him!"—and Murad quietly thrust the point of his sword down the sleeper's throat, and quitted the place.

The first thing he had to do was to cross the gardens. It seemed as if he had never seen them before. The fountains falling back into their basins made a silvery tinkling, which formed a ravishing accompaniment to the song of the nightingales. The bats, which looked like great leather birds, wheeled in circles through the air upon noiseless wings. The trees, allowing the moonbeams to filter through their foliage, flung mosaics of light and shade upon the sward.

Murad fancied he saw one of the marble lions move, and started back, but speedily seeing his mistake, was heartily ashamed of himself, although he knew there was no one near to laugh at his alarm. If a real lion had chanced to pass at that moment he would have had to pay for the fright which the statue had cost Murad. As soon as he had recovered the first feeling of surprise at the novelty of the scene, Murad, who was not exactly of a poetic temperament, hurried on. What he wanted to see was not the garden—fine enough in its way, but only a prison, beyond the walls of which he had never wandered at liberty—where every step he set was on a well-kept lawn. He wanted freedom of space and chance adventure. He sprang over the wall and fell into the midst of a detachment of Nubians going their rounds.

These gallant fellows at once took to flight. They were only ten in number, and a cloud obscured the moon for a moment; but when they found they had only a child to deal with they retraced their steps.

Murad kills a Nubian.

You will have observed that Muraci did nothing hastily. His was a deliberative mind. When he saw the guards coming he said to himself, "These people have run away once, so they may do it again. Ought I to wait for them to come? No! My best plan is to rush upon them."

He did so. They met. The first who encountered him had reason to regret it, but his regret did not last long. In two minutes he was dead. Murad flung some silver to the others and plunged into the thicket.

The Nubians left their dead comrade on the ground, but they picked up the money. It is, however, a matter of time to find coins in long grass, even by the bright light of an Eastern moon, so that Murad could escape at leisure, and at last reached a sombre and dense wood. When, however, the Nubians had divided the spoil, their captain called them together, and said—

"You are a pack of cowards and fools. This was but a lad we had to do with—some precious young rascal, who has just been making a hole in the royal treasury. Why, he's a mine of wealth, that boy—a stream of riches, which glided away between our legs after besprinkling us with a few silver drops. We must track it to the fountain head. He escaped in this direction. Our own interests, as well as our duties, point out plainly enough the course we should take."

The nine guards set forward, marching carefully, and trying the bushes with their spears.

Murad heard them approaching, but remained quite still in his hiding-place.

At last they had to cross an open glade flooded with moonlight. They held a brief consultation as to the direction in which they should prosecute the search. The leader, picking out the darkest nook at the edge of the wood, pointed it out to his men. The unthinking and inexperienced always pitch on the darkest spot for a hiding-place, overlooking the fact that it is sure to be the first to be searched. At the moment when the officer was indicating to his men the direction they should take, Murad, who was crouching in the underwood, felt a warm breath upon his neck and ten sharp claws on his shoulders.

If I said he was not frightened I should tell a falsehood, especially when, on turning his head, he saw two eyes—two glowing red stars—gazing on him in the gloom. But fear did not abide long in the breast of Murad. He saw, however, close by him another group of stars, an

The cubs.

alarming constellation; in short, the young prince had hidden himself in a den with three young lions.

Unseen danger could make him tremble, but when he knew what he had to deal with he recovered himself, and began to reflect on what he had to do.

"Here I am, between three lions and nine Nubians, armed to the teeth; which should I dread most? The latter, of course, for I frightened them, and I killed one of them. They have two things to avenge on me. If I kill one of the lions he will roar, and at his voice these birds of night will run away."

Murad then seized by the throat the brute which was still tearing at his flesh, and drove the yataghan into his breast. But he miscalculated for the cub paid the penalty of his life without uttering a single growl.

Still the little army of invaders continued to advance, only instead

Murad the lion-killer.

of coming on steadily they did so at the double. The child sprang to his feet, seized the second of the lions, and flung him straight in the teeth of the advancing band when it was but a few steps from the copse. This new style of projectile had a most telling effect. The Nubians retraversed in ten seconds the ground it had taken them five-and-twenty minutes to get over in the first instance.

The field was Murad's. Of the three lion whelps one was dead, and a second one was struggling on the ground with a huge wound in the flank. He did not emulate the taciturnity of his brother, for he filled the air with piercing yells. The third was squatting under some thick boughs, uttering a low growling.

And now Murad was seized with a third whim. It was not a bad one for a beginner.

He wished to carry off the third cub as a memento of his first expedition. He re-entered the bushes and searched about. Before long the two youngsters came face to face. The cub, warned by the fate of his brothers, stood on the defensive, and, as soon as Murad came within reach, plunged his talons into his neck. Murad smiled. He would not have cared to bag his game without some trouble, so taking his captive by the throat he made him loose his hold. The lion gasped, choked,

Flight of the Nubians.

The lioness.

and at last, half-strangled, fell on his side, whereon the son of Marsillus took him by the scruff of the neck and carried him off.

The wounded cub continued its moanings, which were soon answered by a fierce and formidable cry. The mother was coming to the rescue of her young! Murad saw that flight was impossible. The lioness came to a halt on a neighbouring height, relieved in profile against the pale sky.

She searched with anxious and terrified eyes the glade whence the cries proceeded. Perceiving the wounded cub she made but one bound to it, rolled it over and over, licking its wounds, trampling and tearing the ground with her claws. At intervals she raised her head, and gave utterance to a menacing roar. Her fierce caresses hastened the cub's death. When she saw he no longer stirred she devoted herself to searching for some one on whom to avenge the great calamity which

The death of the lioness.

had overtaken her. Then she heard the complainings of the other cub which was being carried off, and she stood astonished at the audacity of the robber. You would have declared she knew Murad could not fly. Without hurrying herself at all, she advanced towards him in narrowing circles, of which he was the centre, lashing her sides with her tail, lowering her head, laying back her ears, and opening her terrific jaws.

Murad availed himself of the delay to drag off his clothes, and roll them round his left arm; and then, scimitar in hand, awaited her attack, determined to make a stout defence, but feeling certain he had but few minutes to live. He continued to retreat, fixing his eyes on those of his terrible adversary, until he reached a rock, against which he placed his back.

The discomfited sentry.

47

On arriving within a few paces of the lad, the lioness sprang upon him. Murad sank on one knee, and thrust nearly the whole of his left arm down the monster's throat. The pain he suffered was horrible, and drew from him so savage a shout that even the lioness was terrified. Then, not knowing what he was doing, mad with rage and pain, and guided less by presence of mind than instinct, he drove his steel into the creature's belly, and ripped it entirely open. Then, bathed in blood, he sank beneath the corpse of his victim, and lost consciousness.

He espies a slender stream of blood.

And now, my young friends, we will no longer stop out of doors at this time of night, but re-enter the palace, and see what is going on there.

Every hour the guards went the rounds of the building. One of the soldiers, in passing the door of Murad's chamber, slipped, and fell at full length on the pavement, to the great scandal of his commanding officer. Picking himself up, he beat a retreat to the guard-room, amid the jeers of his brothers-in-arms.

The guard-room was dimly lit by a smoky lamp, which, however, gave enough light to enable the soldier, on approaching it, to perceive that his hands were covered with blood. Thinking that he was wounded, he felt himself all over, and found that his clothes were similarly discoloured.

"This is odd," said he to his officer. "I am not wounded, and yet look at the state of my hands and my uniform!"

The officer seized a lantern, and hastened to re-traverse the rounds of the palace. On arriving at the door of Murad's apartment, he paused in alarm, for he perceived a slender stream of blood, which took its rise within the chamber. He rushed off in haste to inform the commandant in charge for the night. The commandant, terrified at the news, flew to inform the governor of the palace of the discovery. He, in turn, hurried off to the lord chamberlain, who, dreading the responsibility of waking the sultan, went, at the top of his speed, to find the prime minister. The prime minister ran, out of breath, to break the alarming intelligence to his master.

Hastening to the sultana.

Marsillus dressed in a twinkling. Pale and trembling, with his eyes but half open, and his clothes huddled on anyhow, he hastened to the sultana. She, not expecting such a visit, and never having seen her lord in such trim before, gave a loud shriek, at which her fifty attendants rushed in in alarm. On hearing the news Marsillus had to impart, the lovely Hadrama and ten of her ladies-in-waiting fainted away.

"By the beard of the Prophet!" said the sultan, impatiently, "this is no time for such monkey tricks! We have not a moment to lose. That one of you that is last to recover her senses shall receive fifty strokes of the bastinado."

In an instant all were on their feet, and prepared to depart. The sultan, the sultana, the prime minister, the chamberlain, the commandant, the officer of the guard, the sentry, the fifty ladies-in-waiting, the fifty life guards, and the eunuchs, set forward, preceded by twenty black slaves bearing torches. The procession arrived at Murad's apartment; the door was burst open; his majesty perceived who was the victim, and breathed more freely.

"Really," said the fair Hadrama, "this tutor has given us a most unnecessary alarm."

"This is your stupidity, vizier," said the king, frowning. "How dare you disturb us for a trifle like this?"

"Sire, it was your lord chamberlain who roused me, and stated that the prince was murdered. If I had for a moment supposed—" but at

The Sultana's shriek.

this the chamberlain, seeing himself in danger of losing the royal favour, threw the blame on the governor, who turned upon the commandant. The commandant passed on the charge to the officer of the guard; and he, being a man of action, promptly ordered a hundred blows of the bamboo to be administered to the soldier who was the prime origin of the mishap.

The procession, reassured, was about to resume its progress, when the queen suddenly uttered a piercing shriek.

"What's the matter now?" said Marsillus, giving a start, which was repeated by all around him.

"Do you not see that the room is empty? They have killed my child. There is no doubt about it: I was dreaming of a cat when you woke me! My child is dead!"

"Then," said the chamberlain, "the tutor must have killed him."

"You don't know what you're talking about," said Marsillus; "and as for you, madam, you're a fool. Retire to your apartments. And do you take notice, governor of the palace, that if my son is not found by sunrise, you will be honoured by immediate impalement. Go!—I rely upon your zeal and activity!"

Marsillus retired to bed again, flung himself on his pillow, and slept till nine, which was a thing he never did before. On waking, he saw the governor of the palace seated motionless at the foot of his couch. "Oh, there you are! You bring good news?"

"Sire, the young prince is found!"

"There!" said the sultan to the fair Hadrama, who had just come in, "you see you were too ready to alarm yourself."

The sultana only answered by wiping away a tear.

"And pray where did you find Murad?"

"In the olive-grove which borders the royal park."

"Oh, ho! so my young eaglet is trying his wings. What was he doing?"

"The prince was taking a nap, surrounded by a lioness and three young lions."

"That is impossible, governor. I know you too well: you would never have gone to look for him *there!*"

"My lord, the lioness was dead, and so were two of the cubs. The third, failing to obtain any other nutriment from its dam, was breakfasting off her."

"And pray who had done all this slaughter?"

"I!" said Murad, who entered, pale and gory, followed by two slaves dragging the young lion along in chains.

The Prime Minister's report.

Marsillus rose, ran to his son, clasped him in his arms, and covered him with caresses.

His son did not return them, for he had fainted, overcome with pain and loss of blood. I need hardly say he was tended as became the son of a king, and the slayer of lions.

A few days after, the prime minister submitted a report to the sultan, proving in the clearest manner that the prince's tutor had committed suicide. Marsillus smiled.

"Well done, vizier! I see how to reward you: you shall take the place left vacant by my son's tutor."

Murad grew up. He and the young lion were never separated. They were seen together every-where—even on the field of battle, and thus it was that in course of time they made their appearance in the lists at Fronsac.

Now that you have made the acquaintance of Murad Henakyeh Meimoumovassi, we will return to Charlemagne.

Murad and his pet.

VII. A Formidable Friend.

When the Saracens had entered the lists they formed in a semi-circle, and the two ambassadors rode forward.

Murad was spokesman.

"I come to thee Charles, King of the French, on the part of my father, Marsillus, King of Portugal, Valentia, Leon, and Castile. My name is Murad Henakyeh Meimoumovassi; that of my companion in arms is Angoulaffre. He is governor of Jerusalem, and direct lineal descendant of Goliath. We come to challenge to combat *à l'outrance* your peers and barons, for whom, we here declare to you, we care no more than for the pip of a pomegranate. We will compel those who hear us to reverence the name of Allah and his prophet Mahomet. We offer combat singly against twenty, thirty, forty, on foot or on horseback, armed or unarmed, accepting in anticipation all the conditions which you or your knights may choose to make. If you decline the meeting, we here proclaim our intention of holding you up to the scorn and derision of all quarters of the globe, regarding as felons and cowards those who refuse to measure their strength with us. In support whereof, there lies my glove!"

Murad flung his gauntlet into the midst of the lists, and Angoulaffre did the same. A low murmur ran round the assembled multitude, but Charlemagne silenced it with a motion of his hand, and spoke as follows: —

"I thank King Marsillus of Saragossa for the honour he has done us in sending his son among us. But his son is a young man, and his words are the words of youth. He appears to be ignorant of our history, our tastes, and our customs. Nothing delights us more than to do battle in a righteous cause, and it was not therefore necessary to accompany with threats an offer which would be well received on its own merits, and which, too, would have lost nothing by being conveyed in courteous terms. We accept your challenge, glad to fight for the love of Heaven and the Trinity, and to the confusion of Mahomet. None of us, it is true, is accompanied by wild beasts as a guard, but we have all hunted large game—the bear, or the huge-horned buffalo, so that we do not fear the cautious master or his attendant. Neither is any one of us descended from Goliath, or any other misbegotten child of the Evil One; but we all know how to show ourselves worthy of the divinely-favoured David. What brave and good men, animated by the love of God and their country, can accomplish, we will do, relying on Him who disposes the victory."

The escort of Charlemagne on this uttered loud shouts of approval, which were answered by the Saracens with cries in honour of Mahomet.

Charlemagne appointed his uncle Bernard, and Maynes, Duke of Bavaria, marshals of the list, to arrange the conditions of battle. Murad selected Priamus, King of Persia, and Garlan the Bearded, alcalde of Valentia. While this was going on, Murad's lion, who was called Oghris, which is, in the Saracen tongue, "Throat of Brass," had ceased to roar; and, marvellous to relate, his eyes, usually filled with fire, had become as gentle as those of a lamb. Everything about him grew mild. He gazed as if fascinated at Aude, who, ignorant of the charm her beauty had wrought, was talking with Roland. The lion approached her softly, never taking his eyes off her, and growing ever more submissive as he came near her.

Every one was so pre-occupied that the monster had reached almost to the spot where Aude was standing before any one noticed him. But the horses shied as he came near, and began to tremble so violently, that the jingling of their accoutrements attracted the attention of Charlemagne and his suite. Their eyes fell on the lion, but he, lost in contemplation, continued to advance, more submissively than ever. The knights, perceiving his object, drew their swords and shouted at him, but he continued to advance without regarding them. Murad, in astonishment, called to his lion; three times did he utter the call which always brought the animal to his feet, but the lion continued to advance without paying any attention to his voice. Murad,

The lion in silken fetters.

pale with fury and disappointment, sprang on him, and struck him with the flat of his sword, but the lion continued to advance without turning his head.

Aude, who was surprised;—Aude, who only did not tremble because she had Roland and Oliver at her side;—Aude, who took pity on the poor fascinated monster that came towards her, docile and trembling, had the courage to dismount and approach the lion. When he saw her near him how great was his delight! You would have vowed that in order to reassure her and make her forget his power he made himself as small as possible. When she came up to him he lay down and licked her feet. Aude bent down and ran her fingers through his mane. The great brute licked her hand tremblingly. Then the fair one took her scarf and bound it round the neck of Oghris, who, rising gently on his feet for fear of alarming her, allowed her to lead him in a string.

Great was the astonishment of the spectators; but the most astounded of all was Murad. He did not pride himself particularly on gallantry and good manners, so, dismounting from his horse, he seized the lion by the mane, and, without taking the least notice of the slight bonds by which Aude the Fair held the lion, strove to drag him with him. But the lion, furious, showing his teeth angrily, began to roar in such sort that a terrible confusion ensued.

The horses reared, unseating knights even who were usually firmest in their saddles. The spectators, on hearing it, took to flight in every direction, and for two leagues round the startled peasantry looked with astonishment at the clear sky, convinced that the sound was that of thunder.

After a time the uproar subsided, and they beheld with horror Murad extended on the ground. They did not, however, so much recognise him as guess that he was represented by fragments of flesh and broken steel, and a few fluttering rags of cloth—all that remained of the son of Marsillus.

The lion had squared accounts for his family. The son had avenged his mother.

The death of Murad.

VIII. WHEREIN THE GOVERNOR OF JERUSALEM BEGINS TO SHOW HIS TEETH.

Angoulaffre, who up to this had remained unmoved, now began to choke with rage. He rushed at the lion, who had again laid himself at the feet of the mistress of his choice, and, catching it up by the ear, as one would serve a rabbit, began to twist its neck. On this Oliver stepped forward.

"What ransom do you set on the lion? It is a pet that my sister has taken a fancy to, and I should like to present it to her. Will you take a ransom in gold or precious stones?"

"In the land I govern, on the shores of the Red Sea, I have a palace of turquoise, built upon pillars of crystal. It is so vast that the best walker cannot make the circuit of it between sunrise and sunset. There a hundred silver towers rise into the air; on each is a choir of singers, or a band of musicians. In the centre is a gigantic dome of embossed gold, surmounted by a diamond so huge and so bright, that even at night it can be seen thirty leagues off at sea. It is called 'The Diamond Beacon of Safety,' because it guides our sailors as surely as the north star."

"I have," said Oliver, "a sword called Glorious. Galas, Munifican, and Ansias laboured at its forging two years each. You are aware that they made nine other swords—three each. Ansias made Baptism, Florence, and Graban for Strong-i'-th'-Arm; Munifican made Durandal for Roland, and Sauvagine and Courtain for Ogier the Dane; and Galas made Flamberge and Joyeuse for Charlemagne, and Hauteclair, the third, for Closamont. When the ten swords were made, the three brothers summoned a giant, and bade him smite with Glorious against the edges of the nine others. Glorious came out of the trial triumphant, and hacked each of the other blades about a foot from the pommel. Give me the lion, and Glorious is yours!"

56

Angoulaffre smiled, showing his double row of teeth, yellow as brass, and sharp as pikes.

"What could I do with your arms? Look at me, and tell me if I need them. See these nails!—they pierce deeper into wrought steel than your weapon can into flesh. Behold these teeth! what engine of war is so powerful? With them I can with one gnash divide a knight in half at the waist. Look at these hands!—they can snap off an oak as you would pick a violet. Re-gard these arms, and tremble! With these, one day, while out hunting with the King of Persia, I strangled an elephant. Observe these feet, and dread to come near them! In Nubia a mad rhinoceros dared to attack me; he struck me in the calf; the horn broke off, and remained in the wound, while I trampled the huge beast to death under my feet. What use would your weapon be to me?"

Angoulaffre strangles an elephant.

"Nevertheless, I must have that lion; and, since you will not accept any ransom for it, let it be the prize of our combat."

"And do you suppose you can encounter me alone?" asked Angoulaffre, grinning so horribly that the lion thought his last hour was come.

"Does it want more than one to kill a dog?"

The giant, furious, let go the lion, which hurried off, crouching behind Aude for shelter, like a chastised cur.

"Well! I am in good humour to-day," said Angoulaffre. "You see I am disposed to smile. Be thankful for it. I shall be happy to show you how the dogs of my country bite."

During this discussion the spectators, whose curiosity overcame their fears, had resumed their places. The knights, by the aid of their squires, had remounted their horses, and the mangled remains of Murad had disappeared. Charlemagne, reaching the royal seats, gave the signal for the commencement of the tourney.

The trumpets again resounded, mingling their music with the discordant notes of the Saracen instruments. The heralds scoured the lists, arranging all in their places. Then Angoulaffre approached Charlemagne.

"Are you, then, he whom they call the king? What sort of people are these French, who are satisfied with such a sovereign? Is it an emperor I see before me, dressed in silk like a woman? You call us dogs, accursed Christians, and you dwell in burrows, as if you knew you shamed the sun, that deigns to touch you with a few unimportant beams. In my land the king is king not only by birth. If he were disguised amid a multitude, you would say, on beholding him, "This is the king!" He clothes his limbs in steel, and would blush to be seen in soft attire when his faithful knights are going to do battle. Coward and effeminate! You have allowed a hero, the son of a king, to be slain before your eyes without attempting to rescue him. You have had more regard for yourself and your knights than for your guest; and indeed you, all of you, have reason to rejoice at his fall. Mahomet has summoned him to his presence, ashamed to see that there were two of us to defend his name against such wretched adversaries. I alone am sufficient for such a task. Send, therefore, your peers and knights against me, either in a body or singly; and if they dare undertake the adventure, believe me, you had better give each a farewell embrace before you part." Then pointing to Oliver, Angoulaffre continued—

"This pigmy here has dared to challenge me. Give him a guard worthy, if possible, of my attention, and I consent to waste a few seconds upon him!"

Angoulaffre's defiance.

Charlemagne was not accustomed to hear such language. His blood boiled with rage, and, coursing wildly through his veins, made him at one moment red as fire and the next pale as death. It must be held a final proof that a man cannot expire of rage that Charlemagne continued to live. His nobles were not a whit less moved than he. As for Angoulaffre, he continued to smile savagely.

"It is by sword-stroke and lance-thrust that such words are answered," said Charles, "and you will receive a hundred blows for every syllable you have dared utter."

"Ill-said, paltry kingling!" replied the giant. "*Our* warriors never need two blows at a foeman."

"Enough of parley, sir," said Roland. "Do you not see how you are delaying us?" and then he added, aside, to Oliver, "My brother and dear friend, you admire, I know, my castle on the banks of the Seine. Take it, and let *me* fight him first."

"No," said Oliver, "not for the crown would I resign this chance of earning my passport to heaven."

"Take my horse, and give me up your place," said Ogier the Dane. "You know that Tachebrune is a horse without peer."

"You are mad to persist in asking me. You do me a wrong. Neither of you would do what you ask of me."

And saying this, Oliver, having kissed the king's hand, assumed his arms, and ran to take his post at the extremity of the lists, opposite to Angoulaffre, who continued to grin horribly.

Angoulaffre's smile.

IX. Wherein the Eagle Stoops, the Raven Croaks, the Wolf Howls, and the Lion Roars.

Large tears coursed down the cheeks of Charlemagne, as he gazed sadly on his nobles and knights, and asked himself if Heaven would permit such heroes to fall ingloriously by the hand of a miscreant.

Charlemagne's tears.

Oliver crossed himself, and rode at the giant. All trembled; Oliver alone trembled not.

It is hardly necessary to say that the usual conditions of this class of duel were, perforce, somewhat modified on this occasion, for they forbade any blows except at the body, and permitted only cuts, not thrusts. As Angoulaffre was six times the height of Oliver, it was impossible they could be strictly adhered to.

The two combatants rushed at each other, and quickly disappeared in a cloud of dust. Then came the clash of steel, which sent a chill to all hearts. Was Oliver unhorsed? Could that be the noise of his fall? No! the dust cleared away, and Oliver was seen firmly seated in his saddle at the end of the lists, prepared for another course. His lance had broken the buckle of Angoulaffre's sword-belt. The huge weapon, in falling, had made a great dent in the soil.

Frantic cries of "Hurrah for the brave knight!" rent the air.

"Charge!"

Again they dashed forward, and disappeared in the storm of dust. This time, too, Oliver escaped unharmed; but the giant, confused by the limited area of the lists, and miscalculating his distance, came down full tilt upon the public gallery. His terrible lance made a deadly

The first course.

passage through the crowd, and smashed the timber-work, which fell in upon the sitters. In the crash Angoulaffre's horse lost its breast-piece.

Ganelon had never been so delighted. He hated Oliver, whose friendship for Roland was proverbial. "This evening," said he to himself, "these boasters will sleep between four planks."

Wolf was as pleased and malicious as Ganelon.

The Duke of Aquitaine, you must know, had been struck with Aude's beauty, and had demanded her hand; but Gerard de Vienne had rejected the offer with scorn, and Oliver had said, with a laugh, "Go and ask Roland for it."

Wolf and Ganelon were made to understand each other: they did not fail to joke together in a whisper while Oliver was doing battle.

Now Charlemagne was never particularly pleased to see people jesting on such occasions, and he was not slow to perceive their smothered laughter, and grew very angry at it. This sarcastic sniggering enraged him.

The words of Angoulaffre still grated in his ears, and he fancied that he was the subject of pleasantry for his vassals. Turning round, delighted at a chance of relieving his anger, he said to Ganelon and Wolf—

"The wolf and the crow, Heaven help us! dare to laugh at the eagle! Has he sunk so low that he must submit to this?"

"Nay, His Majesty must not misunderstand us thus," said Wolf. "Our recent submission to his commands should place our loyalty beyond suspicion of that sort."

"What, then, is the reason of this unwholesome pleasantry? When the wolf is pleased, the shepherd should be on his guard."

"An awkward blow of Oliver's made us laugh," said Ganelon, scowling at the combatants.

"Oho! so that gallant knight must serve you for a laughing-stock? In truth, you would have done better to laugh at me. Am I no longer Charlemagne? Did that miscreant say true? Because a giant dares look me in the face, these dwarfs must snap at my heels! One of my bravest knights undertakes, out of regard for me, an enterprise, the very thought of which is enough to turn one's head; he is in danger of his life, and people dare laugh at him under my very eyes! You have done ill, let me tell you; and, since the venture which Oliver undertakes is such good sport, you shall, both of you, take part in it at once. Now,

Oliver unhorsed.

63

raven!—now, wolf! to your prayers for this hero; for I swear by Heaven you shall take his place in the field!"

Then, leaving Ganelon and Wolf dumb with confusion, Charlemagne resumed his place. Angoulaffre and Oliver, who only awaited the monarch's return, ran another course. This time Ferrant d' Espagne arrived alone at the end of the lists. The giant had adopted surer measures.

The two champions.

He had couched so low in the saddle that his face had touched his horse's neck. Oliver, taking advantage of this, had thrust his lance into his left eye, whereon Angoulaffre had seized him in his mighty grasp, and had gripped him so hard, that his armour, bent and bruised, forced itself into his flesh. Then the giant was seen to rise in his saddle, and hurl the luckless knight to the ground, where he lay without stirring, his armour broken, and bathed in blood. Cries of horror resounded on all sides, but they were speedily drowned by the shouts and music of the Saracens.

Charlemagne sat motionless, with his eyes fixed on the body of Oliver. His bravest knights pressed round him, imploring him to send them to fight the giant, but he did not hear them.

They brought a litter; the surgeons entered the lists, and soon the cry was raised, "Oliver still breathes!" Then Charles roused himself, and, with tears in his eyes, exclaimed—

"Blessed St. James! I have ever had full faith in you. Save this gallant champion, and I promise you a chapel in the land of the Saracens. It shall be so lovely, it shall be the envy of all the calendar."

Then, turning to Ganelon and Wolf, he said, "Now, as for you, Count of Mayence, and you, Duke of Aquitaine, if you do not accept the combat, I swear by Heaven that to-morrow you shall be degraded from the order of knighthood on the very spot where this brave knight has just fallen."

"So be it," said Ganelon, "'twill be strange if we do not let you see we are of as gallant and noble a lineage as your favourites!" and, followed by Wolf, he descended into the lists.

64

X. Angoulaffre the Merciful!

When Angoulaffre saw these new adversaries approaching he frowned.

"Aha! for what do you take me, and why do you send these brats against me? By my faith, Kingling, I do not thank you. If this be a sample of your court it is but a poor one, and it is no wonder you are foremost in it. But, in truth, I believe you are but sending me the refuse of your knighthood, which you are not sorry to be rid of. You hope thus to tire me, and to rid yourself of these small fry of warriors. I shall not satisfy your wishes. I should blush to deal seriously with these puny creatures. By the Prophet, my father would be astonished to see the task I have had set me!"

Shrugging his shoulders, Angoulaffre took his post at the end of the lists. He refused the lance which was brought him by thirty squires.

Wolf and Ganelon
are taken up.

"It would be a rare jest if I needed arms to fight these pigmies," said he, as he rode forward at an easy pace. Ganelon and Wolf charged upon him, lance in rest, but instead of aiming at the giant they aimed at his horse.

"Cowards and bunglers!" shouted Angoulaffre. "Oh, Charlemagne, I shall not do you the pleasure of ridding you of such knights. I intend to spare them, and let them go in peace for your disgrace for ever after."

So saying, the giant stooped, and, seizing the two as he had done Oliver, he looked at them quite unconcernedly.

"Faugh! the wretched Christians! it would be a murder to put them to death;" and with these words he rode off towards the chapel, still holding Ganelon and Wolf in his grasp.

You have, of course, my dear readers, not forgotten the chapel of which I spoke at the beginning of the story. It was surmounted by a huge iron cross. Angoulaffre went up to it, and without injuring his prisoners, he hung them by their belts, one on each limb of the cross, like a couple of rings on a ringstand.

"Gallant defenders of the cross," said the colossus, as he rode back to his place in the lists; "become its guardians also!"

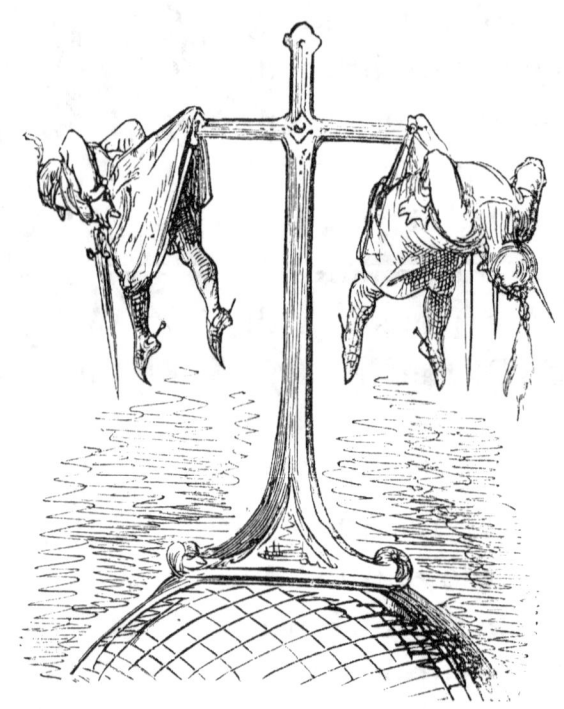

The suspended champions.

XI. How Angoulaffre Had an Attack of Toothache, Which was the Death of Him.

Roland heard no further. The insolence of the giant had aroused in his heart one of those fits of fury which, when coupled with strength and courage like his, nothing can resist. The dishonour done to Ganelon and Wolf enraged him, for he no longer saw in them either rivals or unworthy opponents. They were knights—they were Christians, and he felt a share of the insult offered to them.

He sprang on the back of Veillantif, and clashed into the lists. A murmur of applause saluted his entrance. People felt that the real struggle was only now commencing, and that if Roland were vanquished there was no one to take his place. The honour of the French name was the stake of this contest.

Three pages ran to pick up the gauntlet which Angoulaffre had flung down in defiance, and dragged it with difficulty into the middle of the lists. Roland stooped, picked it up, and flung it in the giant's face.

On receiving this insult the Saracen lost his self-possession, and gave vent to an oath so terrible that all the assemblage crossed themselves. You will not, therefore, be surprised, my friends, that I do not repeat it, although it formed the entire speech of the Governor of Jerusalem. He felt himself in the presence of an enemy worthy of him, and understood that the time for words was gone by. As an habitual drinker likes wine that is rough, warriors delight in foemen who smite hard.

This time the giant assumed his lance and his vast shield. The spectators had not a drop of blood left in their veins, and many prayers were breathed to Heaven for the success of the Christian knight.

The signal was given. The combatants dashed forward and encountered half way. Angoulaffre had stooped down to await Roland, but he, with superhuman activity, avoided the fearful blow which was aimed at him, and struck his adversary on the face with his lance.

Angoulaffre's fall.

The spear lodged between two of his teeth and broke.

The greatest courage is often accompanied by little weaknesses. The hero who sports with life on the battle-field will often shrink at the sight of a spider. Angoulaffre, now, had a horror of a dentist—as, my young readers, is the case, I conjecture, with most of you. A decayed grinder had given him considerable pain for the last six weeks. Imagine his rage, then, when he received a tremendous blow from a lance on that particular tooth. He ceased to be a man—to be a giant: he was a wild beast, mad with fury. He lost his presence of mind, which until now had lent him double strength. Flinging aside his arms he flung himself blindly upon his foe.

But Roland, whom danger never stirred, evaded him craftily, and harassed him. He seemed to be playing with his formidable adversary. A cleft stroke severed the girths of Angoulaffre's horse; the saddle turned round; the giant lost his balance, and fell to earth amid shouts

68

The Brazen Teeth in pain!

of laughter from the spectators. Roland approached him, gave him his hand, and assisted him to rise. Then he asked him if he required rest.

"I never leave a fight half finished," said the giant; "but I am thirsty, that is all."

Charlemagne, hearing these words, ordered his pages to roll a hogs-head of Spanish wine into the middle of the lists. Angoulaffre broached it with one blow of his fist, emptied it at one draught, and then, flinging the cask beyond the barriers, remounted his steed.

The combatants selected fresh spears, and, having taken their places on the field, rode at each other once more. This time they smote one another full on the breast. What a terrific crash, my young friends No iron-clad of our day could have resisted it. Angoulaffre was driven back on his horse's crupper; he stuck his knees in so tight, to save himself from a second fall, that the unhappy animal had all the breath knocked out of its body. It was a misery to hear it cough.

Roland had bent beneath the stroke. His back had touched the crupper of Veillantif, but the brave knight did not lose his seat. The spear had glanced off his excellent armour from girdle to shoulder, and he escaped unhurt, though the blood flowed from his mouth.

"I should be loth to kill so brave a knight," said the Governor of Jerusalem. "I offer you your life; take it at my hands."

"I can accept nothing from you but blows," said Roland, quietly; "because I feel certain I can give you as good as I take, and perhaps even throw in a little over."

"As you please," said Angoulaffre; and once more they resumed the fight.

69

The last charge.

The giant flung aside his lance, and took a battle-axe, the sight of which gave the spectators a fit of cold shivers. Roland also laid aside his spear, and drew Durandal from its sheath.

Veillantif seemed endowed with human intelligence. The brave creature divined the slightest wish of its master. Now it bounded, now it scoured the plain; anon it charged or it reared, and ever it went unhurt through the shower of blows. The horse of the Saracen was not worth half of Roland's. Its size and weight rendered it difficult to manage. For some minutes it coughed incessantly, and scarcely obeyed bit or spur. Roland, by a clever turn, took the giant in flank, and with one blow of his tremendous sword clove in two the horse of his opponent.

Angoulaffre came to earth, seated between the two severed halves of his steed, and bellowing with astonishment and anger.

The Saracens had left off laughing now. Their music was silenced. Garlan the Bearded, who commanded them, foamed with rage; he tore out a good tenth of his beard by the roots. The Alcalde of Valentia foresaw the fate of Angoulaffre, and was asking himself whether he and his men should ever see Spain again.

Roland was loudly cheered; but, without taking any heed of it, he dismounted, and, approaching the colossus, who had not yet regained his feet, he said—

"Keep your seat, governor, and while you rest yourself, send some of your warriors to me; there will then be no time lost."

70

The musicians are disconcerted.

"May I be struck by a thousand thunderbolts, if I give you a moment's respite! Mount, and defend yourself!"

"I am not in the habit of taking any advantage in a combat. Since you are dismounted, I will continue the contest on foot."

During this conversation ten horses had drawn from the lists the remains of Angoulaffre's steed.

Then began a combat yet more terrible than any of its predecessors. The marvel was how Roland escaped the rain of blows aimed at him; but the bold knight managed so admirably, that he got close to the monster, and cut off his right leg at the knee.

You will guess, my friends, how sad a figure the Governor of Jerusalem cut with such a very ill-assorted pair of legs. He fell, biting the ground with rage, and rolling to and fro in his attempt to rise, until he wept at his own impotence. Roland approached him.

The end of Angoulaffre's charger.

"You cannot continue the struggle. Your life is in my power. Accept Christian baptism, and I will spare you."

Angoulaffre, without answering, rolled himself to the place where his axe had fallen, seized it and cut off his left leg at the knee. Then raising himself on his stumps, he gazed sternly at Roland, and said, simply—

"I am ready!"

At the sight of this act of Spartan heroism both Christians and Pagans applauded. Charlemagne himself was touched.

"Governor of Jerusalem," said he, "desist from this useless struggle. What greater proof could you give of your courage? Believe me, when you appear again before your king in this guise, and tell him, 'It is Roland who has conquered me,' you will not see him sneer at you."

"You—you Christians, then—can live after the shame of having been vanquished? That, and that only, is beyond our power. Behold, faint hearts! You have seen how we can fight; see now how well we know how to die!"

I will not, my dear young friends, relate to you the end of this fearful conflict. It was no longer a battle—it was a butchery. Blows followed one another without pause. Roland was covered with wounds; his armour was hacked away piece by piece, but he did not give ground. He felt his strength failing, and desired at any price to bring the contest to an end. Without regarding the almost certain death to which he exposed himself, he closed with his foe, and dealt him a tremendous blow, which stretched him at his feet.

There was one short minute, during which the impressed spectators kept silence. The respect which bravery always commands restrained the burst of the general rejoicing; but, these first few seconds past, every one felt himself relieved of an immense peril.

The sight of Roland, to whom Charlemagne had hastened, was the signal for an outburst of frantic cheering from every side.

The king embraced his nephew, and said—

"I would reward you for so splendid a victory. What would you have? My gratitude is unbounded: let your desire be without limit. Which of my provinces shall I bestow on you?"

"I am yet more ambitious. When I wish to own a province, I will go win it with my sword."

"What would you have, then?"

Aude had just left Oliver, who had no longer need of her care. She felt that the triumph of her lover would not be complete if she did not share it.

Roland gazed at her so meaningly, that Charles turned to Gerard de Vienne, and said—

"Here is an ambitious gallant, who seeks his reward at your hands. What say you, Gerard, and you, Lady Guibourg? Does it not seem to you that your niece will be fortunate in having for a spouse my friend and nephew, Roland? I ask her hand of you for him."

"Sire," said Gerard, it is doing us too great an honour."

"Aude could not have a nobler husband than Roland, who comes of your royal line, sire," said the Lady Guibourg.

Angoulaffre brought to his knees.

"I was not rich enough to satisfy this grasping soul," replied Charlemagne, "and I thank you, Gerard, for coming to my help. Ah! Turpin, here is work for you. No other is worthy to celebrate such nuptials as these. Have ready a splendid sermon for the occasion, for the wedding shall take place on our return to Cologne."

Angoulaffre's death-agony.

XII. The Last Will and Testament of Angoulaffre.

Angoulaffre was stretched on the ground, surrounded by his companions in arms. When the surgeons came to dress his wounds, he rejected their aid.

"Go to the Evil One, vile concocters of drugs! My soul is not foolish enough to dwell in so dilapidated a mansion as that which I have to offer now. All your remedies will but drive her away the sooner. Come hither, Alcalde of Valentia, Corsablix, Margariz—all of you—come round me, that I may die while looking on the faces of friends. Tell to King Marsillus the manner of Murad's death—and mine. Tell him that with my last breath I called for vengeance on Roland. I bequeath to you a hatred so fierce and strong, that it cannot but survive me. I leave all my property, without exception, for the furtherance of vengeance. If bribery can help you, spare nothing: there is no human integrity that could withstand the sight of the wealth you have to

74

offer. Swear to me you will spare no means of hastening the downfall of this accursed one, and I shall die more happy."

"Rely upon us," said Priamus. "We inherit your hatred; and whether it be ten years, or whether it be twenty years hence, rely on it, this Roland shall perish by our hands!"

"We will hew him into as many pieces as he has given you wounds," said Garlan the Bearded.

"His death shall become a tradition," added Abysm, the favourite of Marsillus. "I swear to you, people shall speak of it when the recollection of this petty Charles shall be extinct."

"You had better implore the aid and protection of the Prophet in your undertaking, for he who has vanquished me is not to be lightly overcome," said Angoulaffre.

"If we have to unpeople Nubia, Persia, Egypt, the Atlas, the Caucasus, Scythia, and Spain, to swell our forces," said Ecremis of Vauterne, "as sure as Mahomet is greater than St. Peter, Charles and his knights shall perish ere long."

"Before a year elapses we will sleep at Cologne," said another.

Priamus promises.

"Enough, babblers and boasters!" said Angoulaifre, who felt the chills of death approaching; "do your best to carry back your carcasses whole to Spain, and if Mahomet grants you that favour, renew there these promises. In the meantime, take care of your precious hides in to-morrow's tourney. Death grasps me by the throat— farewell! Ah, dog of a Roland!"

These were the last words of the Governor of Jerusalem.

Sixty Saracens, marching in two files, bearing thirty spears between them (a soldier holding each end of a spear), extemporised a litter, on which the dead body of the giant was placed.

Two hours before, he had entered the lists, mounted on his steed, followed by a brilliant suite of kings, emirs, and alcaldes, and preceded by a band of barbarous music; proud of his strength, relying on his own bravery, boasting, and threatening. But if Heaven does not favour the cause of the lion, it not unfrequently happens that the lamb gets considerably the better of him.

The enraged Garlan.

The treacherous wolf.

XIII. THE TWO ROGUES RELEASED.

The whole assembly was so full of other matters, that no one gave a thought to Ganelon or Wolf. Pinabel, the nephew of the Count of Mayence, was the first to recollect them. Approaching Charlemagne, he inquired if it would not be proper to release the two suspended knights, and if the king would entrust the task to him.

"That concerns Roland," said the king; "he has achieved their deliverance, and therefore they are his property. Go, then, nephew, and take down the two heroes, who are cutting so very sorry a figure up yonder. You will, of course, think it proper to give them the use of their wings."

Roland was talking with Aude, and was not particularly pleased at the interruption. However, he went to the chapel, where he arrived in a very bad humour.

"It is very hard," said he to Ganelon, "to be put to inconvenience every minute for people who are not the least grateful for what one does. When a man hasn't the strength to carry out an enterprise, he should not attempt it. This is the second time that I have had to release you from a state of suspense, and for no fault of mine. For

Heaven's sake, in future don't put the credit of France in jeopardy lightly. Remember, you are not the only Frenchman in the world, and also that I cannot always be close at your heels to repair your blunders." And, without further delay, he restored the two suspended knights to the ground, and returned to the fair Aude.

"Well," said Wolf to Ganelon, "are you in the humour to digest affronts like those?"

"I fancy, my lord duke, you have had your share of them too, and they don't seem to disagree with you."

"It would be only right to chastise him for his insolence."

"And pray what hinders you?" said the count, smiling.

"The same reason that teaches you patience. This Roland is a brute and a—"

But here the idlers congregated around the two vanquished knights, and mocked at them unsparingly. Not being anxious to supply public amusement gratis, they thought fit to retreat, and returned to their tents, where they passed the night in the formation of projects that were far from Christian, though they originated in Christian brains.

The released champions.

The sleeping camp.

XIV. The Corselet of Cambric.

It is nine o'clock. All is quiet in the camp. The fires have been extinguished as a measure of prudence, and only the moon is allowed to gleam.

In the plain, however, a few tumblers displayed their feats by torchlight to a few spectators, but ere long, losing their public, they were fain to pack up their traps and seek repose beneath some forest tree. By degrees every noise died away. Hardly a chirrup was heard to give life to a lovely night; still, now and then, one heard from afar the ringing of steel. It was some watch on its rounds. The armour glittered a moment in the moonbeams and then disappeared, and that was all.

Let us, too, go our rounds, and see what is passing in the camp. We will begin with the Royal tent. If you were not with me, my dear young people, I would defy you to enter it. Never was treasure or sacred relic so carefully guarded. Charles slept in a great bed of state, and a hundred of his bravest and stoutest men were appointed to guard him. Forty knights kept watch, changing guard three times a night, according to the muster-roll—ten at the head, ten at the foot, and ten on either side, each with a drawn sword and a torch.

Aude, too, had retired to her pavilion. She could not sleep, however, for thinking of all that had happened during the day—a day that had been at once hateful and glad: hateful, because it had nearly deprived her of her dear Oliver; joyful, because it had decided her marriage with Roland—her dear Roland. Her waiting-women surrounded her. Ten Moorish maidens sang to her Spanish ballads, which she preferred to all others, but to-night she heard them not—she was lost in meditation. Four Saxon damsels combed her long tresses, waiting for the signal to dress it for the night, a signal she forgot to give. Eight Lombard girls had made ready a perfumed bath, but it had been three times prepared already, for it grew cold while she was musing. Oghris was not more fortunate. He had gently placed his head in her lap, but she had not bestowed on him a single glance. He was a guard that made a mockery of the precaution taken to put sentinels at the tent-door.

Roland and Oliver
reposing.

Roland slept beside Oliver. The two gallant fellows had fallen asleep hand in hand. The friends were now virtually brothers.

Meanwhile Ganelon and Wolf had concocted a murderous undertaking. "Don't you think Marsillus would give a handsome price for Roland's body?"

"I believe you," answered the Duke of Aquitaine; "but it would be better to deliver him up alive, and let the king manage him. It is by craft we must oppose him; as to force, we must not dream of that, for neither you nor I could do anything with him in that line."

Let us take a stroll now beyond the camp, and see who they are that wander in the skirts of the forest. A delightful couple are whispering together. Mita, the worthy sister of Aude, whom we remarked at the head of the royal *cortége*, and who was called "the little knight of pearls,"

Mita was walking along, leaning on the arm of Miton of Rennes, the friend of Roland. They were followed by a waiting-maid and a page.

"My sister is fortunate in having for her knight such a man as Roland."

"Cannot you see how it breaks my heart to hear you speak so? To win your favour must one be the only knight who has no equal in the field?"

"I know my own value, and it seems to me that I deserve to have prodigies of valour done to win me. Listen, Sir Miton. You would wed me: is it not so? You repeat, over and over again, you would achieve miracles for my sake!"

"It is true."

"Then I shall seek a proof of this to-morrow. At daybreak you will receive my commands. If you carry out well the enterprise I shall plan for you, I will be yours—yours devotedly. If you attempt it, but do not succeed, I shall be your friend as heretofore, but nothing beyond. If you draw back, never speak to me again, for I should speak to you as to a poltroon."

They had now reached the camp, where they must part.

"Farewell, Miton; may you succeed to-morrow. I go to pray for your success."

She reached out a hand, which trembled in that of the knight, and which he kissed respectfully. Miton returned to his tent, but did not close his eyes all night. Every time a footstep passed near his tent he rushed to the door, expecting to receive the message from Mita. At early dawn an attendant came with a packet, which she gave to him, and said—

The corselet of cambric.

"My mistress sends me to you to communicate her wishes. 'Go seek Sir Miton,' she said to me, 'and bid him rejoice if he be truly desirous of proving to me that he is worthy of my love, for I am going to give him an opportunity of proving it. Give to him this cambric garment of mine, and bid him wear it to-morrow in the fight. If he loves me he

81

will consider it a talisman more potent and more secure than steel, and, full of confidence, will present himself at the tournament without any other armour except his greaves, his shield, and his helmet. If he does this and triumphs, I shall be ready to give him any proof of my love that he may demand. If he does not succeed, he shall none the less have my esteem and friendship for having essayed it. If he should fall, I will wear mourning for him and die in a convent. If he refuse, I shall despise him as the falsest and most cowardly of men.'"

Miton, who had sunk on his knees to receive from the messenger of his love the packet, which he covered with kisses, rose smilingly, and spoke thus to the attendant:— "Return to her whom you have the honour to serve, and tell her that I am happy and proud that she has given me an opportunity of dying for her pleasure. Without her, life is nothing to me; and this is putting me to too easy a trial, for I feared she would send me away from her, and that would have been to put me to a slow and lingering death. I feel truly blest now, since I can devote to her openly every minute as it passes to her service."

Miton gave all the gold and silver he possessed to the messenger, dismissed her, and prepared himself for the battle.

He put on the garment sent him by Mita, and I assure you he looked very well, and not at all ridiculous, when he was equipped as his lady had commanded.

I ought to tell you, my friends, that our knight was about twenty-three, and had a handsome face, framed in long yellow locks. He was second to none in either elegance or strength.

The cambric corselet which he had assumed, bound round his waist with a rich girdle, came down to his knees, leaving bare his neck and arms, which were very white.

Milton and Turpin.

Thus equipped he visited the Archbishop Turpin, related to him his adventure, confessed to him, took the sacrament, and then gave himself up to prayer until the hour for entering the lists.

The Mêlée.

XV. Montjoie! Montjoie! St. Denis!

It was nine o'clock in the morning. The heralds went about every-where, shouting aloud, "Lace your helms, brave knights! lace your helms!"

The combatants got ready for the conflict. They examined for the last time with the greatest care every minute point of their armour, and made sure that their horses were properly equipped and saddled. These precautions taken, they hurried off to the lists; the Saracens by the southern gate, the Christians by the northern.

Charlemagne took his place in the Royal pavilion, with Himiltrude by his side. Aude placed herself on the throne reserved for the Queen of Beauty. Oghris laid himself at her feet, surveying the crowd with wondering eyes.

The benches were crowded. The knights took their places. Trumpet peal and shout rent the air. The Emperor was in his place.

The heralds next proclaimed silence, read the conditions of the tournament, and called on the knights to do their duty, for the honour of

Heaven, the Emperor, and the ladies. Then they called the two leaders, Christian and Saracen, to take command of their forces.

Garlan the Bearded rode forth, and reviewed his men. Miton did the same, and advanced into the centre of the lists. His novel style of armour attracted some attention.

"What is this?" said Charlemagne. "Is Miton out of his senses, or does he come here to seek certain death? Go instantly, and command him to quit the lists."

Love on the pillion.

Ogier the Dane darted forward to convey the Royal command, but was stopped by Turpin, who had heard Charles's exclamation.

"Pardon me, sire, for thus suspending the execution of an order you have given; but Miton is performing a vow. Your Majesty would find it vain to forbid him the combat. Heaven alone is able to preserve him."

The severe eye of the bishop met the supplicating looks of Mita, and her eyes sought the ground.

Aude understood all, and wished to interpose.

"Sire, you will not suffer so brave a knight to be slain—"

Charlemagne shook his head sadly. "I know Miton, and nothing will prevent him from carrying out his enterprise."

Then turning towards the suite of the Queen of Beauty, he said—

"I have among you, ladies, a cruel foe, who thus devotes to death one of my bravest knights. Let us say the prayer for the dead on behalf of the victim of this relentless beauty."

All rose, and repeated the supplication in a low voice, Turpin leading them. The terrified Mita alone had not the power to rise. She sank on her knees, and would have remained there motionless and overcome, had not her sister raised her.

In the meantime Miton, ignorant of what was passing, and not even hearing the shouts of the crowd, or the entreaties of his comrades, who begged him not to devote himself in this way to destruction—

Miton, gay and proud, to think of the trial he was subjected to, had made all his dispositions for the combat.

There were a hundred horsemen in the field—fifty on either side. Their leaders drew them up in two lines of twenty-five. It was truly an imposing sight—these brave fellows, clad in their glittering arms, in firm and compact lines, planted well in their war-saddles. One might have called them a column of iron. The horses, no less impatient than their masters, whinnied and pawed the ground.

At last Charlemagne gave the signal.

"Charge!" shouted the heralds.

Scarcely were their voices heard ere the first rank of combatants dashed forward. The two parties met halfway with an alarming crash. In vain did the spectators attempt to make out the result of this first onset. They were obliged to wait till the dust had blown off. The heart of Mita beat very fast during those few seconds, but at last she beheld her knight hand-to-hand with Garlan the Bearded. One-half of the combatants were stretched on the earth; some so sorely wounded, that their squires had to come, raise them, and drag them out of the *mêlée*. Others, however, got up without aid, and went to seek fresh adversaries.

Priamus had his spear broken, but he had kept his seat in the saddle. Seeing Girars of Roussillon engaged with Corsablix, a wild chief from the Atlas, he rushed towards them with uplifted blade. But the Burgundian knight perceived his approach, and rapidly dashing at his first opponent, he seized him by the throat, made him do service as a shield against the blows of the King of Persia, and finally flung him, a bleeding and mangled corpse, under the feet of the horses. Then, having but one enemy to deal with, he determined to seize Priamus's horse, and made such good use of his feet, nails, and teeth, that in a twinkling he was in the saddle; while the King of Persia, rolling in the dust, yielded up his impious soul through twenty gaping wounds.

"Allah Akbar! Allah is great!" cried the Saracens.

"St. Denis, Montjoie! Montjoie!" cried the knights; and, lo! the second rank flung itself into the conflict.

85

The blare of trumpets and Saracen horns, the beating of drums and gongs, drowned the noise of groans and imprecations.

The dead and dying were once more dragged out. The wounded sought shelter as best they could. Forty warriors yet remained to contest the field—twenty-five Saracens and fifteen Franks.

For a quarter of an hour Miton and Garlan had fought together, with no advantage on either side. With his keen blade the Count of Rennes had cleft the casque of the Alcalde of Valentia, and would have split his skull open but for the turban, which deadened the blow. Garlan had hacked in pieces his adversary's shield, and the corselet of cambric began to be marbled with streaks of gore. Miton saw that the ranks of his warriors were thinning, and was anxious to make an end of his foe in order to hasten to their aid. He closed with him, knee to knee, foot to foot, and, regardless of the danger to which he exposed himself, seized Garlan by the gorget of his coat of mail, dragged him from his horse, and then passing him from his right hand to his left, held the point of his sword to his throat, and compelled him to yield to his mercy. Then he sent the miscreant a foot beyond the barriers, and gave his charger to Thierry, Duke of Ardennes, who had just been unhorsed.

Cha'chaân el Da'djah, Emir of Toledo, entertained the presumptuous idea of avenging Garlan the Bearded, as if, because he had strangled a few lions in the desert, ripped up a few elephants, and cut in pieces a million or so of enemies, he could pretend to hope for the conquest of a French knight. He shouted his war-cry, and darted forward to meet the Count of Rennes, brandishing, as he did so, a huge flail with seven chains, the same with which Attila armed himself when fighting the legions of Aétius. But the blow was delivered in empty air—dragged the Emir forward, and made him lose his balance. Miton took advantage of this miss to seize Cha'chaân el Da'djah by the leg, and dragged him from his seat with such violence as to break the saddle, entangle him with the harness, and throw the horse down on its side. Then the spectators beheld a strange sight. The Count of Rennes grasped his foeman by the ankles, rose in his stirrups, and, using the body as a mace, swung it round his head, dashed into the thick of the fight, and began laying about right and left at the Saracens with the Emir. Every time this novel arm fell it encountered some weapon of defence, so that before long little was left of it but shreds. After a time the mortal instrument of war lost its weight, and became useless. When Miton flung it away it had stretched eight Saracens on the plain.

He cast his eye over the field. Marganice, Governor of Carthagena, was fighting with Roard of Limoges and Itiers of Clermont; Garnaille, King of Ethiopia, confronted Lambert the Short and Humbert, Count of Bourges; M'kamat Haddada, Caliph of Mecca, was showing a bold front to Riol of Mans, Hoël of Nantes, and Bazin of Geneva. Alis, King of Morocco, was engaged with Pinabel; while Sangaran, who ruled at the source of the Niger, Baimalanko, chief of the tribes on the borders of the Dead Sea—each one of these two blacker than the other—and Zumzum-Kalakh, King of Garbe, pressed hard on Aimery of Narbonne, who was, however, giving them two blows for one.

Miton flew to his rescue, and in three minutes, and with twenty strokes of his sword, had ridded him of his foes. Sangaran and Baimalanko fell before his arm, and went to rejoin the Evil One whose livery they wore.

"Thanks, I owe you a similar service," said Aimery to the Count of Rennes. "I shall have finished with this villain in a few seconds. I am not afraid of a single encounter, so leave me and go succour Pinabel, who has scarce blood enough left to keep him alive."

And, in truth, the nephew of Ganelon was fighting in the dark, for he was blinded with his own blood. The King of Morocco, who saw a new foeman coming towards him, determined to abandon the contest with Pinabel and charge at once on Miton, a manoeuvre he accomplished so rapidly that he took the latter by surprise. For four seconds the Count of Rennes was exposed defenceless to the fury of Alis, and this unguarded moment cost him a gash which laid open his left arm from shoulder to elbow, and marked him with a purple chevron on the wrist. Mita uttered a shriek as if she had received the blow, and hid her face in her hands.

"See," said Himiltrude, "what interest the little Mita takes in the combat, sire. The wound the Count of Rennes has just received makes her heart bleed."

"Keep your nonsense to yourself, madam," said the Emperor, who hated to be interfered with at the wrong moment. "When men wield the sword, women should not wag the tongue;" and he abruptly turned his back on his consort. In point of fact, it was not a well-chosen time for talking.

And now Riol of Mans had, with a dexterous back stroke, sent the head of M'kamat Haddada flying, and this new kind of projectile had struck Marganice, Governor of Carthagena, in the face, and so confused him that he neglected to parry a furious blow aimed at him by Itiers of Clermont. This really excusable oversight cost him his life. One sharp thrust pinned him to his horse's crupper like a butterfly on a cork.

Garnaille also perceived his end approaching. Lambert the Short gave him no respite.

"It shall never be said," cried, fiercely, the King of the Ethiopians, "that I received my death-blow from a Christian hand." Thereupon, resting the pommel of his sword on the ground, he flung himself on the point and expired shouting, "Allah!"

Aimery of Narbonne, a lad of sixteen, seemed to be playing with his opponent.

"Dog!" exclaimed Zumzum-Kalakh, "cannot you fight more steadily?"

"I will give you a lesson in politeness," said Aimery, still smiling. "First of all, I don't approve of people addressing me without baring their heads." As he spoke, his sword sent the King of Garbe's helm flying. It was one of the famous casques of the ancient tribes of Beni-Ad.

"Bravo, Pagan. Are not you afraid of getting sunburnt?"

A blow of the battle-axe, which shivered the Count of Narbonne's shield, was all the answer vouchsafed by Zumzum-Kalakh.

"Bless me! he's getting vicious," said Aimery, without being in the least put out. "We must teach him to say he's sorry."

His sword whirled in the air and smote off the wrist of the King of Garbe, and so brought the combat to a close.

The King of Morocco alone continued to make resistance. Miton hastened to dispatch him, for he felt his strength failing him. However, he would receive aid from no quarter save Heaven. His shield was riven, his left arm, laid open with a terrible gash, hung powerless by his side, and every blow he dealt his enemy cost him five in return.

Mita had no eyes for any but the Count of Rennes. She lived with his life, she suffered for his wounds, and she would have fallen dead had he perished. How she blamed her cruel commands, and how she hated the King of Morocco! In truth few men's deaths have been as fervently prayed for as his was.

Miton felt a cold sweat seize him; a mournful singing in his ears made him fancy his end was approaching. He struggled against death, and gave one last blow at his opponent, then fell senseless under his horse's hoofs. That blow was the last the Moorish king received. The sword pierced his bosom, and the steel remained fast in the wound. He was immediately

The moribund Moor.

seized with the death shudder, flung wide his arms, dropped his weapons, and uttered so terrible a cry that his frightened steed ran away at frill speed straight ahead until he dashed against the walls of the lists. His rider rolled in the dust. The King of Morocco was no more.

Charlemagne sprang up beaming with joy.

"Ogier," said he to the King of Denmark, "go bring me news of Miton, and tell him how I prize his valour. I am, moreover, not the only one who prizes him here, it appears. Well, little one," he added, turning to Mita, "you have perilous fancies. For this once all has turned out well, but you must promise me not to tempt the devil a second time."

Mita flung herself at the Emperor's feet, and kissed his hand in silence. Charlemagne smiled.

"Come," said he, "rise, Countess of Rennes."

89

The discomfited band.

XVI. A Funeral March.

Thus ended this brilliant passage of arms. Was I not right, my children, when I told you that its equal was never seen? The wounded Saracens were conveyed to hospital, and I need hardly add, they were as well cared for as if they had been duly-baptised Christians.

The dead were buried; they were sixty-three in number, neither more nor less. There were, after this tournament, a great many thrones to let in the East.

The surgeons declared that the wounded would not be fit to move for a month at the very least.

Charlemagne loaded the survivors with rich gifts, and then, after four or five days of rejoicing, he prepared to depart, leaving Fronsac strongly garrisoned. He wished to spend Advent Sunday at a town anciently called Durie, in the diocese of Julliers, and the Feast of the Resurrection at the Cathedral of St. Lambert, in Liege.

The crescent
in distress.

When the Saracens were left alone, they determined, after a long consultation, to inform King Marsillus without delay of the melancholy fate of his envoys, and to bear to him the mortal remains of his son. Nobody, however, cared to be the bearer of such tidings, and one and all professed to suffer horribly from their wounds. In short, of all that brilliant expedition, there were none left to perform this duty except the band.

The solemn procession set out for Spain. The drums, covered with mourning, preceded the hearse about twenty paces.

Thus it was that Murad Henakyeh Meimoumovassi re-entered his father's dominions!

Book the Second.
The Prophet's Paradise.

The lion's latest love.

I. How Croquemitaine was Christened.

In turning over the last page, my young friends, you have grown nine years older. You see time flies quickly when you read my writings. Do I ask too much in begging you to make a hasty flight with me, in five minutes, from the year 769 to the year 778?

Charlemagne, after having, as I said just now, performed his religious duties at Duren and at Liege, returned to Worms at the beginning of the year 770. There Miton and Mita were married, and there, subsequently, the latter gave birth to a lovely little girl, who was called Mitaine—a lovely little angel, plump and soft, with large black eyes, and golden locks as bright as the glory of a saint, Charlemagne saw the infant one day in its mother's arms, and believed he beheld a vision.

Mita and her baby.

93

"Surely," said the good Emperor, "this is Our Lady with her holy babe!"

When he came nearer, he recognised the Countess of Rennes.

"You are too blest, Lady Mita. You are favoured of Heaven indeed. It is not possible but that this little angel should bring good fortune to all who approach her; and, if she has not already been christened, I should like to be one of her sponsors. Would you wish me to be her godfather?"

Charlemagne took one of the child's tiny hands, and kissed it, the little arm disappearing entirely in the monarch's bushy beard and moustache.

Then, radiant with joy at this meeting, which he looked upon as a good omen, the Emperor hastened to an assembly of the people that he had convened. He was so happy and devoid of anxiety, that he yielded to the intercession of his mother, Bertha of the Big Feet, who had long been trying in vain to bring about a reconciliation between him and his brother Carloman.

During this same year Himiltrude bore a son, who was charming in face, but, unfortunately, deformed in figure. Charles christened him Pepin, but the people nick-named him Hunchback; and when the populace takes upon itself to act as sponsor, the names it gives do not die out.

This son and heir was not calculated to flatter the Emperor's dignity. His father did not receive him very favourably, and determined to divorce Himiltrude.

Aude and Roland, less fortunate than Miton and Mita, were not yet married.

"Sire, is it not time to celebrate our nuptials?" said the Count of Mans one day to Charlemagne. "For eight months I have been waiting your pleasure, and I trust you will at last fix a day for the marriage."

The Emperor had just had a dispute with his queen about the child, so that he did not just then regard marriage very favourably. He did not listen with a very good grace to his nephew's entreaty.

"By my beard, I consider you're in too great a hurry:—know that! Your beard is scarce grown, and yet you want to be at the head of an

Roland's request.

establishment. That is not what I consider proper. You have to make a name for yourself before you think of transmitting it to others. Besides, a man never fights so well if he has a wife and family; so don't bother my head any more about it. You are, both of you, young enough to wait—wait!"

Queen Bertha, who had no more affection for her daughter-in-law than Charles had for his wife, set out for Lombardy to settle a fresh alliance, and before long returned with Desiderade, daughter of Didier, King of Lombardy. Himiltrude, I should add, was divorced, despite the threats of the Pope, Stephen the Third.

Charlemagne spent his Christmas this year in Burgundy, and Easter at Valenciennes, in Hainault.

The reconciliation of the brothers had never been more than a formal one; so that when, about the second week in December, 771, Charles heard of Carloman's death at Samoucy, a royal palace in the old diocese of Laon, he did not waste any time on tears. He called together a full court at Valenciennes, announced to his lords the death of his brother, and led them into Neustria. He encamped on the royal farms of Carbonac, in the midst of the forest of Ardennes. The formidable appearance of the forces he commanded induced the nobles and bishops to do fealty to him. Gerberge, daughter of Didier, and widow of Carloman, endeavoured vainly to assert her children's rights. She was compelled to fly with them and a few attendants, and seek refuge at the court of her father. Charlemagne was then proclaimed sole ruler of all the realm of the Franks.

Queen Bertha's choice had not proved a very fortunate one. Desiderade, sister of the dethroned Queen of Neustria, did not make a very sprightly appearance at the Court of France; so Charles determined to get rid of her.

Roland, who was ever lamenting the indefinite postponement of his marriage, once more addressed his uncle on the subject.

"You do not intend, I am sure, sire, to do me a wrong, but you inflict more suffering on me than I can express by thus perpetually adjourning my union with Aude."

Charlemagne, who had just been having high words with the queen, was not favourably disposed to marriages. He replied, in an ill humour—

"Do you want to drive me crazy, my fine nephew? Marriage is a folly, take my word for it. Besides, I have a fancy to ravage the land of Saxony. I hear that in a town they call Eresburg—I

Roland's rejection.

don't know why—they worship an idol named Irminsul, and I have set myself the task of burning this impudent divinity. I count on your assistance. On my return we will talk about your marriage."

Roland went away sadly to find his Aude.

In the year 771, the Emperor spent Easter at Herstall, and Christmas at Attigny. About the beginning of the year 772 he convened his nobles at Worms, placed himself at their head, and invaded Saxony. This land, subdivided into numerous petty states, was inhabited by Westphalians, Osterlindsi, Sclaves, Hungarians, &c. All these tribes were driven back to the Baltic, their idols were destroyed, and their lands devastated. Compelled to sue for peace, they came in and did homage on the banks of the Weser.

Charlemagne, who was no less terrible to his wives than to his enemies, got rid of Desiderade, his second queen, and determined to marry a third. He was of this mind when Roland once more sought him.

"Sire, since you have given me encouragement to hope, I come to remind you that I love Aude, the niece of Gerard of Vienna, your friend, and that you have promised her to me in marriage as a reward for conquering Angoulaffre. You desired me to follow you to Saxony, and I did so; no one can say, surely, that I was sparing of my person in the campaign. You have often spoken severely against marriage, but I understand you have changed your views, since you are, for a third time, going to do yourself what you used to say was bad for others. I am your sister's son.

A royal roar.

I have served you to the best of my ability, and every one agrees that the ability of Roland is no trifle. Will you not please to fix a day for my nuptials?"

A kick for Cupid.

Charlemagne was in a particularly good humour that day. He burst out laughing at his nephew, and said—

"By my beard and sceptre, I believe this youngster is going to set me to school. My friend Ganelon was right when he had me beware lest this rogue should lead me by the nose. So-ho! my warrior, have I not made you Count of Mans and peer of the realm? Have not I granted you the Marches of Brittany? And must I now reward you for the blows you have struck in defence of your own precious hide? No, my fine nephew; I don't approve of people who try to force my game. Besides, I have a notion, after my marriage, of making an excursion in the direction of

97

Lombardy. You will accompany me. When we come back we will see what is to be done."

This year (772) Charles kept the festivals of Easter and Christmas at Herstall, on the Meuse. About this period Didier, King of Lombardy, invaded the states of St. Peter. Coming at the head of ten thousand stout lances, he laid siege to Rome. Pope Adrian did not lose heart for a trifle like that. He closed the gates of the Eternal City, carefully inspected the walls, and manned them with troops, determined to perish amid the ruins of his capital rather than surrender.

Then he sent a deputation of bishops and men of distinction to Charlemagne, to remind the son of King Pepin that he was a Roman noble, and that it was his duty to defend the Church in the person of its supreme head. The Emperor was not desperately fond of his ex-father-in-law, at whose court all his enemies found refuge. He had long meditated an expedition in his direction, and so, accepting with joy this providential chance, he convened a full court at Paderborn. The expedition was resolved on enthusiastically, and Geneva was chosen as the rendezvous of the forces. The army was divided into two sections. Bernard, Charlemagne's uncle, had command of one column, with orders to cross Mount Joux (St. Bernard), and open a campaign in the plains of Milan, while the Emperor led his half of the army over Mount Cenis.

In vain did Adalgisus, son of Didier, attempt to defend the passes of the Alps. He was everywhere repulsed, and was hemmed in at Pavia, where his father joined him (October, 773). Pavia was then a castle, which would well have deserved the reputation of being impregnable if it had not (as is the case with all impregnable places) been taken several times. Nevertheless, it displayed some coquettishness in the matter, never permitting itself to be captured till after a wearisome war; for it required no less than a whole winter to scale its walls, which were seventy feet high, to carry its seventeen gates, and make oneself master of its sixty-two towers.

Charlemagne went to Rome to spend the Holy Week. He entered it in triumph on the 2nd of April, 774. A grand procession of bishops and nobles went out to meet him at Novi, and accompanied him to

Pavia in peril.

St. John at the Lateran, where Adrian waited to receive him. The crowd hailed him as a preserver. He was surrounded by banners and crosses; people of distinction vied for the honour of carrying his victorious arms; and little children, dressed in ancient costume, strewed flowers in his horse's path. The Pope and the Emperor embraced, and the latter, after having taken the sacrament, visited, attended by his suite, all the sacred spots in the great capital of the Christian world.

A council was called, at which one hundred and fifty-three bishops and priests assembled to assist the Pope in conferring on Charlemagne the most extensive powers and privileges.

During this time famine was making fearful havoc in Pavia. Every day people died of starvation in hundreds, but the town did not surrender. Charlemagne was not one who liked to see work long about. He quitted Rome and assumed the command of the army, and a few days after Didier was forced to surrender. Neither his courage nor his submission could appease the Emperor, and the conquered prince, his head sprinkled with ashes, had to kneel to his new lord. The last of the Lombard kings became a monk, and finished his days, under the name of Brother Desiderat, in the monastery of Corbie. Ansa, his wife, the two sons of Carloman, and Gerberge their mother, with

Desiderade, the divorced wife of the King of the Franks, all fell into Charles's hands, and he condemned them to the cloister. Lombardy was thus made the property of the crown of France.

Aude and Mita had retired to Paris, where they awaited mournfully the return of Roland and Miton. Here the Countess of Rennes gave birth to a marvellously beautiful boy, who was christened Mitis. Never was a baby made so much of. Nothing was good enough for him. The two women, left to themselves, formed endless projects, and counted with impatience the hours which seemed to pass so slowly. But one day the weeping attendants made their appearance, bearing the dead body

Brother Desiderat.

of the little cherub. They related that a knight, with his visor closed, had attacked them and snatched the child from his nurse; that, without regarding their cries or supplications, he had made his way at full galop to a neighbouring stream, where he had dismounted, and, thrusting the child into the water, had held it down with his foot for some minutes. Despite the threats he uttered they came up with him, but too late. The monster, having lifted the corpse ashore with his foot, remounted his horse and fled.

The drowned darling.

The despairing ladies.

The two sisters were for a long time like a couple of mad women. So excessive was the grief of each that one might fairly have asked which was the mother of the murdered babe.

Now it happened that on the day of the murder Ganelon had passed through Paris on his way to Brittany.

The Saxons, taking advantage of Charlemagne's absence, had invaded the territory lying between the Rhine and the Weser. The Emperor, but just returned from Lombardy, sent against them four formidable armies; then, having held an assembly at Duren, he placed himself at the head of a fifth column and crossed the Rhine (775). He made himself master of Eresburg, and left a garrison there to hold it, and next defeated at Brunsberg the masses of Saxons that endeavoured to stop his passage of the Weser. He advanced as far as the Oder, cutting the Westphalian forces into pieces on his route, and then marched back after having reinforced the garrison of Eresburg, which was to serve as a prison for his Saxon captives.

This year Hildegarde presented Charlemagne with a daughter, who was christened Rotrude. The Emperor was so delighted with her that Roland ventured to renew his request.

"Sire, you bade me share the campaigns in Saxony and Lombardy, and I did my duty to the best of my power. Is it not time—"

"My dear nephew, spare your eloquence. I see you coming, and begin to know your petition by heart. Well, by St. Nazaire! I will grant you the request you press so warmly. In one month you shall be wed."

Five days after they had to mount, and march for Italy again. Rotgause, Duke of Friuli, and Adalgisus, son of Didier, had resolved to attack Rome and Italy by sea and land (776). Charles once more crossed the Alps, took Rotgause a prisoner, and, having cut his head off, handed over the government of Friuli to one of his French nobles, the Count Markaire. Then he set out for Worms.

One day the Emperor was riding at the head of his army, with Roland beside him. They were marching alongside of a splendid corn land. The reapers, terrified at the sight of the soldiers, had flung down their sickles, and fled; but, their curiosity restoring them their courage to some degree, they ventured to watch the column from a safe distance.

"Have you never, sire, envied the lot of these peasants?" asked the Count of Mans.

Charles looked at his nephew in wonderment, thinking he was gone mad.

"When once their work is over," continued Roland, "they return to their homes to find a wife waiting on the threshold to embrace them, and a bevy of children who storm them for kisses; while we—"

"I understand you, nephew mine. This is a new way of putting it that you are trying, and if I let you have your talk out, it would infallibly end in the old question, 'When is the marriage to be?' I am not more hard-hearted than most people; and, by the mass! on my return—"

The Emperor paused. He had just caught sight of a whirlwind of dust a long way off. By degrees the whirlwind lessened to a cloud—the cloud turned into a horseman—the horseman proved to be Hugo of Cotentin.

The haste of Hugo.

The Count Palatine had spurred fast to tell Charles that the Saxons were again in revolt, and were ravaging the banks of the Rhine.

Roland sighed. "Aude—dearest Aude!" said he, "shall we never be united except in Paradise? If I thought so, I would hasten the period, and get myself killed in the very next fight."

102

The lion and
the assassin.

But I should never finish my story if I were to relate to you all the expeditions of Charlemagne against the Saxons. He was always crossing the Rhine, sweeping away whole nations, receiving their submission, and taking hostages; but scarcely had he turned his back before he heard the growlings of a fresh eruption. You will learn all this from pages more serious than mine. I will only add, that in 777 Charlemagne assembled the Saxons and their rulers at Paderborn, and that a great many came, and were baptised.

I must now resume my story.

Charlemagne is at Paderborn, surrounded by his Court. Hildegarde had borne him a son, who received the name of Carloman. Aude was more lovely than ever. Miton was now thirty-two, Mita twenty-seven, and Mitaine eight. Oghris was growing old now. His coat was turning silvery. He now required a long ten minutes to quarter an ox, but his claws were still good. He had taken a mighty fancy to Mitaine; and often, when they had tried to separate them, the lion had grown so thin, and the child so melancholy, that they were compelled to abandon the idea.

The god-child of Charlemagne had often been made the aim of assassins, and, without doubt, the same fate was intended for her that had befallen her brother. But Oghris was always at hand, and the murderers had to take to flight. On one occasion, however, one of them had not got off quickly enough, and so paid the penalty for the others.

"Now, at last," said Miton, "I shall understand the meaning of all this!"

Unfortunately, the lion had not thought of this, and his victim was reduced to such small fragments that nothing could be discovered from them.

Charles flew into a great rage on hearing of the attempts to which his god-child had, more than once, nearly fallen a victim.

"By Joyeuse! he who touches my god-child is a bold man. Tell me, Mitaine, have you no indication to give me which might put us on the track of this devourer of babes?"

"None, my lord; the monster appears and disappears as if by magic."

"Well, be he fay, ogre, or vampire, I swear to Heaven I will deliver him into your hands. But until it is in our power to hang, draw, and quarter him, how shall we distinguish this monster, who wishes to devour you, by name?"

"Let us call him Croquemitaine!"

"So be it. Well, then, Croquemitaine shall be hanged: take my word for it."

In the year 777 Charlemagne celebrated Easter at Nimègue.

II. The King of Beauty.

One chronicle which I have discovered, and which is only known to me, assures us that Charlemagne was devotedly fond of children. It was his pleasure one day to call a couple of hundred of them together, in his royalty of Paderborn, and say to them—

"You are the masters here, and my servants are at your disposal. Make hay of all the flowers in my gardens, and my gardeners shall assist you. Plan a dinner tremendous enough to kill my friend Guy of Burgundy with indigestion, and my cooks are under your orders. Ransack my illuminated books; and if by chance you tear them, Eginhard will restore them so that it can't be detected. Break the silver strings of the queen's harp, and they shall be replaced before she suspects mischief. Command, bully, pillage, if you like, to your hearts' content. There is but one thing I forbid"—and Charles, knitting his great brows, spoke in a voice of thunder— "one thing I forbid, do you hear? I forbid you to put yourselves out of the way in the slightest degree."

This speech was calculated to raise the wildest enthusiasm. In a moment the palace was ravaged. Mad with liberty, the little folks rushed hither and thither, pillaging everywhere at random, and to no purpose, like silly butterflies. The happiness of being free to do what they pleased was enough.

It was indeed a deafening tumult, an unequalled outburst of jollity. They tore down the hangings; they broke open the aviaries; they smashed the statues; they ransacked the sideboards; they tore up the flowers— until, at last, by degrees, their impetuosity wore itself out. At the end of an hour the children, left to themselves, and having nothing more to destroy, could not invent any means of amusing themselves.

When the Emperor returned he found his little visitors scattered throughout the palace, tired, idle, and melancholy. Charles called them

105

Charlemagne at his capitularies.

all round him, and inquired if they were all enjoying themselves. The children hung down their heads without answering. He repeated the question with the same result. At last Mitaine, more confident than the rest, opened her mouth—

"God-papa—not to keep anything from you—we don't know what to do, and were never so bored in all our lives."

"My children," answered Charlemagne, "let this be a timely lesson to you. In pleasure, as in war, everything goes wrong without a clever commander. To play well, just as to fight well, you need a captain. Choose some one who shall be general of your games; and, by my beard! you will see that all will go well."

"Beloved sire!" said the children, trooping round him, "choose our general for us."

"I will," said Charles; "but you must at least promise me to obey him whom I select."

"We will! we will!"

Charles perceived a fair boy of twelve in the crowd; and, taking him gently by the ear, he led him out, and presented him to his small subjects.

A wounded warrior.

"Here is the little king I offer you. Obey him as you would me; and as for you, Joel the Fair, will you take my advice?"

"I permit you to offer it, cousin," said the youngster, drawing himself up grandly.

"Then, sire, since you deign to listen to me, accept this hint. Would you rule without discomfort, sleep without fearing some evil dream, and live at ease?"

"That would suit me nicely!"

"Well, then, Joel the Fair, make yourself beloved!"

"We will take care to do so," said the boy, and immediately gave one of his subjects a rare buffet for leaning too familiarly on his royal shoulder.

Charlemagne withdrew to rejoin Eginhard, Theodulph, Leidrade, and Alcuin, with whom he had shut himself up to work at his code of laws. But he had hardly been in his closet half an hour when a great hubbub was heard under the windows; shouts, laughter, and cries were mingled together, and soon rose to such a pitch that the Emperor rose, curious to see what was the cause of the tumult, and went to the window.

I can assure you, young people, that he was not a little astonished to see Mitaine fighting with a big boy, whom she had just thrown down and was kneeling upon.

The lady and her knight.

107

"So, Master Joel, you have a strange way of ruling," said Charles, opening the window. "Is this the way in which you ensure the peace of your dominions? What is the meaning of this?"

The tumult ceased. Mitaine released her victim, and Joel advanced and addressed Charles.

"I must remind you, sire, that you promised us uninterrupted liberty, and I have therefore some right to feel astonished when you interfere with my kingdom. What would your Majesty say if the King of Saragossa or of Persia were to question you about your doings in your own realm? However, I have not forgotten that it is to you I owe my crown, and as I am a gallant prince, I will consent to answer your questions. We had determined to hold a tournament, and in order that it might be done in a manner becoming my state, I first chose myself a court. It is composed of those whom you see yonder, half-inclined to quarrel over the scrag-end of a pie. I armed my knights— those are they on the lawn yonder, where they are now holding gallant encounters, which will prove to you I have chosen well. I improvised arms as I had invented knights. The ladies chose their gallants. Mitaine was unanimously elected Queen of Beauty, and she selected for her knight that big boy to whom she has just been giving such thumps. The trumpets sounded, and I took my place on the throne with a majesty that could not have failed to please you. The jousts commenced, and all went well enough. Riolet received a blow on the eye from Charlot, which lends quite a martial air to his visage; Loys has had two teeth knocked out; and Ode has left two handfuls of hair on the field. We did not expect it to stop here when Berart, the chosen cavalier of Mitaine, entered the lists. He presented himself proudly, and arrogantly defied Odille, who, without disturbing himself, gave him a kick on the shin, so dexterously applied that the unhappy youth lost heart and ran away. At this sight Mitaine was transported with anger, and jumping quickly down from her throne, she rolled the astonished and terrified Berart in the dust; and then, turning on his opponent, upbraided him for his cowardice—in short, you can see what has befallen poor Odille. For my part, I abstained from placing any obstacle in the way of Mitaine's triumph. She was hitherto our queen by virtue of her rank and beauty: now she has won the title by her courage also."

Charlemagne laughed for seven minutes without stopping—so says the historian—as he had never laughed before. Then he called his god-child to him.

"By my sceptre! this is the conduct of a heroine, and you shall be well rewarded. It seems to me that a triumphant march would be about the right thing at this period. What thinks our brother Joel of the proposal?"

"Excellently said, sire. Let there be a march of triumph."

"There's only one thing that puzzles me. If we crown Mitaine for her valour, we shall have no Queen of Beauty."

The Emperor
laughs!

"By my beard, sire," said little Joel, stroking his smooth, twelve-year old chin, and aping Charles to the best of his ability— "by my beard, sire, you are puzzled about trifles."

Then he went in search of his friend Riolet, whose eye was getting blacker every minute.

"What do you say to a King of Beauty like that? It is but right that both sexes should have their part in the triumph as usual.

"What a philosopher he is!" said Charles, laughing till the tears ran down his face. "Let Oghris be brought—he is the only animal worthy to carry my courageous god-child. And you, rival and discomfited knights—it is to you, Berart, and you too, Odille, that I am speaking—go, conduct your conqueror in triumph. But now, what are we to do with the King of Beauty, brother?"

Joel, without answering, called on four knights to volunteer, and placed Riolet on their shoulders, the pain and confusion making him pull some very strange grimaces. In this fashion the procession set out amid loud laughter and cheering.

In the evening Charles took Miton aside with him, and said, "Learn, my friend, that our Mitaine is not intended to wear a petticoat for

109

long. A sword will suit her hand better than a needle. The secret attacks from which, thank Heaven, she has till now escaped unhurt may be renewed, and I would fain have her under my own guardianship. I have an offer to make to you, Count of Rennes. Give her to me for a page, and I will have her brought up to the use of arms. I am greatly mistaken if I do not thus rear a staunch supporter of my son."

The offer was accepted, and from the next day Mitaine, to her delight, took rank with the pages, whose male attire she adopted.

Mitaine a page.

III. How the Emperor Charlemagne Saw a Vision.

Charlemagne only took repose in order to give others an opportunity of resting. The chronicles tell us that he used to break off his slumbers four or five times during the night, rise, dress himself, and dispatch some matters of business. At Paderborn he occupied a chamber on the ground floor, and was often seized with the inclination to go down into the park, where, being alone with his thoughts, he used to allow himself to become lost in reverie.

Charlemagne
at his prayers.

One beautiful night in the spring he perceived in the heavens what seemed like an immense causeway, paved with stars, which commenced above the Gulf of Friesland and disappeared about the Galician frontier, passing over Germany, Aquitaine, Gascony, and Navarre. Little by little there seemed to him to glitter an unusual number of luminaries; they increased in size, changed their forms, and began to move all in the same direction from the north-east to the south-west, and presently he beheld, moving across the heavens, crowds of armed warriors. He had mistaken for stars the glint of the moon upon their armour. For a whole hour troop succeeded troop; the horses, excited to a mad ardour, galloped among the clouds, raising a dust of star-sparkles with their hoofs. Then all became motionless as at first. The night grew dark and silent, and Charles, lost in reflection, turned his eyes to earth. The sight he saw froze for some seconds the blood in his veins. It appeared like a moving light, which had assumed a human shape—a lingering sunbank

111

Charlemagne's vision.

forgotten by the twilight, and animated by some supernatural power. It advanced slowly, its outline showing clearly against the darkness of the park. At last the Emperor could distinguish a form more beautiful than is granted to the mortal inhabitants of the globe. The figure spoke, and the air became laden with odours. Its voice hushed the songs of the nightingales, who perched on the boughs to listen.

"My son, why have you forgotten me?"

"My lord, who are you?" inquired Charles.

"I am St. James, the apostle, the brother of St. John the Evangelist."

The Emperor fell on his knees.

"You called upon me at the tournament of Fronsac, and promised me a chapel In exchange for Oliver's life, and I heard you. Oliver lives, and nine years have passed and still my bones lie in Galicia, forgotten by Christians and given up to Saracens. You have led your legions to the Roman shores, to the ocean, and to the Gulf of Friesland. One part of Europe only have you omitted to visit: it is that where my bones are laid, and to which you swore to me to make an expedition in my honour. I am sent to you from above. If Heaven makes you the most powerful among the mighty ones of earth, it is that you may accomplish its designs. Arise, then; rescue my remains from profane hands, and open the route for pilgrims to my shrine. Arm your brave Franks, Lombards, Saxons, and Austrians, and march straight for the Saracens of Spain. I shall be with you in danger, and by-and-by you will find me ready to conduct you to Heaven."

The vision vanished. Two hours later Eginhard, coming to seek Charlemagne, found him still upon his knees in the park praying, with tears in his eyes.

Murad's nightmare.

IV. How King Marsillus Saw a Vision.

A short time previous to the foregoing events, Marsillus had a vision at Saragossa.

Come with me now to Spain, my young friends. Do not murmur, for there exists nothing so lovely as Spain, unless it be "the terrestrial paradise," of which I am not in a position to form an opinion.

There the sandal-wood, the spikenard, the saffron, the ebony, and the clove, the most extraordinary flowers, the most delicious fruits, all grow wild. The streams prattle more gaily there than anywhere else, joyfully sprinkling with dewy drops the ever-verdant banks. On all sides trees, clothed with luxuriant foliage, provide shelter for the most musical birds in the world. The choir numbers the tomtit, the nightingale, the phoenix, the turtle-dove, and a thousand others.

Must I, at the risk of making your mouths water, mention a few of the fruits of this marvellous land? What do you say to the fig, the grape, the pomegranate, the almond, the lemon, the pine-apple, the olive, and the orange?

And the flowers!—clumps of roses everywhere, lilies, chrysanthemums! Here, grow ox-eyes; there, spring violets; yonder bloom the narcissus and the balsam. The cool brooklets, abundant and limpid as glass, flow over pebbles as bright as crystal and topaz. There are gardens like those of Persia, minarets like those of Bagdad, a blue sky like that of no other part of the world.

The nights are so delicious, one is sorry to go to sleep. Everywhere are seen wealth, beauty, joy, and plenty! Such is Spain.

All this, however, was ruined by the presence of the Saracens.

Marsillus was taking a nap. He was lying on cushions of priceless material. The pavilion in which he had sought repose was of stained ivory, inlaid with gold. In the midst a joyous fountain diffused coolness around it; while an incense, compounded of musk, ambergris, and camphor, made into a paste with distilled otto of roses, burning in marble bowls, filled the air with sweetness.

All at once the daylight turned sickly pale. A chill like that of the tomb succeeded the agreeable coolness, and the perfumes yielded to

The ghost of Murad.

sickening odours like those of the grave. The flowers faded; all that was brightest became dull and tarnished; and a corpse came and seated itself beside the King of Saragossa. It scarcely retained the human form, being made up of shreds and rags of flesh, and rendered only the more hideous by the gay robes in which it was enveloped.

"My father!" said the corpse, "have you, then, forgotten me?"

Marsillus opened his eyes, uttered a shriek, and after gazing round vainly for some way of escape, sank back motionless, with haggard eyes and bristling locks, and bathed in a cold sweat.

"Is it thus you receive your son, after a separation of ten years? Open your arms to me, beloved monarch, for I hunger for your embrace!"

On seeing Murad approaching him, the terrified Marsillus sprang to his feet, and strove to get out of his way, but in vain. The corpse caught him in its arms, folded him to its bosom, which cracked in a ghastly way with the force of the hug, and covered with cold and clammy kisses the face and white locks of the King of Saragossa, on which they left gory stains!

"Leave me—depart!" shrieked the old man. "What have I done to you, or what would you have me do?"

"I would be avenged on Roland of France."

"I will avenge you, Murad. But now leave me, if you do not wish me to perish on the spot." And Marsillus, putting forth all his strength, freed himself from the embraces of his son, and rushed to the other end of the chamber.

"In truth, my lord, you are not altered. As I left you nine years ago I find you now. You have just asked me two questions. I will answer them. You have asked what I would have you do? To that I answer, Avenge my death! I would see this accursed Roland and his friends punished in a way that should never be forgotten by the rest of mankind. I am astonished that so affectionate a father and so just a king should have been so long thinking about vengeance. Your other question was, 'What had you done to me?' Those words, by the Prophet! should have died away on your lips; but since your conscience does not assist your memory, I will take its place. You do not question, of course, my dear lord, that death reveals everything to us? One has reason to complain of it not so much because it takes us from this world, as because it places the past before us in naked truth—brings in review before us all our errors and our beliefs—and teaches one, for instance, that one has had such a father as you."

Marsillus dug his nails into the wall, against which he had placed his back, as if he would fain scoop out for himself some place of refuge.

Murad continued:— "While I was a child, happily for me, I did not occupy any place in your life; but from the hour when you saw me return the conqueror of the lioness and her cubs, you began to keep an eye on me. I grew up under your personal superintendence, and if the queen, Hadrama, my mother, had not at times pressed me to her bosom, I believe I should have become a wild beast, and not a man. My name became famous; the prodigies of my valour, my wisdom, and bravery won you many kingdoms. In a short time I had doubled your empire. Your jealousy increased with my fame, until, unable to look undazzled at the glory of my renown, you determined to make away with me. From that moment I had to encounter a thousand plots—a thousand treacheries, over which I triumphed by a miracle, but of which I never once suspected the origin."

Marsillus would fain have denied this, but his voice stuck in his parched throat.

"Your slaves one day found a huge snake, a venomous monster, which they at once slew. It was a female, and would have left twenty little ones to lament her loss if you had not considerately ordered the destruction of the whole family. The father alone escaped. Once in possession of this little stock of poison, you asked yourself how you could best dispose of it, and being neither selfish nor thoughtless— you see, I do you the fullest justice—you were not long in remembering me. Your creatures took the twenty young snakes and scattered them from their nest to my room, where they concealed the mother's body under my bed. As soon as night came, the male snake traced from corpse to corpse the path you had so obligingly mapped out for him, and, full of fury, arrived almost at the bed where I was sleeping. I will spare you the recital of what followed, for it would wring your heart. All I have to observe is, that on my making my appearance before you next day, you knitted your brows; you were even put out when I laid at your feet the two serpents, one only of which owed its destruction to me. It was fortunate for you that on the previous night I had struck one of your slaves, for it was at once decided that he had attempted to revenge himself on me, and, in your anxiety to see me righted, you sliced his head off before he had time to utter a word in defence."

Marsillus sank on his knees.

The King's revenge.

Murad's maddened steed.

"I shall only briefly recall to you the horse, which, maddened with some noxious drench, almost leaped with me into a bottomless abyss. Thanks to Allah, I did not lose my self-possession, and gave the animal such a blow behind the ear with my fist that he dropped lifeless, sending me rolling within a few paces of the gulf which you had intended for my grave. Next day, on rising, I beheld a startling sight. You had, in your stern sense of justice, ordered the impalement of all my faithful grooms, who were devoted to me, and you replaced them by creatures of your own."

Marsillus hid his face in his hands.

118

"Finally, after ten years spent in futile efforts to get rid of me, you determined to send me to the French tournament, where I met my death. Now I might certainly desire, and insist, that you should pay dearly for your past vagaries; but I offer you pardon, and only ask one thing in return; but that I must and will have."

Marsillus raised his head.

"Angoulaffre, Priamus, Corsablix, and all the other victims who shared my fate, speak to you with my lips. We demand the death of Roland and the knights of Charlemagne. Swear to avenge us!"

"I swear!" murmured the old man.

"Give me your hand on it!" And Murad strode towards him. But at that Marsillus shouted so lustily, that his guards rushed in. They found the King stretched on the ground, his robes dishevelled, and his lips uttering disconnected sentences.

Impalement.

"Don't leave me!—don't leave!" he cried, dragging himself to the feet of the guard. "I have seen Murad! He calls for vengeance! His kisses have chilled my very marrow. You won't leave me?—promise me you won't! If you do, I'll have you all put to death!"

The most experienced physicians were at once sent for. They agreed that His Highness was suffering from brain fever. But as nobody had the courage to convey this intelligence to His Majesty, no attempt was made to cure him; to which circumstance he owed his recovery.

By degrees the dreadful scene vanished from his mind, and in a month he had almost forgotten it.

Marsilus meditates.

119

"Go to war at my age!" said the King to himself. "What nonsense! I have the finest kingdom in the world. Charlemagne leaves me alone: why should I provoke him? Not I, i' faith! I must have had a bad dream, and I must mind I don't get an unpleasant waking-up by going to tweak Charlemagne by the beard. Sleep sweetly, Prince Murad and let me live in peace!"

From that time Marsillus never passed a day without receiving a visit from his son. He had a guard constantly in his presence, but it was no use. Then he tried to discover some means of ridding himself of this frightful spectre; and, at length, one night determined to await its approach resolutely, yataghan in hand.

Marsillus with
Murad's bones.

Murad came as usual, and approached his father but he, with four blows of his sword, sliced off the head, legs, and arms of the corpse. Then he breathed more freely. But the head immediately burst out laughing, while the right arm politely picked up the weapon Marsillus had let fall, and handed it to him.

"Take this yataghan, sire; it is one I wore for a long time—the one, in short, you gave me as a boy. Have you forgotten it?"

The King, more driven to his wits' end than ever, tremblingly flung his son's limbs into a mat, and tied the four corners together. Then he ran at full speed into the garden, accompanied by roars of laughter from the head, which did not cease to move as he bore it. Arrived at the end of the park, he dug six deep holes; put the head in the first, the right arm in the second, the left arm in the third, the right leg in the fourth, the left leg in the fifth, and the trunk in the sixth. Then he threw the earth in upon them, and ran in again, without daring to look behind him.

Marsillus by this means gained a month's respite. But, at last, the Sultana one day begged him to accompany her to the bottom of the grounds, where she had discovered some unknown description of flowers, which gave out an odour so sweet, it was almost impossible to tear yourself away from them when once you had gone near them. The King refused with such evident horror, that the surprised Hadrama only persisted the more, and he had to give way. As he approached nearer, his blood froze in his veins; his eyes were blinded with mist; his teeth chattered horribly. Walk slowly as he would, he *must* at last reach the terrible spot where his son's remains were concealed.

On arriving there, the Sultana said, "See how thick the turf is! Did you ever see anything like it?"

Marsillus at Murad's grave.

To the terrified Marsillus it seemed as if human hair was growing and covering the ground on which he trod.

"Is there anything more delicious than the scent of these flowers?" But Marsillus could only smell the foul odours of a grave.

"See what flocks of birds perch in the branches! Hark! how sweetly they sing!"

But Marsillus seemed but to hear a laugh that came from under the ground. He saw that the leaves of this strange tree were shaped like human tongues, and when the breeze shook them, low voices murmured— "Revered sovereign, avenge my death!"

The King of Saragossa fell on his knees and to his prayers. The big tears ran down his white beard.

121

"Sow sin, and you will reap remorse!" he exclaimed, with his eyes fixed on the earth.

The next day he called together his nobles, and announced to them his intention of avenging the death of Murad!

The delighted Saracens.

V. THE TWO ALCALDES.

Marsillus commenced his address in the following words:—

"May Allah enlighten you, and shed his glory on you, for I have assembled you to a council. Listen to this brief recital, and give me your opinion on it.

"A lion, full of youth and strength, was gaping and yawning enough to put his jaws out of joint. He had done nothing for the day, but yet, wholly given up to idleness, he stretched himself on the warm sand, roasting first one side and then the other in the hot rays of the sun.

An ant happened to pass close by him, painfully dragging a small fly. Seeing such great labour bestowed on so small an object, the lion burst out laughing. 'It is not very becoming in you to make a jest of me,' said the toiler, without ceasing from his task; 'I am weak, but I make full use of the little strength Heaven has given me, while you, who might do anything, are giving way to slumber before you have earned it by fatigue. Leave off smiling, for you are in the wrong. I am stronger and braver than you. Remember, *a busy ant does more than a dozing lion.*'

"Mahomet, who was leaning on a cloud, and happened to hear them, greatly approved of the ant's remarks.

"By the divinity of the Ka'abah, by the shrine of Mecca, are not we like this lion? We pass our lives in sloth and luxury, while the ruler of the Franks is hard at work extending his domin-

Mahomet's approving smile.

ions. The day before yesterday he was in Aquitaine—yesterday he was in Lombardy—to-day he is in Saxony—to-morrow he may be in our kingdom. But do you, the sons of those whom Mussa led along the banks of the Rhone and the Saone—do you feel inclined to sit still and wait his coming? If, gorged with prosperity, you have forgotten the past, the people of Nimes and Arles, of Narbonne and Bordeaux, of Toulouse and Chalons, do not forget it when they gaze on their ruined cities, their desolated cathedrals, their overthrown fortresses. Children of Alsamah, of Abdel-Rahman, Ambissa, and Marsufle, have at the descendants of Charles Martel, Eudes, and Pepin! If these victorious names do not make your hearts leap, will they quail at the recollection of our disasters at Poitiers? The bones of our sires enrich French soil—the harvests the Franks reap have been fattened by the blood of our bravest, which fed the fields. They are ours, but we have been robbed of them. Let us go and win them back again!"

The assembly received this harangue with terrific cheering. Shouts, observations, threats, and warnings were mixed in such inextricable confusion that Marsillus did not know what to listen to. He remarked, however, that two of his emirs held themselves apart and maintained silence. When the tumult had subsided, he beckoned to them to draw near.

"Why do you keep aloof instead of sharing in the general enthusiasm? Answer, Abiathar—answer, Ibn al Arrabi, You are generally more lively when there is a prospect of war."

"Sire" said Abiathar, the Alcalde of Huesca, "I grieve to behold you undertaking an enterprise which will bring you no credit."

A threatening murmur ran through the assembly.

"This is a fearful responsibility you take on yourself," said, in his turn, Soleyman Jaktan Ibn al Arrabi, Alcalde of Saragossa. "Is it not possible you may have reason to repent having called down upon yourself the wrath of the King of the Franks?"

This speech caused such an outburst of anger, that some of Marsillus's knights drew their swords and threatened the lives of the two emirs.

"Verily, I feel no gratitude to you," said the King of Saragossa. "I hope I may attribute the cowardly expressions you have just uttered to your increasing years!"

"In spite of our age, we lack neither strength nor valour," said Abiathar, who turned a ghastly white with sheer rage; "and we prove that, I think sufficiently, by having the courage to talk reason to madmen!"

Several chiefs rushed at them with drawn swords.

"We don't in the least lack strength," said Ibn al Arrabi, as he seized one of the

Marsillus enraged.

most violent of his assailants by the throat, and flung him twenty paces away. "Any one who doubts it can easily try the experiment."

Marsillus descended from his throne, and placed himself between the contending parties.

"Do you," he said to his knights, "reserve your ardour for a more fitting occasion. I thank you for having proved that I was right in relying on your support. As for you, Abiathar, and you, Ibn al Arrabi, I feel obliged to you for your frankness. But your prophetic powers will, of course, have enabled you to guess that I shall confide the defence of Huesca and Saragossa to others. Having, then, no office under the crown, you will be enabled to hear without regret the plans about which you are so full of caution and prudence."

With that he gave them the signal to withdraw. The two emirs bowed and departed. One month after they presented themselves at the Court of France.

The escaping emirs.

VI. CHARLEMAGNE IN SPAIN.

Abiathar and Ibn al Arrabi found Charlemagne at Paderborn, where he immediately accorded them an audience.

"Sire," said Abiathar, "we come, accompanied by a hundred followers, to do homage and service to you. The report of your unrivalled glory has reached even us, and we have arrived at the conclusion that he who accomplishes so many great things must be the favourite of Heaven. We have studied in secret the teachings of your faith, and we have found in them the springs of truth and virtue. They have, in short, convinced us, and inspired us with an ardent wish to become Christians. We would then strive to make proselytes, and, trampling the crescent under foot, would raise the cross on high. Martyrdom in our case almost preceded baptism. Marsillus is in pursuit of us, and has commanded that when taken we shall be subjected to the most hideous tortures. But Heaven has been our aid. We have escaped the executioners who were on our track, and here we are at the feet of the most powerful monarch in the Christian world, asking of him to baptise us!"

These falsehoods made the greatest impression on Charles.

"We come, moreover, sire," said Ibn al Arrabi, "to announce to you that Marsillus is busily preparing a religious war, and is ready to invade your realms. We do not bring, it is true, the ordinary gifts of envoys—gold, jewels, and fine merchandise but we do what is better,

127

we bring you Spain as a present. The chief people of Huesca, Valentia, and Saragossa are yours. These cities are devoted to us and wait but our signal to tear down the crescent and erect the cross. We announce ourselves from this moment to be vassals of the Crown of France, and we undertake to show to you the only four practicable passes of the Pyrenees which exist—those of Barcelona, Puycerda, Pampeluna, and Toulouse. The Christians in Aragon, Castille, and Leon, are ripe for revolt. At the first hint they will descend from the inaccessible fastnesses in which they find shelter, to join your triumphant armies. In Asturia and Catalonia the standard of the cross is ready to be displayed. Call together, therefore, a large army, and hasten to anticipate the measures of those who wish to take you by surprise."

Charlemagne was so delighted that he clasped the two emirs in his arms, and kissed them on the cheek and chin. Subsequently he presented them to his peers, knights, and bishops, and invited a new recital of the intelligence they had brought him. They acceded to his request.

"It is St. James who has sent them," said the Emperor; adding, "he shall not have to wait, I swear by Our Lady!"

The war had been resolved upon more than a month, when the two alcaldes arrived at Paderborn. They soon beheld the forces which Charles had called together marching in from all quarters.

You must know, my young friends, that the nobles who held fiscal territory—that is to say, belonging to the Crown lands—were bound to hold themselves always in readiness for warfare, to present themselves at the first summons, with their contingents of men-at-arms, at the place where the sovereign ordered them to assemble. Charlemagne had never made such gigantic preparations as he did for this Spanish expedition. He called together the whole of his faithful vassals of Neustria, Burgundy, Austrasia, Germany, Bavaria, Septimania, and Provence; he even summoned the Lombards, although they had only just been reduced to submission.

It was the beginning of spring, a time which the Emperor thought favourable for commencing his campaign. He set out for his country estate of Casseneuil, in Poitou, whence, after celebrating Easter, he marched to Spain at the head of the most wonderful army he had ever led.

The two Saracens, who were present at the inspection of this vast force, were astounded at it. There passed before them two hundred thousand soldiers, armed in a hundred different styles, according to the fashion of the country from which they came, — and they had come from every part of Europe. Then followed the machines of war — towers, balistae, onagri,* scorpions, and catapults. Next rode the paladins, the nobles and knights of the realm, followed by the bishops, priests, and clerks of the Chapel Royal. When Charlemagne appeared, clad in his panoply of war, the Saracens shook with terror.

"All is over with Spain," said they, shedding abundant tears. "What people, what cities, what fortresses could resist such armies? An iron tempest is about to burst over the heads of the children of the Prophet. What could we do in this world after that? Let us return and die in the land that gave us birth."

And the Saracens, without waiting to see the end of the spectacle, rode off at full gallop. At a later period they were recognised among the slain before the walls of Saragossa. The Emperor divided his army into two columns. One, consisting of the Lombards and Austrasians, marched from Narbonne under the command of Count Bernard, entered Spain at Perpignan, marched along the coast to Barcelona, and overran Catalonia as far as the Ebro. The second column, composed of the flower of the army, knights and nobles, and commanded by the Emperor in person, crossed the Pyrenees from Gascony and Navarre, and sat down before Pampeluna, whither in his turn came Count Bernard.

The siege lasted three months, and was carried on with great losses on both sides, until one day Charlemagne, being at prayers, petitioned Heaven to allow him, since he had entered Spain for the glory of the Christian faith and the destruction of the Saracen race, to take this stronghold of the infidels, which he would purify, and where sacred

* Onagri were machines which discharged large stones. Scorpions flung showers of arrows, darts, and small missiles.

chants should rise instead of incense offered up to false deities. "Saint James," said the Emperor, "if it was really you who appeared to me — if I have rightly obeyed the orders you gave to me — intercede for me that I may win this city."

He rose, comforted in his mind, ordered an assault, and on that day Pampeluna fell. One hundred thousand Saracens received baptism; all who wished to persist in error were put to death.

The Franks marched along the banks of the Ebro and laid siege to Saragossa, which made as stout a resistance as it could; but it was fated to fall, as Pampeluna had done. The Saracens, growing alarmed at Charlemagne's success, submitted. Alcaldes and emirs came in from all sides to render homage to the Frank monarch; even those who could not come sent him hostages and tribute.

Charles overran the whole of the north of Spain with his victorious army. From Catalonia to Galicia, and extending to the line of the Ebro, he was everywhere received by, rather than took possession of, cities and fortresses. Arriving at Compostella, he paid a devout visit to the sepulchre of St. James, according to his promise, and had baptised there those of the Galicians who had forsaken the faith of their forefathers for the service of Mahomet. He established priests of the Holy Church in all the chief towns of Spain, and assembled in the month of July a council of sixty bishops and a parliament of peers, by whom it was decided that all the archbishops, bishops, kings, and princes of Spain and Galicia, present or future, should recognise the authority of the Archbishop of Compostella. The church was dedicated to St. James, Turpin officiating. It was endowed by means of a tax of four deniers per annum imposed upon the innkeepers, and was released from all feudal service. The King also declared it to be his wish that all the bishops of the country should be ordained, and all the kings crowned, by the archbishop of the diocese.

In this way the King discharged his obligation to the saint. This done, he pursued his route to the southern extremity of Spain, now known as Cape Finisterre. There, finding he could advance no further, he flung his lance into the sea, and returned thanks to Heaven and St. James for having aided him to bring his expedition to a successful issue. The gold and silver which the Emperor brought back with him from Spain enabled him to restore and found many churches—to wit, one to Our Lady at Aix-la-Chapelle, and also of St. James; a second of St. James at Beziers; a third at Toulouse; a fourth in Gascony, between the village of St. Jean de Sorgeat and Ax; and, finally, one at Paris, between the Seine and Montmartre, of which nothing remains but the lofty tower known as the St. James's Shambles. The Emperor divided his new provinces into two Marches, called those of Septimania and Gascony. The first, which consisted of Catalonia proper, had its capital at Barcelona; the second, embracing Navarre and Aragon, had Saragossa as its seat of government. To Louis of Aquitaine, Charlemagne's son, was committed the task of keeping the country in submission as far as the Ebro.

"Pass on!"

The one-eyed assembly.

VII. THE TRAP.

Mitaine had followed Charlemagne into Spain. She was now so skilful in the use of her sword that her want of strength was not noticeable. She rode well, and easily bore the weight of hauberk and suit of mail, casque and greaves of steel. She only needed wings to be so like, as to deceive the spectator, one of the armed cherubs who accompany the Archangel Michael.

Charlemagne who had not forgotten the attacks of which Mitaine had more than once been the object, gave her a command of twenty men, under pretence of rewarding her for her good services. It was, in reality, a body-guard which he established about her.

From this moment, then, please to picture to yourselves our fair young friend marching proudly at the head of her twenty veterans.

The precaution was a wise one. It happened, however, that Mitaine one day wandered forth beyond the bounds of the camp. Night overtook her in a forest, which, however lovely by daylight, was not at all an inspiriting spot at night.

She dismounted in the midst of a glade, where she resolved to await the return of day rather than venture further. It was so dark that the Old Gentleman himself—sharp-sighted as he is—could not have seen his tail before him or behind him.

Mitaine stretched herself on the sward, sleeping with one eye and waking with the other. Before long the moon showed herself above the horizon, but her light could scarcely penetrate the thick foliage, and only lighted imperfectly some portions of the thicket.

Mitaine heard approaching footsteps, and was instantly on the alert. "What a fool I am!" she said to herself, after listening for a few seconds; it is my horse trampling on the broken branches." Again she heard it: it was impossible for her to close her eyes. All was now silent, but the silence alarmed her more than the noise. Three times she called her steed— "Vaillant, Vaillant, Vaillant!" A distant neigh was the only response. She rose and went on tiptoe to inspect the spot where she had tied up her horse, but her horse was gone. Then she fancied she could make out under one of the trees a human form—a little further off another,—a third—in short, she counted eight. She saw them move, and come towards her in a circle, which narrowed every moment. She drew her sword, and rushed on them; but soon found herself seized by powerful hands, which grasped her like a vice. Nevertheless she did not lose heart, but began to fight and struggle, to bite and hit out to such effect that, if the night had been less dark, one might have seen a writhing mass of human forms struggling fearfully. Every time when they thought they held her prisoner she contrived to break loose. It was no easy work for the attackers or the attacked, for none of them could see a bit. One would have declared it was blind men quarrelling over their booty.

"Why don't you use your weapons?" said a sinister voice. The speaker was merely a spectator of the combat.

"It is easier to say use your weapons than to do it," answered one of the ruffians. "One can't see a bit, and the young demon goes on so that we don't know how to get hold of her."

Mitaine continued to lay about her on all sides until one of her opponents cried out, with a fierce oath, "Curse the girl! she has stabbed me in the eye!" And the wounded man in his fury, listening only to the voice of rage, struck out wildly and hit one of his comrades, whereupon ensued a general *mêlée*, of which the young girl availed herself to escape.

"Farewell, Croquemitaine!" she cried; "he will have to be swift of foot who overtakes me in running." But instead of making her escape she climbed into a tree, and hid herself among the branches.

"Follow her! I swear by the Evil One that I'll hang every one of you if she escapes!"

Mitaine now heard her enemies groping among the underwood, trying the holly and juniper bushes with the points of their swords, until at last the sound died away, and she heard no more. However, she determined on remaining in her place of concealment until dawn.

"I shall know how to recognise you this time, Master Croquemitaine! One of your fellows has lost an eye, and I have noticed that they have a Westphalian accent," said the brave girl, as she reached the ground. "If Heaven conducts me safely to the camp of my royal sponsor, you shall be uncloaked, I will promise you on my faith!"

She knelt down, breathed her matin prayer, and resumed her way, trusting to Providence to recover her right path. When she had walked for about an hour she heard distant shouts, and the blast of a horn.

"Who can tell what I may have to encounter now? Prudence is not cowardice; so I had better conceal myself, and reconnoitre."

Again Mitaine climbed into a tree, and watched. Before long she saw a party of soldiers approaching, exploring the forest, beating the bushes, and shouting to the full extent of their lungs. She then heard her own name, and recognised her father, who, in great alarm, headed the searchers in person. She was not long in descending from her perch, I assure you. How delighted she was to fling herself into Miton's arms!

For a minute they occupied themselves in exchanging embraces and broken sentences, to which neither thought of listening, and which had to be begun afresh as soon as the first outbreak of joy was over. The Count of Rennes related his

The meeting of Miton and Mitaine.

fears at not seeing his beloved child return on the previous evening, his alarm when Vaillant returned home alone, and how he had spent the night in searching the forest. Having said thus much, he allowed his words to give place to renewed caresses.

When they were once more on the move, Mitaine informed her father of the dangers she had escaped. She also recited her adventures to Charles.

The Emperor listened attentively, and then said to Miton—

"Count of Rennes, send out in every direction, and bid them bring before me, dead or alive, all the one-eyed men within ten leagues round."

Bodies of cavalry were dispatched in every quarter, and acted with such vigour, that by the next morning early forty blind men awaited His Majesty's inspection. They were of all races—Franks, Jews, and Saracens. Charles examined them carefully; and when he had rejected those who seemed to him to have been blind for a long period, or those whose presence in camp for two days past was established on good evidence, he remarked, with great astonishment, that there only remained ten men in the livery of the Count of Mayence, and that they were all recently wounded in the right eye. The emperor knit his brows, and sent for Ganelon.

"Prithee, friend, can you explain to me how it is that all your men here have become blind since yesterday, and all of the same eye, too?"

"Nothing can be more simple. Because I am short-sighted."

"You dare jest with me!" shouted the Emperor, with a voice of thunder.

"Heaven preserve me if I should!" said the count, with a low reverence. "Your Majesty will perceive that there is nothing in this at all unnatural. Having very weak sight, I am always seeking for anything that will strengthen it. I have tried all remedies, and have found only quacks in France. One physicked me; another bled me; a third invoked the devil; a fourth sent me to take the waters at Aix-la-Chapelle—"

"Speak no evil against those waters!" interposed Charlemagne, who frequently had recourse to them, and believed in them firmly.

"Some put the bones of St. Ursula on my eyes; others wished me to remain for five years in complete darkness. I had quite given up all hope of any good results, when chance flung in my way a Saracen more learned than Esculapius, or even Hermes Trismegistus himself. This wise person explained to me that in all things it was necessary to make the most of your powers; that I had only a certain strength of vision to dispose of, and that in dividing it between my two eyes I employed it without profit. It would be better for me to have one eye that saw as well as two, than two eyes which only saw as well as one; and he recommended me to have one eye put out. His discourse appeared to me so full of logic and common sense, that I gave him his freedom."

"But that does not explain—"

"One moment's patience, sire. The remedy appeared to me good, but extreme; and I confess I hesitated, for fear of committing a mistake which would be irreparable. It was then that I sent for these objects that you observe: they all complained of being short-sighted. I deprived them of their right eyes—"

"And?"

"They can't see any better now than you and I!"

"Speak for yourself, count. If you are short-sighted, I have a tolerably keen vision. It would serve you right, by St. James! if I were to have both your eyes put out for telling me such absurd nonsense. Now, I am neither an Esculapius nor a Hermes Trismegistus; but I am going to prescribe a remedy which will do you a very great deal of good. You will start, with your one-eyed warriors, for Aquitaine, where the air is said to be very beneficial to the sight, and you will take a letter for me to your friend Wolf, and bring me back an answer.

Charlemagne thereupon turned his back on the count, who set out the same night for Toulouse.

The pages' archery practice.

VIII. How Roland Undertook to Carry Saragossa by Storm.

If, my young friends, I have for some few chapters omitted mention of Roland, don't jump at the conclusion that he did not distinguish himself during the war in Spain, for he took the most notable part in it, as you may judge for yourselves.

After three months spent in fruitless attacks, Saragossa still stood as strong as it was on the first day of the siege. The catapults and balistae had become disabled without making the slightest impression on the ramparts.

The scaling parties had been repulsed, and the stormers, hacked in pieces with daggers and lances, had been flung from the walls into the fosse, or fell among the flames of the raging fires—for burning pitch had been flung over the walls until it had covered them with a coating of bitumen as impenetrable as iron.

Roland lost patience. "Prepare everything for the storm to-morrow," said he to Charlemagne. "In one hour the breach shall be made!" And he descended into the fosse with no other arms, offensive or defensive, than Durandal and his shield.

"Whither goes your nephew, sire?" said Turpin to Charlemagne, following Roland with his eyes. "Is he mad, or tired of life?"

"I don't know what he is going to do, but he has bidden me have all ready for the assault, saying that within an hour the breach will be made."

"He will do it, then, sire, as he has said it; and, by my faith! I am grateful to him, for we are beginning to grow mouldy here."

Charles mounted his horse, and began to make his dispositions for the assault. The Saracen sentries on guard on the rampart hardly took any notice of the single warrior who approached the city; but, hearing a great noise, they leant over and saw Roland, who was hammering at the wall with repeated strokes

The wall begins to yawn.

of the pommel of Durandal. The Saracens laughed, and asked one another what the idiot wanted.

"Shall we smash him?" said one of them, preparing to roll a huge stone over the rampart.

"What for?" said another. "Is there any reason to be afraid of him? Shouldn't you like to know what he has come here to do?"

Curiosity is the worst of advisers. The sentinels exposed themselves in order to see better, and four arrows struck them in the face. It was the hour of target-practice with the pages of Charlemagne.

"I am afraid this is likely to make the infidels squint!" said Mitaine, choosing a new arrow.

Roland, heedless of all that was passing around him, continued his work of destruction. The wall began at last to yawn, and the knight to smile, delighted at his success. By-and-by the tremendous hammering excited the curiosity of the besieged, and some of the soldiers, seeing the sentinels leaning over the ramparts and never stirring, were anxious to discover what was so engrossing their attention. They in their turn leant over, and each received an arrow in his ear.

"What do you think of those ear-rings?" said Mitaine, laughing. "Were ever such lovely trinkets seen? Saint Eloi, the goldsmith, could not have fashioned finer!"

During this time Roland redoubled his force. A rent thirty cubits long began to threaten the wall with ruin. Marsillus, who was passing in the neighbourhood, felt the earth tremble beneath his feet. Every blow of the pommel of Durandal made the whole quarter of the city shake to its foundation.

"So, then," said the King of Saragossa, "these wretches have brought new engines of war against us! Why has no one told me of this? Ebrechin, go see what it is, and hasten back with intelligence of what is passing."

The earth continued to quake, and several houses began to tremble to their fall.

"It is not an ordinary balista at work there," said Marsillus. "None of those in use now can deliver such hard blows."

But hardly had the King finished his sentence when a mosque

The fall of Saragossa.

fell in ruins within a hundred paces of where he stood. Then a still more awful noise froze his blood with terror. The breach was made: Roland had kept his word.

The slumbering Prophet.

IX. A TRIP TO MAHOMET'S PARADISE.

While Roland was descending into the fosse of Saragossa, Mahomet was taking his afternoon nap in his Paradise. A houri had rolled a cloud under his head, and he was snoring serenely near the fountain of Salsabil.

The first blow of Durandal's pommel awoke the Prophet

"Come in," said he, turning round, in no pleasant humour at being disturbed. The second stroke put him out still more and he rang for the angel Namous, and inquired of him who dared to make such an uproar.

"Great Prophet," said the heavenly messenger, "it's that Roland at his tricks again. He has undertaken to fling down the walls of Saragossa and I really can't help trembling for the fate of your followers!"

"I must see to this," said Mahomet; "I feel certain you are exaggerating as usual, and that my brave Marsillus will not let himself be beaten by a Christian."

The Prophet stepped down into his observatory, and turned his telescope on Saragossa.

"By the crescent! I never remember anything like it. The dog has the mien of a demigod! I am anxious to see him more closely. Etiquette

141

The Prophet takes an observation.

and propriety will not permit me to go to him. Namous, saddle Borak, and seek Roland. Tell him I shall have much pleasure in seeing him, and don't fail to bring him."

The Prophet's horse was turned out to graze in the Milky Way; Namous called him.

"Come here, Borak. You have browsed enough here; you feed too freely, and will injure yourself A peck of stars ought to suffice you for one feed. We have got to descend to earth, and you can hardly stir. If the Blessed Prophet knew it—" With that the angel sprang into his saddle, and began to ply his spurs. In a quarter of an hour they had left the planets behind them.

When Namous alighted, Saragossa was taken and sacked; and Roland was wondering how on earth to spend the evening. The angel approached him respectfully and said, "I am Namous, the envoy and familiar minister of the Prophet. The Lord of the Ka'abah has noted you chief among the Christians, and he desires a visit from you. Be pleased therefore, to follow me at once."

"Your master does me a great honour, and one of which many of my brothers in arms are more deserving than I. You must convey to him my excuses, and tell him that I lead a very quiet life; that I have my religious duties to attend to; that, in short, I don't go much into society."

"The Prophet will very justly feel surprised and hurt at such an answer. He will demand of me the real reason of your refusal. Are you afraid you may be led astray by the beauties of his paradise?"

"If you had known Aude, my beloved Aude, that foolish notion would never have crossed your mind."

"Are you afraid of a trip through the air?"

"If I thought I might tumble I would set out at once. Fear is a complete stranger to me; but I have heard of it so often that I should be anxious to make its acquaintance."

"You are fatigued with your day's work, perhaps?"

"Offer me an opponent worthy of my sword, and you shall see if it is possible to weary Roland."

The angel bowed, and prepared to spring into his saddle again. The attention of the Count of Mans was attracted by Borak, who fretted, pranced, champed his bit, and pawed the ground, impatient to return to his celestial stable.

"What a fine animal!" said Roland, admiringly.

In truth, one rarely sees one so handsome. Borak was a fine-limbed, high-standing horse, strong in frame, and with a coat as glossy as marble which is constantly laved by a fountain. His colour was saffron, with one hair of gold for every three of tawny; his ears were restless, pointed like a reed; his eyes large, and full of fire; his nostrils wide and steaming, with a white star on his forehead, a neck gracefully arched, and decked with a mane soft and silky enough to make a young girl envious. He had a long, thick tail, that swept the ground.

"It is the Prophet's favourite mount. He has sent it in your especial honour."

Roland was touched at the delicate attention.

"I wished," continued the angel, "to bring you some quieter animal; but Mahomet said you were the best rider he knew, and he was

Roland rides into space.

sure you would be able to master it. At the same time," added Namous, treacherously, "if it be that which stops you, I can provide you with other means of transport."

The Count of Mans simply shrugged his shoulders, and by way of answer leaped into the saddle—despite the weight of his armour—without setting foot in stirrup, or putting hand to mane. Borak swerved an instant, then dashed into space, scaling the cloud-mountains at full gallop. The angel spread his wings, and took the lead.

When Roland recovered the surprise, he was as high as the constellation Scorpio. He felt anger would be out of place; so, assuring himself that Durandal was at his side, he resigned himself to circumstances.

The journey was made without difficulty. Only once was the knight in danger of falling, when Borak, scared by a shooting star, which passed between his legs, almost unseated him with a buck-jump. At

Roland in Mahomet's Paradise.

length, after an ascent of half an hour, the steed paused, while the angel knocked at the largest of the eight gates of Paradise. As soon as it opened Roland uttered a cry of admiration.

How can I—with only human language—describe to you so many superhuman wonders? I ought first of all to tell you that all the faculties of our brave knight acquired an immense augmentation on passing the threshold of Paradise. His sight, for instance, although good enough, had only permitted him on earth to distinguish objects at an inconsiderable distance. Imagine his surprise on beholding clearly and minutely the most tiny creatures six or seven hundred leagues off—and that without the laws of perspective being in the least degree deranged. The same thing occurred with regard to hearing and smelling. He used subsequently to relate the pleasure with which he smelt the perfume of a flower which had just come in bloom in a neighbouring state, while listening at the same time to the song of a bird which was warbling at the opposite pole. His mind, too, had become so enlarged that he felt no inconvenience from this vastly increased acuteness of the senses. At one glance he gazed over two thousand square parasangs of country, each parasang being something larger than a league.

The virgin forests of America are but brushwood compared with those he beheld. On all sides were cities of shining whiteness, surmounted by thousands of spires and cupolas of gold and silver. At the foot of their walls flowed majestic rivers, in which the Rhine, the Euphrates, and the Nile would have been swallowed up. Nothing which troubles the inhabitants of earth existed in this enchanted clime. The lion, the tiger, the serpent, and the leopard were but the ornaments of the forest. They fed upon the green herbage, and submitted to human rule with perfect docility. There was no wind—only a gentle breeze; no storms—only perfumed showers. It was an Italian climate beneath an Egyptian sky!

A winged band, commanded by Israfel, the angel of the resurrection, came to meet Roland.

"The Prophet has sent us to you to announce his approach. Will you follow us, or will you await him here?"

"I will follow you," said Roland, joining the troop. He saw with wonder that the forests retired to make way for him; the rivers changed their courses on his approach. He wished to assure himself that this was not a deception of the mirage, and galloped rapidly towards a lake which lay beside his route. His horse did not refuse the leap, but the water respectfully drew back, and he alighted on level and thickly-blossomed sward.

Israfel, remarking Roland's astonishment, said, "The Prophet has taken care that all here shall do you homage. He is aware that you go through life, as through battle, straight at your mark, and he wished to prove that he knew your tastes and habits."

Roland continued his progress until he met the procession, when he halted to let it pass. The ground, before he was aware of it, rose beneath his horse's feet, and he found himself in a minute on a mound, from which he gazed down on the crowd. Israfel made a sign: two trees at once sprang from the soil, and afforded the knight a pleasant shade. The Count of Mans, in silent astonishment, watched the procession without stirring.

First came a thousand horsemen, each bearing a white and ruby banner, and mounted on a white charger. Next to these came a thousand more, clad in suits of mail, armed with maces, and riding on bay horses; behind them came two thousand Berbers from the regions of Timbuctoo, who brandished lances with green pennons, and bore sword-proof bucklers of rhinoceros hide. Their steeds were as black as their faces. Then followed three thousand more horsemen, with serpent-skin girdles. They carried hide shields, and had bows hung at their saddle-pommels. Long lances, furnished with sharp barbs, gleamed in their hands; their horses were cream-coloured. To these succeeded an army composed of soldiers, as many in number as there are drops in the sky; some were armed with spears or bills, others with javelins or maces. A hundred paces behind these came eight thousand elephants, in ranks of twenty-five abreast, the first line white, the second black, and so on. On the back of each was a tower, containing twenty armed men. Behind these, again, came thirty white elephants, covered with golden stars, and so richly caparisoned you

Mahomet's musicians.

could hardly look at them without winking. On these were borne the favourite wives of the Prophet, twenty on each elephant. Canopies of dazzling whiteness, raised upon silver columns, shielded them from the sun. Ten thousand chosen warriors formed their escort. Last came an endless number of camels, laden with palanquins, whose curtains fluttered in the breeze. Each animal was led by a richly-clad Ethiopian, who held the zimzam, or nose-bridle, in his hands. In each palanquin ten houris, far more lovely than anything you can conceive, fluttered their feather fans. Then followed twenty thousand dancing girls, attired in light drapery, with bare arms and legs. You saw, as they moved, among their tresses and round their necks, coruscations

148

of precious stones, so bright you were compelled to shade your eyes. The bracelets that quivered on their wrists, the bangles that gleamed on their ankles, kept up a musical and enticing tinkling.

Shall I enumerate to you the multitude of female performers on the guitar, the tambourine, and the mandolin, and of the singers as well? Of what use is it to crowd the page with strings of numerals?

These houris were of no common origin. Mahomet had formed their bodies of musk, saffron, amber, and frankincense. Their faces were so radiant with beauty, that they diffused a gentle splendour in the night, like the moon when she mounts above the horizon amid the

The Prophet's elephants.

The houris on camels.

mists of earth. Their voices were so sweet, that every syllable which fell from their lips was precious.

After these beauties came the Prophet, attired in a green robe, and seated on a white palfrey. He was dressed with the greatest simplicity, and far from showily mounted, and yet one felt an inward inclination to bend the knee to him as he passed. On his right hand rode his grandsire, Abd el Motalleb; on his left his father, Abdallah; and he was surrounded by Ali, his cousin and most warm disciple; by Said, his adopted heir; by the four sages of Mecca—Waraca, Othman, Obaydallah, and Zaid; by the fiery Omar, the faithful Aboubeker, and thousands of others just as famous.

A hundred thousand horsemen brought up the rear of the cavalcade.

As the troops took up their positions, the scenery underwent a complete change, unobserved of Roland, who was absorbed in watching the procession. When he cast a look around him, he beheld himself surrounded by mountains whose summits were beyond his ken. These gigantic heights, which were composed of gneiss, mica, agate, onyx, trap, and porphyry, were clothed halfway up by forests whose flora comprised the growths of all climes. The vast baobab spread its branches in close contiguity to an island of palms, which displayed their delicate foliage against the blue sky. The silvery mohonono contrasted well with the dark motsouri; the moupanda-panda of Central Africa, the jacquier of Malacca, the oak of Europe, mingled their boughs. Rivers, whose source was hidden in the clouds, bounded from rock to rock, flinging up at every obstacle crests of feathery spray, spanned by rainbows.

The troops occupied positions on the heights. Roland beheld clouds of warriors proudly occupying apparently inaccessible peaks. The elephants were drawn up in two lines, four thousand in each, and the thirty white elephants of the Prophet's favourites were grouped in front of them. And now angels appeared, who, spreading their wide wings, offered their aid to enable the six hundred chosen beauties to dismount. They alighted close to the Count of Mans, before whom they bowed low, and then took their places on a carpet spread for

The Prophet.

them on his right. The camels came next, and knelt down gently, whereupon the houris sprang from their palanquins with a lightness and grace which astonished Roland more than all. Their feet hardly left an imprint in the sand. Like the favourites of the harem, they also approached Roland, and, kissing the ground before him, ranged themselves on his left. Then like a flood advanced the troop of celestial dancers, tripping along to the sound of castanets, flutes, theorbos, timbrels, guitars, and mandolins, amid loud singing, accompanied by the most lively strains of music.

The animation of their movements increased or diminished according to the rhythm, which they marked by accurate beats of the foot and clapping of hands, in slow or quick time. Their eyes were now filled with soft languor—now darted glances of fire. Balancing themselves from the hips, they swung their bodies and waved their arms with ease and grace. At times a comb, unable to imprison such a wealth of tresses, fell out, and freed locks that were as dark as the night.

But now the Prophet gave the signal: the dances ceased, and the houris flew, like a flock of frightened birds, to take their position opposite Roland, and under shelter of the elephants.

Mahomet, in his turn, drew nearer to the nephew of Charlemagne, who immediately dismounted—an act of courtesy to age he invariably observed.

"May Allah, who has made all things of earth and heaven, of day and night, extend his blessing to you in this world and in the one you inhabit! You are welcome," said the Prophet! "I must ask your pardon for the poverty of this reception, as our meeting has been arranged at such short notice that I have only had time to bring as my suite a few of my immediate followers, and the troops which happen to be my guard of honour for the day. Besides, I feared that in surrounding myself with too great pomp, I might seem to be offering a defiance to a late enemy, whom I only desire to make a friend of. If I have not treated you with more ceremony, it is because I wish to treat you like a brother."

Roland made a wry face, which the Prophet thought it convenient to attribute to the glare of the sun in his eyes, and therefore made a sign to four angels, who immediately flew off and spread a rosy cloud before the luminary.

"I accept your explanation," said Roland, coolly, half doubting whether the Prophet were not making fun of him. "I have equal need of pardon; but if I have come without a fitting retinue, you must attribute it to my desire to answer your invitation promptly."

After this exchange of courtesies, Roland commenced the conversation by saying, "You will forgive me if I beg you at once to inform me what it is that has obtained me the honour of this interview, as I am in a hurry to return to earth. I mount guard to-night in the Emperor's tent, and I never like to fail in the performance of duty."

"Never fear," said Mahomet; "I'll have the sun put back. We have all time for our interview."

"I am all attention."

"There is not a more valiant knight than you living. Your single arm is worth an army. Your judgment is sound, your decision speedy—"

"How much do you expect for this panegyric? I warn you, before you go any further, not to set too high a price on it, as I have a clear estimate of my modest worth."

"I am in the habit of giving far more than I get, so fear not, but suffer me to proceed. In my youth I was called El Amin— 'the Safe Man.' I know that I possess a generous soul, and that none can be more loyal than you."

"This eulogy is evidently the prologue of some treason you are going to ask of me."

"If it be treason to leave a bad cause for a good one, to renounce attempts which are futile, and to accept good fortune when it is offered, I have, in effect, treason to propose to you."

"By the Trinity! but you are putting a high price on compliments for which nobody asked you!"

"I swear by the holy mountain—by the temple of pilgrimage—by the vault of heaven and the depths of ocean—that the divine vengeance is about to fall! nothing can delay it. The convulsed skies shall totter! the uprooted mountains shall move! I swear by the resting-place of the star—"

"Of a truth, here is plenty of fine words!" said Roland, shrugging his shoulders. "When we gallant Christian knights make a statement, they believe us without our having to call in the aid of the sky, and sea, and stars."

"As surely as I overthrew the three idols of Mecca, Lata, Aloza, and Menat, the Christians shall be driven from Spain, and their lands invaded. Their army shall be dispersed, and shall fly shamefully. Their hour is come, and it will be bitter and terrible."

"I have read all that in the Koran," answered Roland, who felt his patience failing him. "But that does not say what you want of me, or why you are thus wasting my time. Since the future is revealed to you, and you are so certain of our approaching overthrow, there can be no obstacle to my returning to my post."

"Yes, the future is ours. You alone delay the coming of the day of glory. We shall conquer, but while you live it will be only at the price of terrible sacrifices that we can purchase victory. Why persist in returning to a world in which death awaits you? I offer you the sovereignty of this realm, its wealth, its women, its warriors. The inhabitants of air, earth, and water, the stars which move in the firmament—all that is gifted with reason or instinct, essence and matter—in one word, everything shall belong to you and owe to you unreserved obedience. If the sun annoys you, the moon shall take its place. Give but the sign, and rivers shall dry up to let you pass. A population more vast than all the nations of earth put together shall live only to serve you. These warriors are brave."

"Of what use is their bravery if they have no enemies to contend with?"

"These horses are more swift than the wind."

"Of what service is their speed, since there is here no goal that I desire to reach?"

"These women are lovely."

"Their beauty is sheer waste, for I do not love them!"

"Durandal is famous on earth, and yet the humblest of these soldiers could cut it in two with the edge of his poniard."

"Enough!" interposed Roland. "I have already told you I am in a hurry. You have not, I imagine, the impudence to suppose you are rich enough in wonders to induce me to commit a base action—your Allah himself would be ashamed of such a thing. You have told me I am the bravest of living knights: should I be so if I feared the death you threaten me with? 'My single arm is worth a whole army,' you add. Have I any right, then, to deprive my comrades of its aid at that moment, of all others, when you profess that they are in danger? 'My judgment is sound:' allow me to offer you a further proof of it by laughing at your menaces, and predicting your complete overthrow. Mahomet and Jupiter will soon meet and shake hands, and the crescent will be sent where the old moons go!"

"You will not listen?"

"I have heard too much already!"

"Behold these lovely creatures, who stretch out their arms towards you!"

"They but make me see how far lovelier my Aude is."

"See the lands I offer you!"

"What is a region of wonders compared with the spot where a man was born?"

"Roland, by the faith of Mahomet! you shall never again behold the land of France!"

"I am a Christian, besides being a Frenchman. The native land to which I aspire is Heaven, and that birthplace you cannot prevent me from beholding once more."

"Infidel hound!" said the Prophet, "I—" But the words were such as Roland could not listen to patiently. Mahomet did not finish his sentence, for the gauntlet of the knight smote him on the mouth.

Roland defies the Prophet.

The sun and the sandy plain.

X. WHEN ROLAND REMEMBERS HIS LATIN, AND THE DEVIL FORGETS HIS.

I am unable to tell you what followed. Even Roland had no clear recollection. When he recovered his senses, he rose and cast his eyes round him, to find himself in the midst of a vast sandy plain, stretching on all sides to the horizon. The sun poured its hostile rays upon him so fiercely, that in a few minutes his armour became insupportably hot. The atmosphere was so charged with electricity, that the plume of his helmet crackled, and gave out sparks. In vain he searched the horizon for a place of shelter—there was nothing to be seen but level plain and blue sky. Gigantic red ants came and went busily—they were the only occupants of this desert. All of a sudden he beheld before him in the distance white mosques, knots of palms, and a seaport with some vessels and others sailing out of the harbour. He saw, too, long at anchor, caravans, which journeyed to the city gates.

Roland felt his courage revive, and set out in the direction of the city. But he did not appear to come any the closer to it; he took to running until he fell down with fatigue on the burning sand. Then the city seemed to turn of a yellow hue, the blue of the sea grew paler, and was lost in that of the sky; the trees vanished, and the Count of Mans found himself once more alone in the desert.

"Why come to a halt?" said he to himself. "Better move forward in any direction at hap-hazard. I can only gain by the change."

He rose, determined to struggle on as long as his limbs would sustain him. What was his surprise to see, in an opposite direction to that he had just been pursuing, a mountain covered with verdure, on the summit of which stood a castle! Three walls of circumvallation surrounded it. At the foot of each flowed a river covered with vessels of war. Three hanging ladders of marvellous workmanship united the three platforms of the fortress, and four bastions guarded the approach to each ladder.

Roland once more pushed on; but as he advanced, the fortress rose into the skies, until, after about an hour's walking, he found himself with nothing before him save the blank horizon of the desert. Then despair seized him. He sank on his knees, crossed himself, and shed four tears, the first he had ever wept. They fell on the sand, and there formed four springs for a stream of cool and clear water. Roland received from this new vigour, and having rendered thanks to Providence, he was preparing to move forward, when he remarked

The phantom fort.

158

Eblis.

with surprise a great stirring of the sand. Little clouds of dust began to rise in all directions, although there was not a breath stirring. Then the sand began to whirl round incessantly, marking a great circle at a short distance from our hero.

As it began to whirl, it heaped itself up, drawn towards the centre by some strange force of attraction. You would have said that some gigantic polypus was sucking up all the sand of the desert. After a few minutes there mounted, still eddying round, a huge column, which grew as Roland watched it, until the summit was lost to sight in the sky.

A hot wind, like the harmattan of the Guinea coast, rose and drove the sand before it in clouds. The sun turned red as molten iron. The pillar of sand at last lost its equilibrium, and fell with a horrible rushing sound. Roland closed his eyes, but he did not recoil. Hearing a great roar of laughter, he instinctively clutched his sword by the hilt. What he saw next induced him to draw it from its sheath.

The sand, in falling, had reared a mound, the base of which formed an enormous circle, in the centre of which Roland perceived, with surprise, a huge monster buried in sand to his waist. It was Eblis, the Devil of the East.

159

His Majesty was a hundred feet in height, which is a respectable size, even for a demon of the highest rank. His black skin, striped with red, was covered with small scales, which made it glisten like armour. His hair was so long and curly, a snake might have lost its way in it. His flat nose was pierced with a ring of admirable workmanship, as you see done to the wild bulls of the Roman Campagna. His white teeth, set with precious stones, gave to his smile a very variegated appearance. His small eyes assumed, one after the other, all the prismatic colours, which made it impossible to sustain his gaze. His ears, which exactly resembled those of an elephant, flapped on his shoulders; but he had, to make up for it, a tail sixty feet long, terminating in a hooked claw, which could have wielded the Monument easily as a toothpick.

Eblis had no other covering than his wings, which were large, soft, and marvellously pliable, and in which he delighted to wrap himself. Conceive, further, that a phosphorescent gleam played incessantly over the monster's skin, and you will easily understand why Roland unsheathed Durandal.

Eblis was writhing with laughter.

"I haven't roared so through all eternity, upon my honour! Here, I say, my little man, do you know you have just done a master-stroke?"

This familiar tone displeased Roland.

"I have just met Mahomet," continued Eblis, "and you have broken five of his front teeth. I have seen a good many prophets in my time, but I vow, on the faith of the accursed, I never saw one in such a rage. I have, in honour of the blow, given three days' holiday in the infernal regions. There will be concerts, balls, hunts, and theatres. I have had written, by one of our best authors, a little comedy in the style of Apollodorus, in the last scene of which Mahomet receives a hundred strokes of the bastinado.

"I have given orders to an army of cooks; you can hear even here a rattle of stew-pans altogether refreshing. I will undertake to let you see we are not so backward in this respect as people pretend. You will meet with many old friends among the guests; we have quite a crowd of visitors just now. My wife, who is a lively one, will be delighted to

160

make your acquaintance. Come, let me present you to her as the best of my friends."

"Babbler!" exclaimed Roland, but little flattered at these marks of friendship. "What right have you to address me in this style?"

Eblis, who was not accustomed to be treated so cavalierly, was dumb with surprise for a moment.

"By my father's horns!" said he, at last, "I must have misunderstood you. Give me your hand, Roland, to disabuse me of the error."

He stretched out his tail to the knight, who, however, only drew back a few steps.

"What, puny wretch!" shrieked Eblis, turning as white with rage as it was possible for one so black to do. "I shall send you back to earth. Do you think I am of the same stuff as Mahomet?"

But here Roland flung his second gauntlet in the demon's face.

"That makes the pair!" said the nephew of Charlemagne, placing himself in an attitude of defence.

"Zacoum Zimzim Galarabak!" shouted Eblis, mad with fury. (You must know that is the most terrible oath that can be uttered in the Saracen tongue.) The earth shook and gaped at Roland's feet. He felt himself launched into space. His armour suddenly became icy cold.

"If I get back without an attack of rheumatism, I shall be lucky," said the knight.

He heard around him the flapping of wings; it was a troop of afreets and djins.

"Reflect, Roland. There is yet time. Mahomet is prepared to forgive you."

All the answer Roland vouchsafed was the intoning of the canticle—

"SUB TUUM PRAESIDIUM CONFUGIMUS."

"In a few moments your body will be dashed to pieces on earth. Remember the wondrous things the Prophet offered to share with you."

"SANCTA DEI GENITRIX; NOSTRAS DEPRECATIONES NE DESPICIAS," continued Roland. And now it seemed to him that, instead of falling at hazard, he was being gently carried. The chorus of afreets and djins was left far behind, but he still heard the sound of pinions.

Roland's descent.

"Set your mind at rest," said a voice so exquisitely musical that Roland trembled to hear it. "I am the Archangel Michael. Our Blessed Lady has sent me to preserve you. She had been touched by your constancy and courage. Repose in safety on my wings, and we shall soon reach earth."

And, in truth, in a few minutes' time the Count of Mans, to his astonishment, found himself before Saragossa. He was at prayer in his tent when he heard the voice of Miton.

"My dear Roland, where are you?" cried the Count of Rennes, anxiously.

"Here I am," said the knight, hurrying to his friend.

"Charlemagne, who knows how punctual you are, seeing you were ten minutes behind your time to take on your guard, has sent to look for you in every direction. You are pale, my dear Count; what has happened to you?"

"I will tell you all about it," said Roland, as he hastened to his post near the Emperor.

Roland hurries to his post.

BOOK THE THIRD.
THE FORTRESS OF FEAR.

The scouts' report.

I. THE FOUR FOES OF CROQUEMITAINE.

Charlemagne had an excellent memory. He never omitted to pon-
der over the dangers to which Mitaine was exposed at every turn. He
had the scene of the late ambush carefully searched by his spies in
the first place, and afterwards by his soldiers. All, on their return,
made the same report. They said the forest was inhabited, and there
was a good deal of talk about a castle called "The Fortress of Fear,"
which was to be found somewhere in the neighbourhood, although
nobody they met with had seen it. None, however, doubted its existence. If a child disappeared, or any cattle were carried off, the trembling peasants said, "The Lord of Fear-fortress had taken them." If a
fire broke out anywhere, it was the Lord of Fear-fortress who must
have lit it. The origin of all accidents, mishaps, catastrophes, or disasters was traced to the mysterious owner of this invisible castle.

"I should like to have the mystery cleared up," said Charlemagne
to himself. "I can hardly resign myself to the belief that it is Ganelon,
my old brother-in-arms."

He called his knights together.

"My faithful champions I need four of you for a perilous adventure. I know not where I am sending you—I know not whether you
will return. Who will risk death for my good favour?"

All the knights at once flung themselves at his feet, each entreating the Emperor to honour him with his choice.

"You place me in a difficult position," said the Emperor, greatly moved; "I see that chance must point out the four champions. I can without fear trust to it, for you are all equally brave."

Mont-Rognon
the Monstrous.

The names of all the knights present were put into a helmet, and Mitaine played the part of Destiny to the best of her power, little thinking she was choosing her own champions and avengers. The first name she called out was that of Allegrignac of Cognac, Count of Salençon and Saintonge.

"The lot suits me admirably," said the Emperor, giving a friendly wave of his hand to the knight. "You know the language of the country, and will be a safe guide for your companions."

Mitaine next named the Baron of Mont-Rognon, Lord of Bourglastic, Tortebesse, and elsewhere.

"This is indeed a capital choice! There is no stouter arm in the Arvennes than yours; and if there be a postern to be burst open by a powerful shoulder, you will be there, Mont-Rognon."

"Porc-en-Truie, Lord of Machavoine," cried Mitaine.

"I am in luck to-day, by St. James! You are known to be experienced, Porc-en-Truie, and you will conduct the adventure, I entrust to

Mont-Rognon in a hurry for his dinner.

you, to a prosperous end, I feel sure. But I am curious to know who is my fourth champion."

"Maragougnia, Count of Riom," said Mitaine.

"Now we have wisdom, strength, and cunning. Maragougnia can give the serpent points at wisdom, and beat him. If I do not succeed with such knights I shall despair altogether."

Charlemagne withdrew with his four champions, told them of the perils to which his god-child had been exposed, the investigation he had instituted, the suspicions he had entertained; and finally, he spoke of the Fortress of Fear, winding up in these terms:—

"I am anxious to square accounts with this Croquemitaine. You will pass through the forest till you arrive at Alagon, a little hamlet on the banks of the Ebro. There you will inquire for the Fonda del Caïman, or, if you prefer it, the sign of the Crocodile. You will there rest yourselves and then set out on your quests. You, Allegrignac, for a short time, striking off from the river, will pursue your course towards Pampeluna. You, Mont-Rognon, will proceed in the direction of Catalyud; and look out for the Saracens, my friend, who on that side are disgusted enough with the trouble we have given them. You, Porc-en-Truie, will make for Fuentes. If you are guided by me, you will travel by night only, and conceal yourself carefully by day. You will appreciate my counsel when once you are on the road. You, finally, my gallant Maragougnia, will have to direct your steps towards Lerida, but you will not go beyond the river Alcander. I have reserved this expedition for you because it is the most hazardous—there, you need not thank me. I understand you! Quarter the country in every direction, and find out for me this Fortress of Fear. He who brings me the head of its dreaded lord shall be created a baron and peer of my realm."

Maragougnia
the Melancholy.

The Emperor replenished the purses of his champions, and took leave of them with an embrace. When they found themselves alone they interchanged looks of bewilderment.

"What do you think of that?" said Porc-en-Truie, with a grimace.

"That I shall be a duke," said Allegrignac, cutting a caper. "This adventure won't take me a minute!"

"To think that we must set out to-night!" said Mont-Rognon, in tones of regret; "and to think that I have ordered a splendid supper for to-night, which my fellows will get the benefit of!"

"To think that we shall none of us ever come back again!" said Maragougnia, in a melancholy voice, as he wiped away a tear with the sleeve of his chain-mail.

"Pshaw! who knows?" broke in Porc-en-Truie, with a smile. "Let us set out, and then we can see!"

They appointed to meet on the borders of the forest, and within an hour afterwards they were all on the spot, equipped for war or for travel.

Porc-en-Truie, Lord of Machavoine, was a great fellow of thirty years of age, more skilled in avoiding blows than in dealing them. He invariably shirked all his military duties, not because he was a coward, but because he was incorrigibly idle. He had been known to tramp three hours afoot to save himself the trouble of saddling his horse, and he had killed his dearest friend in a tournament, in order to terminate a long and fatiguing tilting match. He arrived at the rendezvous on horseback, with no weapon but his sword.

"How imprudent!" cried Allegrignac, the moment he saw him coming. "Are we going to a wedding only, or are you desirous of emulating Miton's great feat at the Tourney of Fronsac?"

"I hate a load of weapons, and I don't mean to kill myself for this Mitaine—for whom, between you and me, I don't care a grain of mustard- seed!"

Allegrignac of Cognac, Count of Salençon, was twenty-five years of age, and six feet six high. He had an open countenance, a stout heart, an untiring tongue, limbs of steel, a stomach of leather, and a very slender patrimony. His hair was curly, his teeth were white. He was as proud as a Spaniard, as brave as a Frenchman, as simple-minded as a goose. He was possessed of a pleasant contralto voice, a cheerful spirit, and a grey horse called Serenade.

Picture to yourself a figure clad in complete steel, and with weapons of vast weight, like one of those armed and bandy-legged giants you see in a procession of trades, capable of lifting enormous weights, not to mention cattle, and any other unconsidered trifles he could lay hands on, and you have a portrait of the Baron of Mont-Rognon, Lord of Bourglastic, Tortebesse, and elsewhere. This huge mass of muscle existed only to eat and drink. He was a descendant of Esau on his father's side, and of Gargantua on his mother's. He once performed a gigantic feat—he killed six hundred Saracens who happened to get in his way as he was going to dinner. He had an elastic stomach, and a mouth armed with four rows of teeth. Having described his stomach and his mouth, I need not go on with the likeness, for all that remained were mere incidental appurtenances. He arrived third at the place of meeting, leading by the halter a mule laden with provisions and bottles.

"What's this?" said Allegrignac, laughingly.

"That!" said Mont-Rognon, offended at his bluntness. 'That's supper."

"What's the use of that?" said Porc-en-Truie.

"Charlemagne has ordered us to perish for him," broke in the Lord of Bourglastic, "but he did not stipulate that we should perish of hunger."

Maragougnia, Count of Riom, was the last to arrive. He was equipped in the most gloomy style. His armour was of browned steel, sprinkled with silver tears. From the coronet that surmounted his helmet sprang a few mangy black feathers, which drooped over his shoulders like the branches of a weeping willow, and all the rest of his accoutrements were to match.

He had one extraordinary quality, which was his strong point—instead of making him lose his head, fear only gave him increased presence of mind. They related deeds of prowess of his which were, in reality, only prodigies of cowardice. He did everything with a profound air of melancholy. His first wife, they say, died of yawning; the second perished of sheer weariness in three weeks.

Behind him came a page, who might be considered to have originated the sombre livery worn nine hundred years later by the page of the Duchess of Marlborough.* This lugubrious squire bore the count's change of arms—to wit: two daggers of mercy; three swords, various; one lance; one helmet; one morion; two daggers, poisoned; one battle-axe; one flail, iron; one shield; one breastplate; one shirt of mail; two pairs of gauntlets; three pairs of spurs.

"Good heavens!" said Allegrignac; "are we going to equip all the nation for war? Look, Porc-en-Truie! the Count of Riom has stripped the armouries of his ten castles."

"I wouldn't stir an inch," said Porc-en-Truie, in the interval of a couple of yawns, "to assure myself that Maragougnia has done something silly. If you assured me to the contrary, I might perhaps be surprised into getting up to see. And yet no! I couldn't believe it; so I should stay where I was."

Porc-en-Truie, I must observe, sat himself down on the grass the moment he arrived.

"You're quite welcome to laugh at my prudence," said Maragougnia, "but I don't forget we are going to certain death."

"Certain death! Fiddlesticks! I mean yet to rival the Methusalems of the period," said Porc-en-Truie, rising. "And now let's be off, if we are to reach Alagon to-night."

"To prepare for death," said Maragougnia, dashing away a tear with his gauntlet.

"To go to sleep," said Porc-en-Truie, with a yawn.

"To try a throw with the dice," said Allegrignac, jingling the money in his purse.

"To make a good supper," said Mont-Rognon, with a hollow voice, gnashing his teeth like castanets.

In ten minutes the four knights had entered the wood. At sunset Allegrignac was hammering with his fist at the door of the Fonda del Caïman.

* *Vide* "Malbrouck:" —

"Elle voit venir son page
De noir tout habillé.'

The four adventurous knights.

Sign of the Crocodile.

II. The Sign of the Crocodile.

The innkeeper was a man of middle size, half Spaniard and half Moor, with a big body and thin legs, a brown skin and grey eyes. He had acquired considerable reputation in the district for his mode of dressing calves' feet with saffron, and his handiness in stabbing people in the right place. He made everything a matter of trade, and used to regret that he had inherited no religious opinions which he could have abjured at a fixed price to be got either from the Saracens or the Christians. For the rest, he was a most obliging host, provided your purse was well supplied; and I believe I shall put the finishing stroke to the likeness when I say he was the biggest robber in all Spain, from Pontevedra to Girone.

Ali Pépé opened the door. One is always forgetting something, and I forgot to tell you his name was Ali Pépé.

"Where's the landlady?" asked Allegrignac, twisting his moustache.

"I want a bed," yawned Porc-en-Truie.

"Some supper!" growled Mont-Rognon.

Maragougnia said nothing. He was absorbed in studying the inn, and the estimate he formed seemed far from satisfactory.

Ali Pépé stood on the defensive, blocking the entrance of the inn.

"Your lordships appear of too exalted a station for me to omit to inform you that you will find the accommodation here very unsuited to you."

"Here's frankness and disinterestedness! But where can we find better accommodation?"

"My inn is the only one in the district."

"Then make way for us," said Mont-Rognon, catching up Ali Pépé by the girdle, and carrying him in at arm's length into the kitchen. "We shall be able to converse better here!"

Maragougnia entered last. He tried all the locks, in order to see whether the doors closed securely. He examined all the outlets, sounded the panels, and ordered his squire to bring him his arms.

Mine host of
the Crocodile.

"We want four beds," said Porc-en-Truie.

"In the same room," said Maragougnia, who had a horror of being solitary.

"First of all we want supper," bellowed Mont-Rognon; "don't let us forget the most important of our wants."

"A modest supper," suggested Maragougnia, who was afraid of the expense.

"A modest supper! " bellowed the Lord of Bourglastic. "Don't you do anything of the kind, landlord, or I'll burn the place about your ears. Empty your poultry-yard, drag your fish-ponds, uncork your bottles; set to work—kill, pluck, draw, and broach,—in short, make ready, to the best of your power, a feast for an emperor or a sultan!"

173

"You will lay for me separately," said the Count of Riom, tearfully, "a few radishes and some wine of first-rate—"

"Cheapness," kindly suggested Allegrignac, with a smile.

"May I know whom I have the honour to serve?" said Ali Pépé, with a bow so respectful that Maragougnia was horrified to see it, fearing it would be included in the bill.

"Nothing easier," said Allegrignac, returning Ali's bow. "The short gentleman you see there is Purveyor-in-Chief to Charlemagne and all the crowned heads of the civilised world, from Armenia to Lusitania, from Scandinavia to Tripoli. He travels from district to district in search of new dishes to delight the royal tables. His dissertation on roasts is in everybody's mouth. He has proved satisfactorily that beef ought not to be taken from the spit until the meat begins to turn brown and show the gravy; that mutton should be taken from the fire as soon as it begins to redden; and that veal should not be dished up until the meat is quite white. This man, who seems so unpretending, has discovered that thirst is fostered by currents of air; that the Scythians have stomachs an inch smaller than the Germans have; but then, on the other hand, deeper by seven times than those of the Cimmerians. He was the first who fried carp in rose-water; and he has, at last, after long and wearisome research, found in an old manuscript the recipe for garum, which was so highly prized by the ancients, but was thought to be lost. He has confided the secret to me, and I reveal it to you, in the hope that it will incite you to give us a better supper. Learn then, profane wretch! that in order to prepare this dainty dish, you must let a hen-mackerel lie in pickle with small mushrooms for seventeen nights at the full of the moon. The inside must be removed carefully, pounded, soaked, and braized with religious care in a bag of rose-coloured silk—and mind, it must be rose-coloured. The liquor thus procured is gathered in a silver vessel, when the weather is fine—or stormy. It must be left to settle for three weeks and seven hours, after having been mixed with a preparation, of which I forget the composition, but which is the chief ingredient, and gives all the value to the dish. You see with whom you have to deal: be sure, therefore, that the repast is worthy of this great dignitary and of us!"

Ali Pépé bowed.

"That gentleman who is snoring yonder travels in the hope of introducing some improvement into the royal sleeping arrangements. No one knows better than he the wisest adjustment of counterpanes, quilts, blankets, bolsters, pillows, and valances. His comparative treatise, entitled 'Lectus cubilaris, Lucubratorius, Emortualis, Genialis et Decubitorius,' has been engrossed on vellum by the monks of Monte Casino. To him belongs the honour of superseding the sack of maize-straw by the down-bed, which he imported from Cimbria; as also that of adding a second mattress to the sleeping-tackle of Royalty, which used to consist solely of a ticken, a pillow, and a bundle of straw. You see, therefore, that you must be careful to lodge us well for the night."

Ali Pépé made another low bow.

"I don't like talking about myself," said Allegrignac, "but for this once I will yield to your importunity, and inform you who I am. You must surely have heard of the great giantess Alcomiroziropoulo-pilousitounitapignac!"

The landlord eyed the Count of Salençon askance for awhile, then, resigning himself to his fate, he made an assenting gesture.

"She was my mother," said Allegrignac. "She perished after six years of married happiness, murdered by my unhappy father, who was never tired of beating her. Disgusted with matrimony—and not without cause—she determined to live single. I came into the world within twelve months afterwards, and chose the profession of arms. My fortune, my noble birth—everything assured me that I must owe everything to my own prowess. I cheerfully accepted my lot, and crossed the Alps to avenge my father. I laid siege to Toulouse. Need I continue to relate my misfortunes?"

"Not on my account, my lord. The particulars you have just related suffice to inform me with whom I have to deal. I have only to ask you who the fourth warrior of your party is?"

"This weeping willow—"

"I am a poor devil of a wanderer in search of fortune," hastily interposed Maragougnia. "My wants are as modest as my means: I know how to be satisfied with little."

"I treat my customers according to their tastes and their purses," said Ali Pépé. "You have, noble sirs, asked for a good many things. I will now give you a sketch of the accommodation I have to offer. I have but one room and one bed to let—"

"I'll take it, then," said Porc-en-Truie, promptly: "I wouldn't sleep out of doors to-night for the world. I shall not resume my journey till to-morrow. In the meantime, though, if either of you wishes to have half the bed—'

"Thanks, I shall push on to-night," said Maragougnia, as he left the room to find his squire, and tell him not to give the horses a feed. "They will find grazing on the road," he remarked.

"As for me," said Mont-Rognon, "I give up the room to you with all my heart. I intend to spend the night in eating. I shall not start till to-morrow morning."

"I'll keep you company till then," said Allegrignac; "we have a few bottles and an old dispute to settle. You owe me a dozen, and I'll bet you that you'll be under the table by the ninth. I feel just in the humour for the trial to-day."

A scornful smile was the only answer vouchsafed by Mont-Rognon, who turned to the host, and asked, "What soup do you think you can give us?"

"Can your lordship put up with pomegranate soup?"

"Let us see the pomegranates."

Ali ran to his larder, and returned with a basket-full of fruit. Mont-Rognon selected a dozen.

"Don't forget to serve it up warm, and with a slice or two of orange in it. What next?"

"If your lordship will leave it to me, you shall have no reason to complain. I have been head cook to the King of Mesopotamia for ten years, and His Majesty told me, only eight days since, that he has no pleasure in eating now I have left him. I would suggest, for soups, pomegranate, water-gruel, and ortolan; for entrées, calves' feet and saffron, and fillet of venison with sweetbreads. For the next course, chicken *farci à la Madame Râpée*, heron garnished with woodcocks, roast sucking-pig with cameline sauce."

"I should like well enough a quarter of whale served up on a layer of eggs," said Allegrignac, carelessly.

"You might have had it this morning. Unfortunately, they had the last of it for King Marsillus to-day."

"You will give us, instead, a peacock. You will stuff it with chestnuts and saffron, and serve it up with fennel and powdered sugar."

"I can also offer your lordships dory with orange-juice, and lampreys with lily sauce."

"Is that all?"

"Yes, sir. The bill of fare is simple, but select!"

"Now, by Lenten fasts! you want to starve us to death," said Mont-Rognon. "You must improve this poor fare, Master Head Cook of the King of Mesopotamia. Let us have ragout of venison, salt quarter of hare, preserved cabbage, purée of foreign' figs *à la Sardanapale*, pigs' chitterlings with sweet wine sauce, and ribs of beef in honey. Now, be off to your kitchen, and if we want anything else, we'll let you know."

Ali made a low bow, and was about to leave the room.

"One word more," said Allegrignac. "Don't forget to send up the roasts on the spit, and, above all, be particular about the wine. Don't be afraid of sending up plenty of bottles."

"And, stay, landlord!" said Porc-en-Truie, "as you go you can show me my room. Farewell, Allégrignac! Your hand, Mont-Rognon! Good luck to you, Maragougnia! I shall be asleep, no doubt, when you start. I trust you will succeed, and take back to the Emperor what he wishes."

"We shall be sufficiently fortunate if we take back a whole skin!" sighed the Count of Riom, preparing to depart.

In the next chapter you will see how the four knights set about the accomplishment of Charlemagne's wishes.

The best bed-room.

III. How Allegrignac, Maragougnia, Porc-en-Truie, and Mont-Rognon Opened the Campaign.

Porc-en-Truie followed Ali, who conducted him to the first floor, where they entered a chamber that was shabby enough in appearance in all conscience.

"Are you silly enough to think of putting me to sleep here?"

"It is the best room in the inn. King Marsillus slept here the day—"

"Come! I hope you are not going to talk more absurdity of that kind to me. Learn to understand better those with whom you have to deal. Where's the bed?"

"Yonder, sir."

"That a bed! By the beard of Solomon! what you have the impudence to call a bed would have horrified Job himself, and he passes for a person not easily dissatisfied. What is all that hanging about the curtains?"

"Those are cobwebs," said Ali, with an air of satisfaction. "We take them down when our customers wish it, but they never do.'

"How is that?" asked Porc-en-Truie.

"Why, you see," said the other, quietly, "the spider is insectivorous."

"And you dare bring me here?" asked Porc-en-Truie, pale with rage.

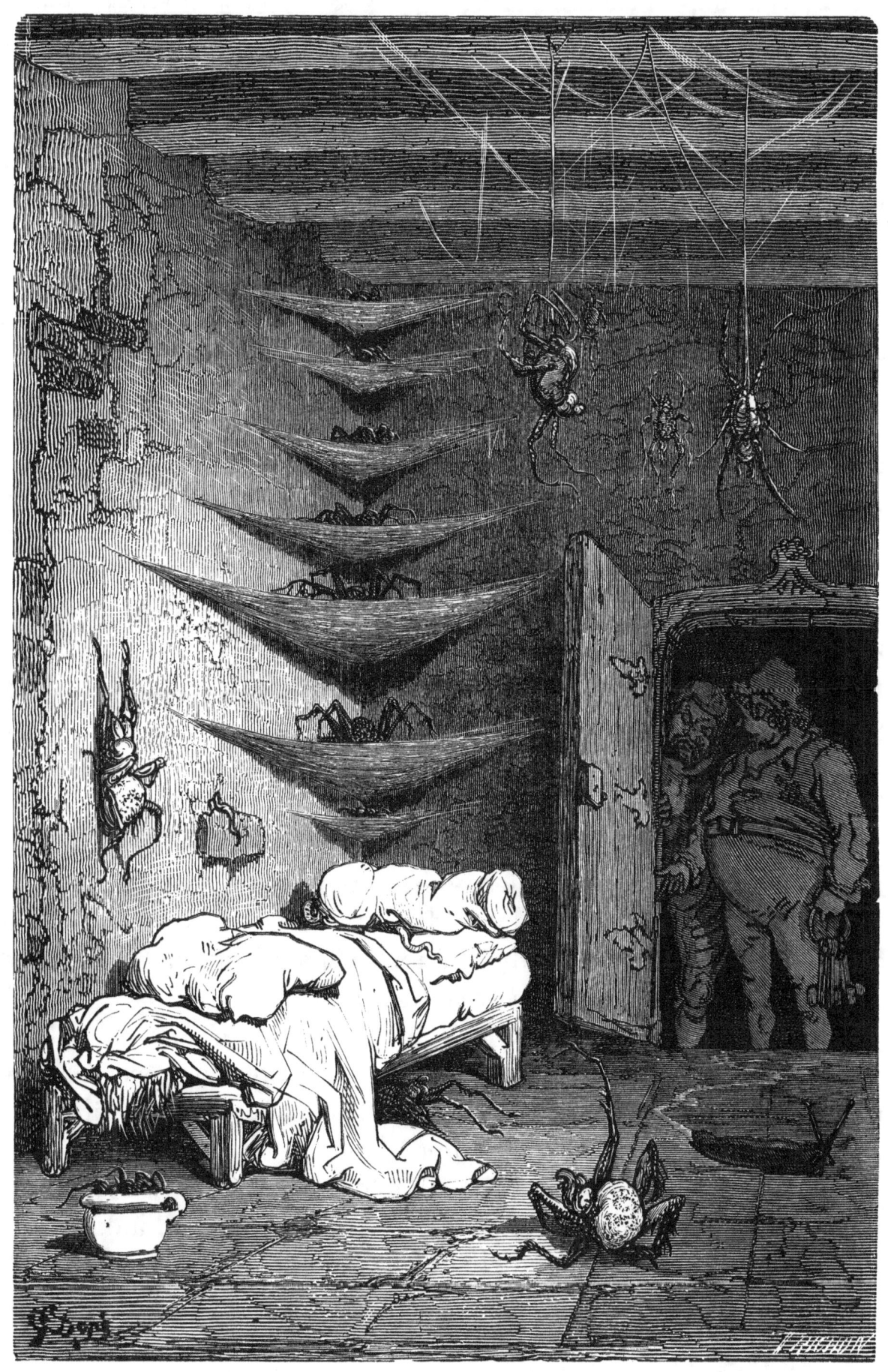

The spare-bed at the Crocodile.

"I dare swear to your lordship there is not a better bed in the house."

"Let me see yours;" and the knight seized the landlord, and made him conduct him to his own bedroom. It was not palatial by any means, but all was clean and neat in the host's room, and the bed looked inviting.

"How, rogue! you would sleep in this lordly bed without a scruple, while I am served as food for the spiders you rear! Leave the room, and thank Heaven that you leave it by the door instead of the window!"

The Lord of Machavoine thrust the landlord out of the room. He, poor wretch! gave up his apartment with a very bad grace, and strove to argue the matter, but he got no answer. The shooting of the bolts, the creaking of the bed, were soon succeeded by a loud snoring, which deprived the defeated wretch of his last hope.

He was going down-stairs in anything but a good temper, when he heard some one moving cautiously at the bottom. The host of the "Crocodile" possessed the courage of those cowards who lie in wait to strike, but who succumb before a hidden danger or an imaginary one, and shrink from an open attack. Porc-en-Truie had kept the lamp—all was buried in complete darkness.

"Who is that?" asked Ali, in a disquieted tone.

"A friend," answered a voice no less apprehensive.

The landlord drew from the folds of his tunic one of those formidable knives which are still the fashion in Spain, and, having opened it, softly descended the last few stairs.

"Who are you ?—what do you want?"

"Don't speak so loud, for goodness' sake? Don't you recognise my voice? I am one whom you supplied with radishes an hour since."

"The knight with the black plume?"

"The same. Can I have a word with you in private?"

"We should find it difficult to discover a more secret and solitary spot than this. What is it you wish?"

"I should like to stop here a month, unknown to my four travelling companions—why, I will tell you later."

180

"Nothing is easier. They will leave to-morrow."

"I want a very humble lodging, which I expect I shall occupy for a month. But what I want more than all is your silence."

"I am as mute as my conscience, and I have a room that will suit you to a nicety." And Ali flattered himself that he had virtually let the lumber-room which had so disgusted Porc-en-Truie.

He retired for an instant, then returned with a light, and once more ascended the stairs, followed this time by Maragougnia. He opened the door, entered first, and putting his hand behind the flame to throw a good light on the scene, turned and said, with the tone of a man who feels he had done the right thing, "There—that's the article for you."

The sudden appearance of the light put to flight a myriad of little black specks, that, hustling, scrambling, and running to and fro over the walls, finally disappeared in the hangings and wainscot.

"I want something more unpretending," said Maragougnia, shading his eyes, dazzled by the light.

Ali could scarcely refrain from expressing his surprise in a shout.

"More unpretending!" said he to himself, utterly disheartened. "These travellers are all alike—there's no satisfying them!" But the landlord of it "The Crocodile" was not the man to let himself be beaten by such a trifle. "If you will follow me, I have exactly what you require. I can let it you for next to nothing;" and he led the knight to a wretched outhouse without either air or light, except such as came to it by reversion from the stable.

"There!" said Ali, briefly.

"This will suit me admirably. The smell of a stable is good for the lungs so this atmosphere ought to be very healthy."

"I let it to invalids," said the landlord, stopping his nose. "Sleep in comfort; the straw is this year's;" and Ali, taking the lamp, left Maragougnia alone with his thoughts.

"Go," said the Count of Riom— "go, my dear fellow-travellers; go and get your necks twisted, and your bones broken. Go and seek a castle in the air for the satisfaction of a royal vagary. I, more wise than you, shall stop here. Who knows, but that fortune may not visit me here?" Thus musing, he fell asleep, and dreamt that his squire had obtained for him a reduction of rent by turning the spit in the inn kitchen.

When the host re-entered the supper-room he was astonished to see the table overturned, with its legs in the air, and Allegrignac and Mont-Rognon making a bed of it. They were sound asleep, far gone in that state of intoxication of which in after years the Templars afforded so many instances. Wrapt up in the most brotherly way in the table-cloth, they reposed on a heap of odds and ends and broken crockery. The lamp had succumbed to the general disaster, and was sputtering and mouldering in the ruins of a venison pasty.

"Bravo!" said Ali, rubbing his hands. "These are the sort of customers I like. Furniture never gets faded with them, for one is always having new." With that he set himself to break whatever had escaped the general smash; he even brought in a few damaged chairs, and distributed them artistically in fragments all over the room. Then, having picked up some gold pieces that had fallen on the floor, he went and lay down in the stable till morning.

Mont-Rognon, whose normal state was semi-intoxication, was the first to wake next day. He gazed unmoved on the scene of destruction in the midst of which he had slept, and then went out into the yard to give himself a washing at the trough. Ali Pépé, hearing him on the move, immediately made his appearance.

An after-dinner nap.

"Listen landlord," said the Lord of Bourglastic, "I like your style of cookery, and your wine suits my palate. I should like to stop here a month; but, for reasons best known to myself, I wish my fellow-travellers not to know that I have put up here. When that drunken fellow who dined with me last night wakes up, you must tell him I started without waiting for him. You will do the same with that sluggard upstairs, and when they are fairly off, come and let me know. I will take your dining-room for a month, and I intend never to quit the table. I shall not stir out, and nobody save you must come near me. I will defray the charges, including this last dinner, but I must insist on being well served. Recruit your forces, stock your larder and your cellar, for by Bacchus! you have got a tough job before you. Only I warn you, if you tell a single soul that I am here, you had better make your will, and order your coffin!"

"What an odd lot!" said Ali, as he went in-doors. Must I send my stingy customer of last night packing? Or must I tell my drunken friend of this morning that he is here? Pshaw! They are both afraid of being seen, and won't stir out an inch. One ought not to miss any profits, how ever small." With this reflection he went into the dining-room.

"Is that you, landlord?" asked Allegrignac, without opening his eyes. "Can you tell me what has become of my friend? It's no use for me to kick about—he's not in the bed."

"He is gone, my dear sir—gone quite an hour ago. He said to me, 'Tell the knight I leave in your room on the ground-floor, that I am sorry I cannot stop to say good-bye, for the heat is coming on, and I don't wish to delay my journey.'"

"Oh, so the drunken dog has gone—wonderful! I suppose he has paid?"

"Not he, sir, truly. He told me you would see to that."

Allegrignac not only opened his eyes at this, but he sat up on end. "At any rate, he paid his share?"

"He has not given me a penny piece; he told me he had won a wager of you." Before Ali had finished the sentence Allegrignac was on his legs. "You're no better than a brigand, and I'll wring your neck for you!"

"I swear to you I have not received a farthing this blessed morning!"

"Well, well," said the Count of Salençon, recovering his good humour, "I'm well enough off not to bother myself about a trifle like that. So you tell me my bed-fellow is really gone?"

"He is."

"And the one who was here last night, too?"

"You saw him go yourself."

"True. Then, if I calculate rightly, there's only one more of us left."

"The one who is snoring in my bed," sighed Ali, spitefully.

"Very well, then; open your ears wide, and listen attentively to what I say. If you let a syllable escape you, you and I shall quarrel. For reasons that I need not state, I wish to put up at your inn for a month."

"He, too!" thought Ali. "What is going to happen to the house?"

"You will choose me apartments opening on the garden. I shall not go out, and nobody must have access to me save you and the sun. You will have the room adorned with flowers. I never grumble at the accounts which innkeepers present to me. I satisfy myself with the explanation that they are not strong in their arithmetic; I am not myself, either. But I insist on being treated well. One word more: you give me the idea of a man who is rather proud of his ears. I always respect people's tastes, but I shall be compelled to deprive you of those ornaments if you mention to a single soul that I have stayed here. You understand me?"

"Clearly!"

"Then lead me to my prison!"

It was not long before Allegrignac was duly installed. His furniture consisted of a bed, a table, some flowers, and a guitar. He ordered breakfast, and desired to be left to himself.

"I am curious to learn what these strange people want here," said Ali, as he went up-stairs. "I only hope the fourth knight won't take possession of my bed for an indefinite period. Let us try and get him out of it at once."

The host gave a vigorous push at Porc-en-Truie's door.

184

"Sir! you bade me call you in good time. The sun has been up some hours. Are not you going to start?"

"Come in " said the Lord of Machavoine. "I want to have a word with you."

"But, my dear sir, I can't come in. You shut yourself in when you turned me out, and I know from experience that one cannot break in the door."

Porc-en-Truie was reluctantly compelled to get out of bed and open the door, jumping into bed again, however, immediately, and turning his face to the wall.

Ali posed.

"Do you know this bed is delicious! I have slept splendidly in it, and I am not such a fool as to go scouring the highways while I can get a good rest here. Listen to me attentively, and don't let me have to repeat anything, for I'm dying for sleep. You will place beside me on a table a venison pasty, two cold dishes, some preserved fruit, and thirty bottles of wine. Thirty—you hear?"

"Only too well!"

"Once a week you will come in on tip-toe, and lay the repast afresh. I am going to take a nap—you may call me in a month's time."

"I trust you won't think of doing so—keeping me out of my bedroom for a month—"

"I warn you that I do not know how much money there is in my purse, and that I sleep so soundly, you might rob me of it without my opening my eyes. Ali, by the way, I forgot! As I don't wish to be disturbed, I command you not to tell a soul that I am here. I don't care a bit if your inn is on fire, if the enemy is coming, or an earthquake happens. I mean to have my sleep out. Above all, don't let my fellow-travellers know of my determination. Nothing less than your life or death depends on that. Now, set everything out properly here, and don't let me hear any more of you for a month"

185

"Sir—sweet sir—dear sir—great sir!" sighed the host, little elated at the prospect of sleeping for the next thirty nights in the stable, "can't you choose some other resting-place? I can assure you, that if you go nearly as far as Montella—about half a day's journey from here—you will find a magnificent hotel, where you will be infinitely better lodged than here. Are you listening to me, my dear sir?

A vigorous snore proved to Ali that he was simply throwing away his eloquence. To make quite sure the knight was asleep, the land-lord began to inspect his purse, but Porc-en-Truie did not stir.

"Well, this is sleeping like a nobleman," said Ali, not half satisfied by the self-appointed award of a handful of gold pieces. "For this amount I can afford to let him finish his nap!"

Porc-en-Truie sleeps.

The landlord's capital.

IV. ALI PÉPÉ'S LITTLE HARVEST.

Allegrignac, Porc-en-Truie, Mont-Rognon, and Maragougnia continued to dwell in unconscious propinquity.

"Who can tell what has become of my companions?" said all four, each to himself. "They have perished beyond doubt, or are prisoners at best. Faith! that's their look-out! Success is very properly the prize of superior intelligence."

For a whole month Porc-en-Truie slept, Mont-Rognon ate, Allegrignac played the guitar in a whisper, and Maragougnia plotted impossible meannesses.

On the twenty-eighth day of his captivity Mont-Rognon greeted Ali with a smile which he struggled to make as gracious as possible. Ali was terrified to see it, dreading lest his customer should ask him for credit on the strength of such an act of condescension.

"Sit down here opposite to me," said Mont-Rognon, growing every moment more agreeable to Ali, who was growing every moment more uncomfortable. "I am tired of eating alone. Besides, I have something to say to you."

The landlord sat down, poured himself out a bumper, and listened.

"Since I have been here I have watched you closely, and the result of my examination is favourable to you. Occupied as I have been, it was impossible for us to exchange much talk, but it was enough to make me appreciate you. I recognise in you one of those bold spirits who, regarding life as a journey, reject from the outset whatever may encumber their progress. Conscience is to them a stranger whose name gives rise to a smile, and remorse a bugbear invented by the weak to restrain the strong. They only require in life that which it is able to offer, but they are not of the kidney to forego one single opening for enjoyment, let the price be what it may. People of my way of thinking are always ready to encourage that spirit. Do you comprehend?"

"That depends on what is to follow. I'll tell you presently. Go on!"

"I travel, as you have been told, in the gastronomical interests of various sovereigns. One of them, whose name I choose to withhold, has sent me to this country with a mission so truly extraordinary that I dread to impart it to you."

"Fear not, sir. I flatter myself I shall understand you."

"The king, whose envoy I am, has a daughter as fanciful as she is beautiful, and he is the slave of her lightest caprice. She has read in some writer of this country that the Saracens owe the clearness of their complexion to a peculiar ointment. I am really afraid to tell you of what it is composed."

"Don't be afraid of anything with me, sir."

"Well, then, they say that one must have, to make it properly, a human head—"

"Ah!" said Ali, pushing back his chair; "you are terribly plain to understand,—rest assured of that!"

"They assert that for this purpose the heads of the inhabitants of these parts are superior to all others. I have unluckily promised to procure one, and if I fail to keep my word, my own head, for lack of better, will have to serve the princess's turn. They persuaded me that to ensure the preservation of the beauty of young girls was an act of philanthropy, and I foolishly committed myself to the undertaking. I offer with all my heart one-half of the sum promised me to any one who will assist me out of my scrape."

"And how much have you been promised?" said Ali, bringing his chair to the table again.

"A hundred ounces. Do you know any respectable man of business who will undertake to supply such an article as I have named?"

"Possibly—but all trouble deserves payment. If I act as your go-between shall I get nothing?"

"Your claim is a fair one. I promise you fifty ounces—twenty-five for him, and twenty-five for yourself."

Mont-Rognon's wink.

"You shall have what you require."

"To-morrow?"

"This evening! But you must pay me half in advance. If you were to change your mind, and leave me with the goods on my hands—"

"Between men of honour—"

"Between men of honour like us it is right to take precautions."

"Well! There's the money."

Ali Pépé took the gold, counted it, tried each coin in succession, weighed them with an air of wisdom, and said, quietly, "The money is quite correct; you shall have just the sort of article you want; and what is more, I'll throw you the sack in!" With these words he left the apartment.

It was Allegrignac's lunch-time; so the host went up-stairs to the count's room, and found him plunged in deep thought.

"Tell me, Ali Pépé," said he, "did you ever happen to be married?"

"Never, sir. I am the oldest representative of a race which will die with me."

"Then you cannot understand my sufferings!"

"Your sufferings, my dear sir?"

"My heart is bursting, and I feel I can trust myself with you. Listen to my history, and sympathise with your unhappy guest. My early life was passed in bliss on the shores of the Sarmatian Sea, till one day I met the daughter of the King of Scandinavia. This marvel of the North had a skin as white as snow, hair as golden as sunlight, and she was as plump as a partridge. Her beauty dazzled me, and I swore I would die to serve her—"

"Your worship will excuse me if I beg you to commence your history at the conclusion. I have several customers waiting below."

"I will be brief. It is the custom in certain cold regions for every young girl who has reached her seventeenth year to make a tour for a couple of months to look out for a husband. Those who make any impression on her, or on whom she makes an impression, accompany her home to her father, who then makes his choice among the suitors. The fair Wahallaaka had just reached her seventeenth year, when I fell in with her at the close of the circuit. My attention was first attracted by the splendour of the sledge in which she rode. It was drawn by thirty wolves, which shook the crimson silk tassels and jingled the steel chains of their harness. Seven hundred and sixty-seven suitors rode behind her. The eyes of the fair Scandinavian met mine, and she felt at once that her journey was completed. Could she meet with a more suitable husband? She was not foolish enough to suppose so; and, giving me a sign to join the *cortège*, she gave the order to return to Khétakous-Mouvoskaïa, which is the capital of her father's dominions. He, a man full of judgment and taste, confirmed his daughter's choice, and it was decided that at the expiration of two months I should become the husband of the beauteous Wahallaaka. For fifty days we had a succession of festivals. Sledge races by torchlight were followed by balls and concerts. White bear-hunting, whale-catching, and a thousand other innocent diversions, furnished me with opportunities for the display of my brilliant intelligence, my strength, my courage, my address, my presence of mind, my grace, my agility, my—"

Ali Pépé threw an imploring glance at Allegrignac.

"I will be brief. Nothing in this world is perfect, and the incomparable Wahallaaka had her share of imperfections. She was given to flirting and fibbing: she was fickle, she was foolish, she was vain, she was rash."

"Sir!" sighed the count's wretched listener.

"I will be brief. You are right; why should I open again these scarce-healed wounds? A page one day brought me a letter from my future bride. 'Go,' it said; 'leave me, to prove your love for me. The ties which are about to unite us are so serious that I wish, before confirming them irretrievably, to assure myself that I have not been mistaken in my choice of you. Go; during your absence I intend to give myself, without reserve, to all the pleasures of society. I shall do everything I can to forget you, and if in a year's time, when you return, I still love you, then, my knight, I will be your bride. You will go to Spain. I do not give you that Eden for your place of exile without good reason. They assert that the men there are the handsomest in the world. Well, my betrothed, when your time comes to return, choose one of the finest of these wretches, cut off his head, and bring it to me, that I may judge with my own eyes of the beauty of the barbarian type."

"Well done!" thought Ali; "here are my four guests beginning again. In everything they do they follow suit, and I feel sure the other two will make the same request. What is to be the end of this?"

"'Should you triumph in this trial,' added the fair Wahallaaka, 'from that moment none shall be as dear to me as you.' When I read this letter my heart was torn with conflicting passions, but I had the strength of mind to leave without seeing my beloved. For a whole year I dragged out my miserable existence in all quarters of the globe. Now, however, my time of trial is past, and I am about to return to my beloved country. One thing alone remains to do. Can I present myself to her, who is so dear to me, without offering her that head which is the object of her desires?"

"But how is it that, brave and mighty as you describe yourself to be, you have not already procured it?"

"The reason is clear, as you will see. I am in the ordinary affairs of life a very lion for courage; the panther and white bear I care not a jot for; but as soon as the idea of fighting presents itself—whenever I find myself in the presence of danger—I tremble, lest I should prove unworthy of the fair Wahallaaka. The thought unnerves my arm, and a child might conquer me. In short—I'll give you forty ounces for your head."

Ali scowled at the knight. "If it be to finish in this manner that your worship has taken the trouble to relate this history, we might both of us have employed our time better."

"If your head appears to me the finest model of Oriental beauty, there is no reason for you to be offended. You appear to be attached to it well, let's say no more about it, but get me for the same price some other specimen of the Asiatic tribes."

"How much did you say you were willing to give?"

"Forty gold pieces."

"You won't get anything worth looking at for that sum! Everything has risen in price since the war."

"Well, then, fifty pieces."

"Say sixty pieces—thirty down, and I'll promise you the best that can be had."

"I am anxious to start, remember."

"You shall have what you want by to-morrow."

"Very well! I rely upon you to keep your word."

Ali, as soon as he had the thirty pieces safe in his pocket, went downstairs, and entered the apartment of the knight of Machavoine. Porc-en-Truie was not asleep.

"I thought so," said the innkeeper to himself; "here's the sleeper as wide awake as a squirrel," and he made as if he would go out again.

"Come in," said the knight, "I have something to talk to you about."

"I am all attention," said Ali, bowing.

"I leave to-morrow!"

"So soon?" said Ali at his long-lost bed with affectionate interest.

"That depends on you. Travellers like to carry away some little remembrance of places they have visited, and I have too much reason to be pleased with my treatment here not to keep up the custom. What do you advise me to get? You see, you must aid me in choosing, for I haven't stirred out, and know nothing about the place."

"Our grapes are very fine here in the north of Spain. Possibly—"

"No. That won't do. I want something that will keep."

"The young girls of our country come from ten leagues round to Alagon to buy plated gold and silver trinkets, and necklaces of seed-pearl and coral."

"You must find out something better than that."

"Your worship puzzles me. The country has nothing else remark-able to offer except its inhabitants; but, of course, I could not offer you one of our people to take away."

"That's a notion! It suggests an idea to me—only it is so peculiar I hardly like to mention it."

"Pshaw! a little shyness will soon wear off."

"I'll give you a thousand guesses, and you'll puzzle your brains over it in vain to all eternity."

"Then, sir, don't let me have to guess."

"You say your knaves here are handsome?"

"They have adorable almond-shaped eyes, red lips, white teeth, and complexions of a delightful olive, covered with black down."

"You only speak of their heads."

"I have a reason for doing so, for it is the only good thing they possess; for which reason our girls are accustomed to say, 'The heart of Castile, the soul of Catalonia, the form of Leon, the limbs of Navarre, and the head of Arragon make a perfect man.'"

"By my faith! the idea is a jolly one, and I must give you all credit for having been the first to think of it."

"Your honour is too good. You accredit me with more spirit than I possess."

"Since you originated the notion, you must assist me to put it into execution. Well, then, how can you get me the head of an Arragonese?"

"What! you wish to take away a real head—a living head?"

"Living is scarcely the word—but a head that has been alive."

"Well, that is an idea that no one has had before you."

"I hope so."

"Our country, sir, is a wonderful one, for this reason—that you can get whatever you want, provided you have the money. If, therefore, you will allow me to manage—"

"Do so, and do so quickly. That is all I require, and I shall leave to-morrow."

"I must have thirty pieces of gold in advance. The game you want is strictly preserved, and difficult to procure. Nothing inspirits the hunter so much as to be paid ready money." So Ali added thirty more pieces to the sixty he had already received, and hastened off to hide it in a secret spot known only to himself. "Now I'll go and see my fourth customer. I am curious to learn what he has to propose to me."

Maragougnia had not during the whole month left the horrid little hole which he had chosen for his lodgings. Anxious to make a profit by his isolation, he had spent the time in *déshabille*, in order to save his clothes. When Ali entered he found the knight patching his shirt with his pocket- handkerchief. "You come just at the right moment; I wish to speak to you."

"I am listening."

"I hope you will not take amiss what I have to say to you, nor misunderstand my intentions. I think I ought first of all to tell you that I am even more wretched than I look. You will understand, of course, that it is not from a feeling of greed that a man denies himself everything as I do. I should certainly not despise the good things of life if I had the means of getting them. Picture to yourself that my misery is such—"

"Excuse me," said Ali, sharply; "I see that you are going to take an hour in framing a demand which could be expressed in a few seconds. I am quite willing to give up my time to those who pay me, but you are either too poor or too stingy to justify my so doing. You want a Saracen's head, and you are afraid to ask for it."

"Good heaven! who could have told you that?"

"You yourself."

"I? When?"

"You talk in your sleep, sir, and are more communicative then than when you are awake. I sleep in the stable close by, and have overheard you. Now that you see I am so well informed as to your wants, let's settle the matter at once."

Maragougnia became infinitely whiter than his shirt.

"I can procure you what you want. But you must understand perfectly that it is not a stock article, so I must have a good price. Fifty pieces of gold down, and fifty more to-morrow on delivery."

Maragougnia fell fainting on the floor. Ali feared for a moment that he had gone too far. The knight's heart no longer beat, his body was icy cold, his breathing had stopped.

"Come, come!" said Ali, "recover yourself. You shall have it for ninety-five pieces, or say ninety, in consideration of my having waited on you for a month."

The Count de Riom did not stir.

"Well, we will fix it at eighty-five, but I won't abate a penny."

The knight opened his right eye.

Miserable Maragougnia.

"Come, I am less hard than I look," said the innkeeper, rubbing Maragougnia's hands. "I will make you an offer."

The dying man opened his other eye.

"Must you have a head? because—I'll tell you what, I have an order for a head on hand, I'll let you have the remnant cheap."

The knight closed his eyes again, and sank back motionless.

"That doesn't suit you? Well! say no more about it. I am going to show you how willing I am to serve you by lowering my demands."

The knight's eyes re-opened, and his heart began to beat again.

"Say eighty pieces, but I shan't come down any lower."

Ali rose to go. Maragougnia gave a heavy sigh, that would have softened the heart of a famished tiger, but made no impression on the innkeeper.

"Eighty pieces of gold! Why, it is more than I should spend in eight years. You'll reduce me to beggary."

"Pshaw! you are no better off now."

"You might as well take my life."

"You may accept my offer or leave it. People don't buy things of this sort every day. Will you have it?—Once!"

"I'd rather die."

"Twice!"

"Ten pieces—I'll give you ten pieces."

"Thrice!"

"Wait a minute! one must take time to think over such bargains."

"Well, I'll come back presently, but I vow you will regret not having taken my offer at once."

Ali went out, leaving Maragougnia pale, trembling, broken-hearted, a prey to a thousand conflicting emotions.

The "Crocodile" at night.

V. How Ali Pépé, Having Done All That Could be Expected of an Honest Man, was Hanged.

That evening the doors of the inn were closed earlier than usual. Ali had given his servants a holiday to go to the fair at Montella, and was thus left alone with his four lodgers. He locked all the doors, put up the chain at the front gate, ascertained that the shutters were closed, all of which were precautions he did not usually take. Then he went down into the cellar, where there was a collection of weapons of all descriptions. He selected a large knife, which he carefully sharpened; put on a shirt of mail, as easy-fitting as silk, but perfectly sword-proof; put on a helmet of extraordinary shape, which completely concealed his face, and went up-stairs again softly. On arriving at the top of the stairs he put out his lamp, and stole forward on tiptoe. He stopped in succession at the doors of the four knights, and peeped through the keyhole to see what they were doing. Mont-Rognon was at his eighth bottle; Porc-en-Truie was asleep; Allegrignac was taking the fresh air in the garden; Maragougnia was furtively counting his money.

196

"Good!" said Ali to himself. "In one hour the gentleman who is at supper will have finished his ninth bottle, and tumbled under the table; the one who is dozing will be snoring soundly; the one who is meditating will be asleep; and as to the fourth—"

The proprietor of the "Crocodile" said no more he had reached the stable, where he flung himself down on the straw.

At midnight Allegrignac woke up in a fright. He thought he heard a piercing cry.

"Somebody's having his throat cut," said the Count de Salençon. He sat down on the foot of his bed and listened. All was silent; you might have heard the spiders spinning their webs.

"I wasn't dreaming, nevertheless—no; I am sure I heard a cry."

He continued to listen, and now the silence made him tremble. He remembered his bargain with the innkeeper. The idea that he was the instigator of the crime which undoubtedly had just been committed deprived him of sleep. He dressed himself, and sat himself down on the side of his bed, with his drawn sword in his hand. In a quarter of an hour two more shrieks resounded through the night. Allegrignac sprang up as briskly as if in obedience to a hidden spring. These renewed cries alarmed him.

Murder a-foot.

"Everybody is having his throat cut!" said he to himself, growing more and more frightened. "My conscience has only to answer for one of the crimes; so, if Master Ali is too zealous, I am not responsible."

As a precaution, he rolled his bed against the door, put the table and chairs on the top of it, and kept watch. The rest of the night passed peaceably and quietly. The moon accomplished her nocturnal round, and when the sun reappeared, Allegrignac, ashamed of his panic, restored everything to its place. At seven o'clock Ali knocked at the door.

"Here is what you want," said he placing a small sack on the count's bed. "Have you the money ready?"

"There it is."

"I should recommend you to lose no time in setting out, for I think I saw one of your companions this morning."

Allegrignac did not wait to hear this advice repeated. He went down-stairs, and, finding his horse ready at the door, he tied the sack to the saddle-bow, set spurs to his nag, and rode off at a gallop. Ali smiled to see him go, and then, when he was no longer in sight, turned into the apartment of the Baron of Mont-Rognon.

"I have obeyed your orders, sir. Here is what you required." And he flung a sack on the table, as he had already done in the case of Allegrignac.

"There is the sum we agreed on," said the baron, tendering him the twenty-five pieces. "Saddle my horse, I am in a hurry to be off!"

"It is ready saddled," said the landlord, taking the money; "your honour will find it at the foot of the stairs."

Mont-Rognon went out for the first time for a month. He attached the small sack to the saddle-bow as Allegrignac had done, and in a few minutes was out of sight. Ali did not on this day enter the two rooms occupied by Porc-en-Truie and Maragougnia. He spent his time in counting his money.

Fifty gold pieces from the drunken knight, plus forty for his keep, will be ninety. Sixty from the talkative knight, plus thirty-five for his board and lodging, will be ninety-five. That makes one hundred and eighty-five pieces in all, if I know anything of arithmetic. Add to this the purses of the lazy knight and the knight of the raven plumes—the one containing one hundred and fifty and the other a hundred and forty pieces, amounting to two hundred and ninety—which I must add to one hundred and eighty-five, leaving a total four hundred and seventy-five pieces of good new money. This is more than one wants

The end of Ali.

198

to begin life with honestly, so I can afford myself that little whim— and will do so!"

Ali Pépé was unable to realise this laudable purpose. He was hanged eight days after, as you, my young friends, will learn, if you continue to read this history.

The friendly dwarf.

VI. Shoulder to Shoulder, Face to Face!

Charlemagne was playing at chess with Naymes, Duke of Bavaria, for a couple of hours, when he was informed that Allegrignac had returned.

The Emperor, who had lost five games out of seven, was in anything but an agreeable mood. The news of the count's arrival completely cured him.

"At last we shall learn the truth about the Fortress of Fear. I feel sure Allegrignac will have acted vigorously and wisely. Fetch him a stoup of wine while I go to assemble my peers, barons, bishops, and clerks. I will hear what he has to say before them."

When these orders had been carried out, Charlemagne caused the Count of Salençon to be summoned into his presence.

"Approach, Allegrignac. You have proved yourself, I doubt not, possessed of endurance and bravery. I shall be glad to have to award the prize to you. Tell us what happened to you."

"I am, sire, overcome at the thought of my great good fortune, and seek in vain for any past good deed of mine which has won for me the favour which Heaven lavishes on me. I will take care not to abuse your kindness, or the patience of so many learned and gallant listeners. I will begin my story from the moment when I left Alagon for the Fortress of Fear. Dawn was breaking when I started. The darkness which was still spread over the earth was beginning to vanish at the

200

The Emperor at chess.

approach of the sun, whose welcome was being chanted by the lark. I was asking myself how so lovely a country could bring one to so dire a fortress, when my horse gave a start, stopped, and, lowering its head, began to snort loudly. I then saw, a short distance from me, a little dwarf, not ill-looking, who sat weeping by the road-side. 'While there is yet time,' said he, 'abandon this insane adventure, and do not disturb the great master of Fear. Seeing you so young and so lovely, I cannot restrain my tears. Did you but know what obstacles you will find opposing you, you would certainly not encounter them.' 'I am the envoy of Charlemagne,' said I, quietly. 'Ask yourself, then, if I am a man likely to draw back.' I had hardly mentioned your name, sire, when I beheld the dwarf flying in alarm. I went on. A little farther on my horse made a second start, and I found myself face to face with a giant, who was in command of a body of twelve armed men. He had a foot placed on either side of the road, like the old Colossus of Rhodes, and his men were drawn up, lance in rest, between his legs, seeking to bar my passage.

"'Whose servant are you, miscreant?' cried I. 'Mahomet has my faith—the Lord of Fear my allegiance.' 'And I will have your life. Hurrah for Charlemagne! 'I flung my lance at the monster with such force and skill that it pierced his body, and lodged in the ground, point downward, fifty paces off. I drew my sword, and rode at his twelve followers, whom I routed. Although charging at

The giant.

full gallop, I had the forethought to recover my lance on the way. By the time these enemies recovered themselves I was already in the midst of other perils. What more need I say? In vain did the elements assist the efforts of men and demons; strong in my loyalty to my king, I overcame all obstacles!"

Charlemagne liked people to talk modestly, and the praises which Allegrignac did not cease to lavish on himself made him frown. "Action is for men, and words for women," said he to himself. "This young man talks a little too much."

"Human strength has its limits," continued Allegrignac; "even mine is exhaustible, and, taking advantage of an interval of quiet, I dismounted to take a rest. I was a short way from the top of a high mountain, on which the Fortress of Fear is built. I had a long time left the temperate zone, and was surrounded by snow. All of a sudden—"

"I'll wager his next words are a falsehood!" whispered Roland to Turpin.

"Nonsense! You're betting on a certainty," said the bishop.

"All of a sudden my horse gave a terrified neigh. I turned round as I sprang to my feet, and beheld an avalanche leaping from rock to rock, and coming to swallow us up. I did not waste a moment. I waited it with feet firmly planted, and arms outstretched. I caught it and held it back for some seconds. 'Quick, Serenade!' I cried to my horse. 'Go along, make haste, poor beast!' The animal understood my meaning, and escaped. It was time, for my strength was just exhausted. I made one final and supreme effort, flung the Titanic projectile on one side, and sank—I confess it—exhausted on the ground. The brave men who hear me will not ridicule my weakness."

Every one looked at his neighbour. They were more surprised at the impudence of the speaker than the strangeness of his story.

"Enough of this sort of prattle," said Charlemagne. "Here be plenty of great deeds—I'll ask for the rest of the story another time. Meanwhile, tell me—and as briefly as possible—have you seen the castle and its owner?"

"I have seen them, and I bring you, sire, the head of the monster as an evidence of my victory."

Allegrignac stooped down to take the bag, which he had placed beside him at the beginning of his story, when Mitaine entered and announced that the Baron of Mont-Rognon desired an audience.

"By my beard! I am curious to see and hear him. Allegrignac, withdraw, and let the Knight of Bourglastic speak. Bid the baron enter."

Mont-Rognon stepped in proudly; he paused at a few paces from Charlemagne, bowed, placed beside him the bag about which we know, and waited to be interrogated.

"I have often reproached myself for having sent you on so formidable an adventure, my brave baron; only the remembrance of your past feats of valour could make my mind easy about you. However, you have returned."

"I know not how to express to my Sovereign all my gratitude for the honour he does me. I always believed that the joy of victory is the greatest in the world, and the beating of my heart assures me that I was not mistaken."

"The joy of victory, do you say? Of what victory do you speak?"

"Of that which I have just won over the Knight of Fear."

A murmur of surprise was heard on all sides.

"Come forward, Allegrignac," said the Emperor, in a severe voice. "What does this mean, and which of you is the impostor?"

The consciences of the two pretended victors were not so clear that they could listen without alarm to the infuriated voice of Charlemagne. They felt that impudence alone could assist them; and Allegrignac coming forward, pointed to the Knight of Bourglastic, and said—

"If, sire, this man pretends that he has vanquished the Knight of Fear, I declare that he lies."

"Lies!" cried Mont-Rognon, blinded with rage. "Who dares utter the word?"

"I, Allegrignac, Count of Salençon."

"Traitor and perjurer! you shall not quit this place alive. A disgraceful death shall be your fate, and the fate of all belonging to you." And he drew his sword. "Yes, you have lied, baron of the realm though you be, and I will teach you to change your note, perjured coward! I shall slay you and yours before the humblest lacquey in my service is the worse by a hair, for all your bravery."

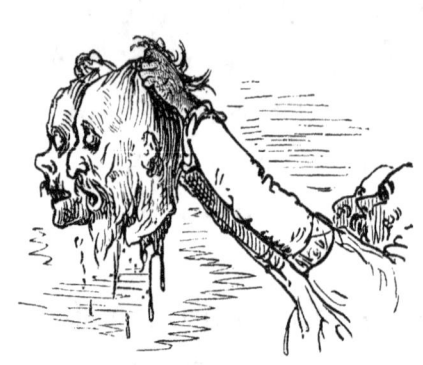

Two heads not better than one.

"These two cocks," said Oliver, "seem to me to crow too long before they begin fighting. It would be mockery to separate them."

Charlemagne raised his voice, and silence was at once restored.

"I find you daring enough," said he, "to deafen me with your clamour. This insolence is insufferable. The first who speaks without being questioned shall be punished; understand that, one and all!" and then he added, after a moment, "What proof have you of the victory you say you have won? Speak, Allegrignac."

"I have the head of the monster in this bag."

"And you, Mont-Rognon, what have you to say?"

"This man is an impostor. I have here what will prove him so." The Knight of Bourgiastic seized his bag, and opened it—the Count of Salençon did the same, and then each held up a gory head for Charlemagne's inspection.

At this sight the Emperor turned pale. He rose, and seemed anxious to speak, but could only utter the one word, "Murderers!"

The whole assembly gave a cry of horror on recognising the heads of Porc-en-Truie and Maragougnia; but the most frightened of all were assuredly Mont-Rognon and Allegrignac, who, letting fall the two accusing heads, flung themselves at the Emperor's feet.

"Sire, do not hold us guilty. We have been the victims of some treason. Yes, we confess it; we were unable to carry out your instructions. Terrified, and at our wits' end, we lost our heads—"

"Then no one will be surprised this evening to see they are no longer on your shoulders," interposed the Emperor, who thus set a-going a horrible joke, which has done service so often since that it has well earned a retiring pension.

The next day, after mass, the Lord of Bourglastic and the Count of Salençon underwent a final examination. By vespers Charlemagne had sentenced them to death. When the bugles sounded they had been beheaded, and flung out to feed the wolves.

Eight days after, Ali Pépé was hanged.

The death of Allegrignac.

Mitaine sets forth.

VII. Mitaine Opens the Campaign.

Charlemagne, on one occasion, committed an act of imprudence; he promised Mitaine that when she performed any remarkable feat of valour, she should be attached to Roland's staff as a squire. From that moment she never rested; ambition constantly haunted her, and, without letting any one know her plans, she was always looking out for some opportunity of distinguishing herself. The Fortress of Fear seemed an object worthy of her labour, and the unfortunate issue of the expedition of the four knights induced her to undertake the adventure. "If my friend Croquemitaine lives in the castle, I will find him, and prove I am not afraid of him."

She set forth early one morning, accompanied by a young page of her acquaintance named Ortez; and when she found herself at what she believed a sufficient distance from the camp to render pursuit impossible, she told her companion to return to the Emperor, and inform him that she had resolved to find the Fortress of Fear.

"Tell him not to be alarmed for me; he shall have no reason to blush for his godchild. I hope before long to remind him of his promise to make me a squire."

The page endeavoured in vain to dissuade her from her plan; in vain he threatened her with the anger of Charlemagne. "When I return," said she, "he will gladly embrace me."

The more he described to her the magnitude of the dangers she would encounter, the more determined she was to face them.

"Well, then, I shall follow you," said Ortez, resolutely.

"If you do anything of the sort I warn you that we shall quarrel."

"Do you think I am wanting in courage?"

"No! I know you are brave; only I do not desire to lessen the merit of the deed I am resolved to accomplish by sharing its dangers with you."

"But it would be dishonourable in me to allow to go alone into danger one whom it is my duty to defend," said the lad, planting his little fists on his hips.

"By the Shrine of St. Landri! you are too importunate, Ortez. Girls like me have beak and talons like fully-fledged falcons. Return, then, to the camp to inform Charlemagne, and if in three days I do not come back, you will pray for a gallant girl who died in the quest of adventure."

The page was obliged to give way; he returned alone along the road which he had just traversed in company with Mitaine, and I will not swear that he had not tears in his eyes.

As soon as she was alone, Mitaine assured herself that her sword was firmly buckled on at her side—that her dagger quitted its sheath easily; then she bent her steps towards a ruined hut which stood in the midst of a vast field of maize. Before long she reached it, and saw a peasant seated on the ground playing with his children. She was struck by his air of profound melancholy, and shocked at the wretched appearance of the little ones that were rolling about in the dust.

The poor peasant.

"Can you tell me the way to the Fortress of Fear?"

On hearing this question the peasant rose hurriedly, and stared at Mitaine with frightened eyes. The youngsters took refuge between his legs as if they expected some calamity.

"Do you know what you are asking?" said the terrified man. "It is doubtless a jest, or a bit of show-off inexcusable in a child of your age."

"You do not answer seriously a serious question. Not being a native of the country, I may not express myself properly; I believe, however, I spoke sufficiently plainly to be understood. Once more I ask you the way to the Fortress of Fear."

"It is the way to certain death."

"What does that matter?—it is the way I intend to take. I feel certain that they belie the lord of the castle, and wish to put his hospitality to the test."

"Here is a madman!" said the peasant to himself, sending the children into the hut; "nevertheless, I must not let him go without having told him the danger to which he exposes himself. For sixty years, my young traveller, I have inhabited this cottage. Not one of those who have put to me the question that you have just asked me has ever returned. At first, the people who travelled along this road came singly; careless, gay, foolish as you, they passed singing before my door: the same evening they were the captives of Fear. When it was found that there was danger in the voyage, there was quite a different sort of procession. Man spends his life in neglecting Heaven and courting death. When Death scowls at him, he believes it is smiling. The procession never returned. Gallant warriors came, and said to me, 'Prepare a breakfast for us to-morrow, good man; on our return we will make great cheer, and tell you our adventures, and laugh over them.' And the feast was wasted for want of guests; and so, later, when reason increased in my brain, as my beard grew on my chin, I made people pay in advance, but I made no preparations for their return. Then came troops of warriors fully armed, amid the flourish of trumpets, and with banners floating on the wind. They pillaged my house, and their horses wasted my crops. Fear made them captives like the others, and from that time I have lived alone in my ruined habitation, which no one dares to approach. I lost my father through his rashness, my wife through her curiosity; she left me these children. One of them wandered away one day when I was in the fields; what happened to him I have never known; he came back to me an idiot. I have never quitted this spot, though it is more like a burial-place than a birth-place. I am a solitary dweller on the frontiers of Death, an advanced outpost, crying to all such foolish people as you to turn back."

"I thank you," answered Mitaine; "but if you had known me, you would have taken care not to tell me this history, for it only redoubles my desire to meet this dreadful tyrant."

The peasant raised his arms to Heaven, as if to call it to witness the efforts he had made; then he again sat down before his ruined cabin.

"You must be poor," said Mitaine, feeling in her purse. "Take this; you will be my heir if I die, which does not appear to me quite so certain. In

The miserable guide.

any case, the money is yours. Pass the night in prayers for my success, and in the meantime point out to me the road that I must follow."

The peasant praying.

The peasant rose, took Mitaine by the hand, and climbed with her a naked height which overlooked the country.

"You see that footpath which borders the forest? That you must follow. Whither it leads no one knows. Heaven be with you! Farewell!"

"Let me embrace you," said Mitaine, holding out her arms to the peasant, who sank on his knees, as if in the presence of the dead. She flung her arms round his neck, and kissed him; the old man wept; one of his tears fell on Mitaine's hand, she signed herself with it as if it had been holy water;— then she departed. The peasant remained on his knees praying until sunset; after that he sought his miserable home, put his children to bed, lit a taper, and again betook himself to prayer until morning.

Vespers.

VIII. THROUGH THE FORESTS.

The sun sank down in a flood of purple, the birds were chanting their vespers. "Come on, Croque-Miton-Mita-Mitaine!" cried the girl. "I would not stir from the spot for the spurs of knighthood."

The sky changed from gold to pale blue, from pale blue to violet, from violet to indigo, from indigo to black. A thousand stars peeped out to see what was going to happen. A waning moon climbed slowly up the heavens, shedding a feeble light and yellow, as if smitten with fever. The air became cooler, a gentle breeze began to stir the foliage, covered with the dust of day, and to awaken it to its morning toilet. Every sound was hushed, except the rustle of the leaves. The grass had grown so thick and long, Mitaine scarcely knew where to set her foot. She was not afraid, and yet, as she advanced, her thoughts became more grave. To be self-collected in danger is one of the signs of courage. A coward loses himself in the presence of peril.

"What am I about to meet with yonder? What obstacles shall I fall in with? I have always heard my royal godfather say that there is nothing one cannot overcome by courage, skill, and perseverance; if he spoke the truth, I have nothing to fear. This Croquemitaine, perhaps, is, after all, only a robber chief, profiting by the public panic to pillage the passers-by. The passers-by?—but nobody does pass by, and, as a rule, people render pleasing, rather than terrible, the paths that lead to a snare. Pshaw! we shall soon see!"

The haunted grove.

All her past life came back to Mitaine's recollection. She seemed as if she should feel less solitary when surrounded by memories of those she loved. She seemed to hear friendly voices. "Be prudent," whispered her mother.

"Be resolute!" said Charlemagne.

"Be bold!" said Roland.

Thus accompanied, she pushed on with firmer tread, and halted not until she reached the border of the forest. As she entered it, her

212

foot slipped upon some round slimy object, and a snake wound itself round her leg. "So the game is beginning," said Mitaine.

There is room in the human heart for Prudence and Courage, they live together like good neighbours, and it would give you, my young friends, a very false idea of bravery to suppose that it cannot exist in company with caution.

Mitaine had put on a suit of mail, and she congratulated herself on wearing her gauntlets, as she stooped down to seize hold of the reptile. She grasped a round and flexible object, and was about to crush it under her heel, when she discovered that what she had taken for a serpent was only a creeper, which broke in her hand. For an instant she felt ashamed.

"This is the result of all the stories I have been so long listening to about this absurd castle. If people had not tried to frighten me, I should not even have stooped down." And she continued her route.

The moon flung her rays over the forest, and Mitaine beheld in the distance a number of white menacing shapes. Some had burst their shrouds, and allowed their skeleton forms to be seen, clattering at every breath of air; others displayed fearful wounds, in which the weapons yet remained; fleshless arms stretched towards her, and the wind bore to her indistinct and threatening murmurs. She allowed herself to be betrayed into a gesture of alarm; immediately the spectres shook their dishevelled hair, waved their arms, and began to move towards her. She saw them approaching in countless numbers, with menacing aspect and hollow moanings.

"By Roland!" said she, "I believe I'm a little frightened. My godfather would blush for me if he knew it." She drew her sword, and rushed on.

Hardly had the sense of alarm left her, when the appearance of all she saw was changed. The spectres vanished, and Mitaine saw before her only a few bleached tree trunks, on which the moon shed its rays. Instead of wounds, she saw inequalities of the bark; instead of outstretched arms, she saw branches; instead of unkempt locks, leaves; while in the place of threatening murmurs she heard only the wail of the wind.

213

"I'm evidently growing foolish," said she to herself; " I have lost my head, and my brain to-night is full of spectres. I must not let my-self be caught again."

Scarcely had the thought passed through her mind when she felt herself caught by the leg; this time there was no illusion. She turned round quickly, and saw with alarm a grim shape, which struggled out of the earth, and flung itself upon her. At the foot of every tree she could distinguish like forms buried in the earth breast high, and writhing in agony.

Mitaine strove, but in vain, to release her leg; the shape clung to it, and its head seemed about to seize her in its jaws.

"Reality or spectre—dead or alive—I will try how you will take this;" and she struck fiercely at it with her sword. The blow fell upon the root of a tree. "How is it that I did not see this at once? I shall never forgive myself this foolish fear. I must admit, Master Croquemitaine, that your jokes are anything but pleasant. Still, I hope you will give me something more serious to do before long, or I shall cut but a sorry figure when I come to relate my adventures."

Observe, my children, that it is almost always thus in life: out of a hundred things which terrify you, at least ninety-five will only make you smile, if you look them boldly in the face.

The sky had gradually become covered with clouds; large drops of rain began to fall; in the distance the thunder rumbled, but so faintly, that it seemed only like the snoring of an elephant or a hippopotamus.

"The greatest danger I run is that of catching cold. The rain has already begun, and who can tell when I shall reach the Fortress of Fear? This coward of a Croquemitaine has so well concealed his abode, that one might just as well look for a pin at the bottom of the sea."

A terrific clap of thunder was the only answer she received, and the glare of the lightning allowed her to distinguish at a short dis-tance the castle, which was perched, as if balanced, on the extreme point of a mountain of eccentric form.

"So this, then, is the precious jewel which they have taken such pains to conceal from all eyes. By my faith! they were right to conceal it, for it appears to me the most hideous in the world."

The gnarled monster.

Mitaine pushed forward. For a long time she followed the course of a ruined wall, when suddenly a flash of lightning cleaving the heavens enabled her to discover a horrible monster gazing at her from its crest. It resembled the skeleton of a horse, combined with those of an ostrich, a whale, and a giraffe. Its enormous head was supported by a disproportionately long neck, and its two claws, armed with immense talons, were seeking on the top of the wall for some point of vantage whence to leap upon her.

Mitaine, taken by surprise, sprang back twenty paces; the monster took as many in advance. She sank upon her knee as it drew near, and felt its hot breath blowing upon her.

"By the Shrine of St. Landri! I am acting like a child, and show myself little worthy to follow Charlemagne and Roland to battle."

She sprang up; the monster immediately recoiled.

"Will nothing teach me wisdom? Every obstacle that I meet boldly disappears, and yet I allow myself to be stopped by this vile form;" and she gave the wall a vigorous kick. The stones fell crumbling, and dragged with them a number of creepers and brambles a century old, breaking a poor harmless tree which had stood for ages, with its branches resting on the wall. Mitaine shrugged her shoulders, and moved on, saying, "As I expected!"

In a few minutes she found herself in the presence of a more serious obstacle. Before her rolled a torrent, which carried down in its rapid waters huge blocks of stone, as any other stream would carry down logs. This new barrier it was not easy either to overcome or avoid. The night was dark, and the moon faint and pale, and half hidden in masses of cloud. It seemed rather like a dying watch-fire than a luminary of the first magnitude. The water of the torrent gleaming in this half light rushed by with formidable violence, and Mitaine felt her brain swim whenever she looked at it. She hurried up and down the bank, seeking in vain for a means of crossing. The lightning, as if to confuse her, redoubled its intensity, and showed her the castle situated at a short distance on the further shore. At length, however, she discovered a tree which lay across the gulf. Every wave as it passed had washed away a portion of the bank; the tree, half uprooted,

Mitaine crosses the torrent.

had held its own well for a time, until at last, weary of the struggle, it had suffered itself to sink to the ground.

Mitaine contemplated this means of crossing not without apprehension. Tremblingly she placed her foot upon the trunk; it shook and rocked. She hesitated, and as her hesitation increased, so the tree became more shaky and uncertain.

"What!" said she, impatiently; "am I so short a distance from my object, and must I draw back because the passage is not quite safe? No! it is fear that makes me awkward; every day I accomplish things far more difficult than this."

She set her foot resolutely on the trunk, and found, to her surprise, that it grew firmer as she went on.

"Why, I am on a wooden bridge," said she, when she got half-way over. "Nay, indeed, it's a fine stone bridge," she cried, as she reached the farther shore.

Of a truth, my children, fear doubles the importance of most obstacles, for it deprives us of half the faculties which should assist us to overcome them. Take away the ape's intrepidity and give it to man, and man will become as agile as the ape.

Mitaine saw before her but one road, and set out resolutely along it, although it was so narrow that she brushed the rock on either side with her shoulders. It was, in fact, less a path than a cleft in the mountain side. She pushed forward on tip-toe, wondering a little what she should find at the other end of this burrow. Suddenly her head encountered an obstacle, and she discovered that the passage had become so low, that she must stoop to continue her path.

"Do they want to bury me alive?" The thought made her hair bristle; and not without reason, I can assure you, for she was in utter darkness, with hardly a breath of air, and every instant she felt the four walls closing in.

"Do your best, Croquemitaine; it shall never be said that I turned back, when I had got so close to you."

She was now compelled to continue her progress on her hands and knees. "You will get nothing by it; I will pay you for this when I meet you."

The Fortress of Fear.

The ceiling was now so low, that she was obliged to drag herself along the ground. "If there be room for a mouse, I'll get through, never trust me!"

At last, she saw with joy a gleam of light, a few paces further on. This feeble ray gave her fresh courage, and she struggled on by dint of nails, knees, and feet so well, that in a few seconds she had reached the outlet. She was about to breathe again, to live again, to move freely! one more effort, and she would be at liberty! She perceived that the opening at the end of the passage was guarded by a strange sort of grating.

"Well, this complicates the situation! I should be curious to know what my long-bearded godsire would do, if he found himself on all fours in this mole-run before these bars. Assist me to get out of this, St. James, and I will offer up to you a prayer of gratitude."

Mitaine made another movement to approach still nearer to the grating; she was about to take the bars in her hand, when she perceived there was nothing before her but a spider's web.

"Thanks, St. James! you have saved me from a terrible danger."

But now the spider came down into the middle of his web to defend his stronghold, and it was with no common insect that she had to deal. Picture to yourselves a body as big as your two fists, bloated and hairy; legs by the dozen, vying with each other in agility and flexibility, with two pinchers like those of a scorpion, and eyes that gleamed in the dark.

If Mitaine had had the free use of her limbs she would not have taken much notice of such a trifle; but you must remember that she was lying flat upon the ground, hedged in on all sides as close as if in a coffin, and that she could

The great spider.

220

only fight the creature by butting at it with her head. The spider, taking advantage of her hesitation, set about repairing its net, adding thread to thread with frightful rapidity.

"It is worth one's while to be the godchild of an Emperor, the daughter of a knight, the friend of a hero, and, above all, a favourite of St. James, in order to run away from a spider. Mountjoy, St. Denis! let's charge the foe!" She lowered her head, closed her eyes, and pushed her way on. The web broke; she felt her opponent glide over her shoulder, and run along her back. She immediately pressed herself with all her force against the roof, heard a sound like the breaking of an egg, and stepped forth mistress of the field. With what joy did she find herself in the open air! How did she rejoice in the rain that beat on her face and the whirlwind, whose violence tore up even the stones in her path!

Before her rose the Fortress of Fear.

The outpost of owls.

IX. A Night in the Fortress of Fear.

I should like, my young friends, to give you a horrible—an alarming—a terrific description of the Fortress of Fear. The subject is a tempting one enough, but I am the slave of truth, and moreover, imagination has built it after such a fashion that every one sees it under a different aspect. I can, however, tell you a little about it.

The Fortress of Fear is only seen at night, and scarcely can its black outline be made out against the black sky. If the moon shows herself, it is only with an evil purpose to bring out more clearly some hideous combination of lines. The stones are leperous, and the snakes that dwell among them seem like worms that feed on them. Life is represented there by the mere refuse of creation—vultures, adders, centipedes, rats, scorpions, toads, woodlice, and owls; and yet one could not help wondering how even such foul broods as these could inhabit such a place. Those who have had the misfortune to behold this ominous sight perceive only an irregular line of towers, half fallen into ruins, and resembling nothing so much as the fangs of some ogress seven hundred years old. The Fortress of Fear is the oldest of all fortresses; that it still stands is a miracle, for a breath can overthrow

222

it;—and yet it is eternal. Each of us reckons an hour in his life in which it has appeared to him; and even the bravest of us must confess to having paid it a visit.

Mitaine discovered a low portal, almost concealed by the ivy; the wood was worm-eaten, the iron was rusty, there was the slimy track

The entrance to Fear-Fortress.

223

of a snail across the handle. In the archway roosted a flock of night birds, which flew out, expressing their disgust at being disturbed, by melancholy hooting. Mitaine pushed the door—it resisted; she smote it with the pommel of her sword—a hollow sound was the only answer; for ten minutes she struggled in vain to force an entrance, then, losing patience, she gave it a vigorous kick with her foot. The woodwork gave way, the lock came off, the hinges parted, and the barrier fell inwards. Immediately she heard a loud noise, and felt several severe blows. The stonework of the arch had given way, and fallen in upon her. Fortunately she was not alarmed; had she shrunk back, she must have been buried in the ruins. A formidable heap of rubbish blocked the entrance. Where Time busies himself in the work of destruction, and Accident assists him to build a barricade, they both do their work so well, that those most experienced in such constructions must bow admiringly to their superior skill.

"Ho! Ho! What do they take me for here?" said Mitaine to herself, not without anger. "Do they fancy by any chance that I want to run away? This is a most needless precaution."

Mitaine was at the foot of a narrow spiral staircase, which led to the top of the castle. The walls, covered with thick moss, distilled an offensive moisture, which, falling on the stairs, encouraged the growth of forests of ferns, lichens, and toadstools, the pleasant homes of hundreds of woodlice, and other creeping things. On the first step was seated a toad; a pale lambent flame played around it, the only light to be met with in this dismal spot. The toad rose on its hind legs like a kangaroo, and began to climb the staircase, leaving behind it on each step a slimy track, which spread out exhaling a noisome odour. Mitaine followed this phosphorescent guide. Hearing a hollow sound accompanying each step, she turned and saw the stairs crumble away one after another as she ascended.

"They are evidently bent on keeping me here, and I confess I shall have some difficulty in tearing myself away."

The toad continued to lead the way. At the sixtieth stair it paused before a door, which opened, although there was nobody to be seen: the toad again moved on, and Mitaine continued to follow it. She found herself in a vast gallery lighted only by the moon. Refreshed by the cool air which blew on her face, and by the glimpse of the open country which she caught through a window, she felt as if she had just emerged from the tomb. On her left hand was a blank wall; before her opened, one after another, a series of huge folding doors; on her right was a large array of columns and arches that flung their gloomy shadows on the floor and side of the chamber. Before her was the toad going on without stopping; gleaming with phosphorescent light, and leaving behind it, as it crawled along, a slimy and shining track. As Mitaine passed by the first column,

The guiding toad.

it crumbled in pieces, and she beheld, standing upright on the pedestal, a corpse wrapped in its winding-sheet, and holding in its hand a lighted torch. It stepped down from its place, and, waiting until she passed, took up its position on her left. The second column sank in its turn, a second corpse descended and placed itself on her right hand, also bearing a torch. The same thing took place throughout the whole length of the gallery; but the attention of our young page was distracted by the spectacle she beheld on passing the first door. She saw an immense hole, the mere sight of which made her giddy; at one moment excessively bright, at the next equally gloomy, it seemed as if lighted by some gigantic forge, whose flame alternately blazed up and died at every successive blast of the bellows. This intermittent glare was insupportable, and for some minutes Mitaine was almost blinded. She heard groans, and, at length, contrived to distinguish thousands of unhappy, wretches with their hands tied behind their backs, and their limbs fractured, suspended by their wrists from the roof. Her heart full of pity and rage, she was about to rush to their aid, when she perceived that the hall was without a floor; a gulf, at the bottom of which a torrent was roaring, yawned beneath the feet of the victims. She turned aside her head, wiped away a tear, and

225

The corpse candles.

hastened onwards. Every door before which she passed afforded her a view of new tortures, and her impotence to relieve these agonies so infuriated her, that, not knowing how to vent her rage, she rushed, sword in hand, upon the melancholy procession that surrounded her; but she encountered nothing but empty air. The corpses, taking no heed, pursued their way without hurrying, without delaying. Then the anger of Mitaine knew no bounds. She rushed on recklessly in search of an enemy. The toad took to flight; the dead, observing their distance, seemed to glide, not walk over the floor. At the end of the gallery a door opened, on grating hinges, and closed again as soon as Mitaine had crossed the threshold. The darkness was impenetrable. She was compelled to halt. The dull flame of the torches flickered up and faded in the gloom without giving out any light. The corpses ranged themselves in an immense circle round the toad; the toad gave a bound at least ten feet high, and Mitaine observed that it increased in size. As it swelled out, the hall became filled with light. Then the beast began to assume airs and graces, to attitudinise, and to ogle; and lastly, to finish these vagaries, it set about its toilet, and commenced scratching itself, emitting, at every touch of its foot, showers of venom and sparks.

The toad
scratching itself.

The hall which Mitaine had just entered was the largest in the world. It seemed like some enormous square, in which met a number of wide roads, whose starting-points were lost in obscurity. The ceiling, which was low, was supported on huge granite cubes, whose sides were adorned with *bas reliefs*, representing the most varied scenes in the dance of death.

The toad took its seat on an overturned column, at the foot of one of the pillars, shining like some baleful meteor. In front of it, beneath a dais of black serge, embroidered with silver, sat the Lord of the

Fortress and his family, while in all the galleries legions of ghosts waited, motionless, the orders of their master.

The throne was of aspen wood; it was no easy task to reach it. Oubliettes, traps, and snares defended the approach. The Lord of Fear was standing up. On either side of him were seated the noble dame Cowardice of St. Panic, and her daughters, Consternation, Fright, Terror, Alarm, Dismay, Apprehension, Trepidation, Timidity, Pusillanimity, Poltroonery, and Dastardy. All were misshapen, and so accustomed to try to look on every side of them at once, for fear of being taken by surprise, that they squinted frightfully. They were all absolutely hideous to behold.

The Lord of Fear was tall, but he stooped and kept his head sunk between his shoulders. His bristling locks were prematurely white; his hollow eye did not remain still for an instant, but wandered restlessly to every corner; his sunken countenance, pale and colourless as wax, was disfigured by green streaks; his purple lips, continually quivering with nervous excitement, endeavoured in vain to assume an air of bravery; his fidgety fingers wandered to his cuirass, his sword, his dagger, as if to assure themselves that they would not be wanting if needed. A cold perspiration bathed his face, in spite of the fever that consumed him. His teeth chattered, and every moment a fit of shivering set all his defensive armour rattling under his dingy cloak; and every time that she heard this sound of steel, Dame Coward gave a terrible jump, and gazed round her upon all sides for the cause of her alarm. She was seated on the very edge of her throne, with her two hands resting on the elbows, so that she might at once jump up and run away. Like her daughters, she was dressed in a material the colour of which was constantly changing. A hare reposed on her knees.

"This little page would be nice to eat," whispered Trepidation to her father; "don't be too severe upon him."

"There you are again with your absurdities! you have no force of character," interposed Alarm. "If one ever listened to you, Heaven knows what would become of us."

"We must, at any price," said Dastardy, "get rid of this young vixen, and I feel sure that by attacking her in the rear—"

The family of Fear.

"I am afraid our last hour is come," said Apprehension, bursting into tears.

"You are always the same," said Alarm. "You would never tire of throwing the handle after the hatchet."

"Why don't you speak, sister?" said Dastardy to Timidity, who was hiding herself. "Let us hear your opinion."

"I—but—I don't know," stammered Timidity.

"You never know anything," answered Dastardy, giving her sister a pinch that nearly brought the blood, and then running away.

Poor Timidity gave a shriek that made all the family jump again. The Lord of Fear sprang back ten paces, and drew his dagger. Dame Coward jumped up and let fall her hare, which immediately hid itself under her petticoat.

"Be silent, idiots, and come round me again; that foolish Timidity has given me a fright. The first who speaks shall be put in the dark cupboard." After this awful threat came the silence of death.

"Well, and what would you do here, little one?" said the Lord of Fear, in the interval between two shivering fits.

"By the Shrine of St. Landri," said Mitaine, clapping her hands on her hips, "it must be admitted you have a strange way of receiving your guests! I have shrunk from nothing in order that I might see you, and my perseverance deserves a better return."

"You do not answer my question. Why do you come here?"

"To drive you away."

On hearing these words the Lord of Fear shrank into himself until you would have thought that half of him had disappeared, and Dame Coward sank back into her chair, behind which her daughters concealed themselves.

"Imprudent wretch!" stuttered Fear, shaking until he nearly fell. "How dare you defy me thus?"

"To judge from your appearance," said Mitaine, smiling, "there's no great merit in that."

"You dare to doubt my courage? You deserve to suffer the terrors of my vengeance." It was not without some difficulty that Fear uttered these words, for his tongue was almost paralysed.

The shriek of Timidity.

"You have no influence over me; and all the absurd scarecrows you have called up to terrify me are only fit to be laughed at!"

"My name is the terror of the universe."

"You libel the universe by saying so. Because a few weak minds allow you to rule them, you consider yourself master of the world. Come out of your den into the light of day, and see how you will be received!"

"The women are on my side!"

"They are not! When they catch a glimpse of you they cannot in truth repress an exclamation of natural disgust. An insect, a shadow, an unusual noise can make them tremble; but when a serious danger presents itself, when a great sentiment animates them, they will, as Christians, die the death of martyrs; as wives, follow their husbands into battle, like the Gallic women; and, as mothers, struggle with lions for the safety of their children. They will, in short, achieve immortality, like Judith, like Lucretia, like St. Genevieve."

"Well, at any rate, I have the children. The little people are my subjects."

"And you dare to tell this to *me*? Why, you actually elevate impudence almost to the position of courage. The children would obey you least of any of us if wicked teachers and foolish parents did not place them in your power. They threaten them with the dark room, and they take care to lock you up there with them. They call the wolf to eat them. Did Romulus and Remus quake at the approach of their wild nurse? I am but a child, but I know how much you are worth, and, by St. Landri's Shrine! I defy you utterly."

Mitaine became aware of a low sound, and noticed a stir among the corpses. At the end of one of the numberless passages that opened into the hall where this happened there appeared some pale rays of light which seemed to come nearer. As their light grew more distinct that of the toad began to die out, and the creature itself commenced shifting uneasily on its seat.

The Lord of Fear seemed more alarmed than ever. His teeth chattered like castanets—he had to make three attempts before he could speak.

"You do ill to deny my power; all these who surround me have acknowledged it!"

"They are ashamed of it now," cried Mitaine; and then turning to them, she shouted, "Can you submit to such a lord? You have only to make one step towards him, and you will drive him and his wretched race from the face of the earth. Your hands are not dead, they are but benumbed for a while. Make one more effort. Fling yourselves on the tyrant. I will show you the way!"

At these words the dead let fall their winding-sheets, and discovered to view a legion of knights in rusty armour with their swords drawn. Alarm gave a shriek, which was answered by screams from Fear himself, from Dame Coward, from Consternation, Fright, Terror, Dismay, Apprehension, Trepidation, Timidity, Pusillanimity, Poltroonery, and Dastardy.

Then was seen a strange sight. The *bas-reliefe* began to start into life, and continued their wild dance along the pillars, to the accompaniment of alarming shrieks. The thunder rolled, and yawning fissures opened in the walls and ceiling. The earth gaped amid deafening clamours, and Mitaine found herself in the dark. She did not remain long thus, for the galleries sank by degrees, and day came on apace. Its first rays glittered on her arms; the cheery voice of Chanticleer resounded, and, as if it had but waited the signal, the Fortress of Fear vanished into air!

Mitaine was mute with astonishment. How fair appeared the country to her! how beautiful the sun! and how softly did the breeze of morning woo her cheek! She fell on her knees, and uttered a heartfelt prayer.

The fields were variegated with a thousand colours, as though they contained specimens of every kind of flower that blows. The birds joined in—never had they chanted a more joyous welcome to dawn. There was nothing left of the castle but the recollection, and that was already growing indistinct.

When Mitaine had finished her orisons and rose to her feet, she beheld an old man and a young woman gazing at her with an affectionate expression. They were but a few steps from her, yet she could scarcely see them, for they were enveloped in a faint mist.

"Who are you?" she asked.

"Your grateful friends. You have delivered us from Fear, who used to hold us captive. For a long time we have ceased to breathe, but, thanks to you, we are about to see once more those from whom we were so hastily snatched away. To-day is the Feast of the Dead, and heaven allows us to pass the day on earth. All those whom you have delivered are going to escort you to Charlemagne's camp to testify to your great courage and noble bearing."

Then Mitaine saw gathered around her from all quarters a number of knights clad in armour that was eaten up with rust. They were of all ages and of all countries, the greater part being mounted. A few women and children followed the procession.

The footfalls were unheard, and left no mark behind them. The figures were transparent, bathed in a strange mist, to which the sun gave an opalescent gleam.

Having ranged themselves in column, they began to march onward, and Mitaine retraversed the places which had seemed to her so terrific on the preceding night: the stone bridge across the torrent, the wall covered with creepers, and almost hidden by acacia boughs, the forest of naked stems—everything, in short, appeared full of gaiety now that the sun was shining.

She called to her the old man who had lately addressed her, and bade him tell her what were the tortures, the sight of which had so roused her.

"Those," said the dead man, "were the halls of nightmare, my child. The Lord of Fear gives his victims no rest. He and Sleep, who delivers them into his hand, understand each other. Incubi, demons, vampires, and ghoules form his terrible executioners, and preside over the punishments. You have seen them at their task, I need not attempt to describe them!

"What can defend us against them?"

"A clear conscience and a good digestion."

In a quarter of an hour Mitaine perceived the hut at which she had stopped on the night before. The peasant was seated on the ground among his little ones.

"Thank heaven!" said she. "Poor old man, your feeble sight will not, doubtless, allow you to distinguish your son as yet. But you, his wife, you can no doubt perceive him."

"We have never ceased to see him since we parted," said she. "There is neither limit nor let to the vision of the dead."

The peasant turned his head, saw the procession approaching, recognised Mitaine, and, with a shout of surprise, at once ran to meet her.

Ere he had reached half-way, his glance fell on his father and his wife, and, overcome with joy, he sank on his knees, stretching out his arms towards them. He would fain have spoken, but could find no language to express in fitting terms the joy he experienced. He scarce dared to move, lest he should put to flight the beloved group he saw before him. When he had ascertained that he was not suffering from an illusion, tears filled his eyes, and, clasping his hands, he fell on his face, saying, "Kind Heaven, I am indeed grateful for this!"

I will not attempt to describe to you the joy of these three, whom death had, for a while, no power to separate. The mother covered her babes with kisses. The peasant, now as aged as his father had been, could not tear himself from his arms. Their white beards mingled at each embrace. The first outburst of joy over, they all three turned to Mitaine, and kissed her hands.

"Who could have forewarned you of all this happiness, my son?" said the father.

"Do you not know, then? My child, who, some years ago lost his reason, has become the cleverest of the family since daybreak this morning. Henceforth there are no saints in the calendar I shall revere as I do you!" said he to Mitaine, who had no small difficulty in freeing herself from the demonstrations of gratitude of which she was the object. She called for the horse which she had left with her host of the previous night, and rode away at full gallop, followed by her fantastic escort.

In about six hours she saw the camp of Charlemagne. The sentinels on outpost duty, seeing a cloud of dust in the distance coming along towards them with such speed, fell back and gave the alarm.

235

"What is it?" said the Emperor. "Who are these that thus fall into our hands? Go, Miton; mount your horse, take an escort, and inspect these new comers."

In a moment the whole camp was alive. Every one put on his corslet, laced his helm, seized his lance, and sprang to saddle. Miton chose thirty mounted knights and led them out.

"By my faith!" said he, "these be strange folks. To judge from their size they ought not to be far off, and yet I can hardly make them out. Can you see them better, Red John?" he asked one of his men.

"Not I! My wonder is as great as yours. But is not that a page in the imperial livery who is riding at their head?"

"By my life, it is Mitaine!" And Miton spurred forward at such speed that in three minutes he was in his daughter's arms. The ghostly squadron halted, and the thirty knights halted likewise, striving to pacify their startled horses, which were snuffing the air, snorting with dilated nostrils, pawing the ground, and neighing as if ready to die of terror.

"Who are these whom you are leading?"

"Those whom I have liberated."

"Liberated! How?"

"I will tell you all in the Emperor's presence. The sun is low already, and we have no time to spare."

Miton and his thirty knights, and Mitaine with her strange followers, rode towards the camp. Charlemagne, surrounded by his peers, came out to meet them.

"By St. James! these people look as if they didn't belong to this world. And if I am not stupidly mistaken, it is my godchild who commands them."

Mitaine dismounted, and approached her royal godsire, who asked her, "Well, little one, what is this strange array? Do you know that I have a mind to punish you, and yet I haven't the heart to scold you, I am so rejoiced to see you again, and so anxious to learn who these are that accompany you."

"My prisoners, sire!"

And the spectres lowered their lances to show their submission to her.

"But whence come they? Have you been to seek them in another world?"

"By my faith, sire, I could almost believe I passed last night there;" and she related her adventures briefly to Charlemagne in the presence of his peers and knights.

"Come, let me embrace you, my darling. So it appears I have promised you something. What is it?"

Exeunt the Fear family.

"You promised me, sire, to ask Roland to take me into his service as a squire."

"It is Roland whom I reward by giving him such a treasure. What say you, nephew mine?"

The only answer Roland gave was to clasp Mitaine in his arms. The little heroine, ruddy with joy, turned to her escort to thank them. They had disappeared! On seeing this, Charlemagne sank on his knees; his example was followed by all the rest, and Turpin recited the prayers for the dead.

Thus ended the adventure undertaken by Mitaine

I wish I could tell you, my friends, that the Fortress of Fear was destroyed for good and all. I am compelled, as a veracious chronicler, to confess that it was rebuilt the same evening.

You will some day or other, my young friends, most assuredly fall in with the Lord of Fear. Call to mind Mitaine whenever you do meet him, and remember that the monster can boast no weapons save those you surrender to him—no power save that which you give him—no courage save that which you lose.

Stung to death by vipers.

EPILOGUE.
RONCESVALLES.
A.D. 778.

RONCESVALLES.
A.D. 778.

You have, I hope, not forgotten, my dear readers, that Charlemagne had dispatched Ganelon to Aquitaine. For the shame and injury of France, the Count of Mayence had turned this trip to good account, by establishing a perfect understanding between himself and our old and little- respected friend, Wolf. They decided on the destruction of Charlemagne and his peers; but as for attacking them openly, they did not dream of that!

"I will undertake," said Ganelon, to lead them into the mountains, if you will only place some twenty thousand Navarrese and Gascons on the heights that I will show you. Then we shall be able in perfect safety to crush beneath the rocks this haughty and hated brood."

About the same period Marsillus had called his warriors together, and was conversing with them, reposing in the shade on the white marble steps of his palace.

"My friends, since this accursed Charles has set foot in Spain, we have never had a moment's peace. Great as has been the bravery we have displayed, we have been everywhere worsted. We can do no more, for each has done his best. I suppose you are none of you less desirous than I to yield this beautiful Spain to these Northern barbarians. Aid me, therefore, by your counsels to avenge our disasters."

Blancandrin, the wisest and most crafty of the Pagans, was the first to speak.

"The fox often passes where the lion cannot. Well, then, since we fail as lions, let us assume the part of foxes, instead of wasting our time in idle laments, and our resources in vain endeavours. Charles is very proud; and when pride is warder, the city is ill-watched. Profess a respectful regard for this crowned bully; tell him you desire to be baptised, and appoint a meeting with him in his own dominions.

Promise to meet him there by Michaelmas, with your principal nobles, to do homage to him, and to acknowledge the Christian faith. Add further, that you will make him a present of three hundred mules, laden with gold and silver; a hundred chariots, filled with a countless stock of rare stuffs; numberless war-steeds; three hundred trained falcons, lions, and leopards broken-in for the chase; besides five hundred fair Saracen damsels, if such be his good pleasure. The invaders have been a long time from home, and have left their estates in the charge of their wives. There is not one of them who would not be glad of a rest. As soon as they have divided the booty, they will all be pressing the king to return, and when once they get home again, he will have no easy task to prevail on them to stir a second time."

"The advice is good, possibly, but Charles is not the man to be satisfied with simple promises."

"Send him hostages—ten, twenty, thirty, if he asks for them. Would it not be better to lose a few women and children than the whole of Spain? I offer to give my son as a hostage, at the risk of his life."

This counsel was considered sound, and was approved by all.

"Go, then," said Marsillus to Blancandrin. "I promise you a splendid escort when you set out, and boundless rewards on your return. Exchange the sword for the olive branch, and be not sparing in promises."

The envoys were accordingly mounted on white mules, with trappings and bells of gold and silver, and before long set out for the camp of Charlemagne.

When the envoys arrived, no time was lost in introducing them into the Emperor's presence. His Majesty of the snowy beard was sitting in his orchard surrounded by his bravest warriors. The younger ones were practising the use of arms; the elder were talking or playing at chess.

Blancandrin, after having saluted Charles with dignified courtesy, delivered his message so cunningly, that the nobles began to shout, "Hurrah, now we shall speedily return home!" Charlemagne, however, remained lost in meditation. It was not his habit to give way readily either to astonishment or disappointment. At last he rose and said, "The news you bring me causes me great pleasure. If King Marsillus is really desirous of securing his soul's safety, let him meet me at Aix-la-Chapelle, and I will welcome him there as a brother."

A tent was prepared for Blancandrin and his suite, on whom every attention and boundless generosity were lavished.

The next day, after mass and matins, the Emperor wisely called together his peers to learn what they thought of the speech of the envoy from the Court of the King of Saragossa. Naymes of Bavaria, a knight of great renown, and one of the king's best counsellors, rose and spoke:—

Charlemagne's meditations.

242

"Sire, you have beaten the enemy wherever he has dared to offer battle. Of his fortresses, not one stone rests on another; his cities have been burnt; his troops have been either killed or converted. You have raised the cross wherever it had been formerly overthrown; what can you desire more? You are offered a ransom for the kingdom in which you will hold the sovereign power; a nation of unbelievers demands baptism at your hands, and offers you hostages. It would be a sin to continue a warfare which has no longer any object. Such is my opinion!"

After this speech, Roland was not slow to spring to his feet.

"So it is you, then, Naymes, whom I hear? and can you give such counsel? Marsillus is your enemy, sire, and you have scarcely treated him in a way to make him very anxious to embrace you. Do not turn your back upon Spain until your undertaking is accomplished; we have been here longer already than was necessary for its completion. Send home those brave soldiers who have tired of war before they have completed their conquest, and I venture to say that with those who remain you shall plant the cross within sight of Africa, if such be your good pleasure. How can you trust the words of a Pagan? Have you already forgotten the fate to which Marsillus condemned two of your nobles, the Counts Basan and Basille? They went on an embassy from you to the King of Saragossa, and he had them beheaded on Mount Hautille. It was your honour, sire, which that day fell beneath the infidel axe. Will you let them trample it under foot because a few prudent warriors would be glad to abandon this undertaking? Go, then, but I must remain! I shall stay here to make my death so glorious that you will all envy me."

During this speech Charles knitted his brows and tugged his long moustache; seeing which, Ganelon rose in his turn.

"These be proud words, forsooth I could not but ask myself when I heard them whether we live in the reign of Roland or of Charlemagne. This sort of thing is easily spoken, and sounds remarkably well, like everything that's hollow. We are told to retreat; are we in the habit of doing so? Does it not look as if Roland had been conquering Spain while we followed at a respectful distance? Forgive

243

my anger, sire, but I cannot help speaking somewhat freely. Take no one's counsel but your own, sire, and you will do right."

Thereupon Charlemagne asked his knights which of them would like to carry his message to Marsillus. All rose and offered to go, Roland being more importunate than all the others.

"You'll deafen me, nephew," said the Emperor. "I shall certainly not send you on a mission you have just condemned. My friend Ganelon shall carry my wishes to the King of Saragossa. To him will I entrust the gauntlet and truncheon."

"That is indeed a wise choice," said Roland, laughing. "You will nowhere find a more cautious ambassador."

"Enough said! By my beard, nephew mine, you will provoke me too far presently. Be seated, and wait until I bid you speak."

"Sire," said Ganelon, "from such a mission one does not always return. I recommend to your care my son Baldwin, who will one day be a brave warrior."

Charlemagne handed the gauntlet to the Count of Mayence, who let it fall on the ground. "A bad omen!" said the Franks, seeing it. "Roland may be right after all!"

"You will hear of me before long, gentlemen," said Ganelon, with an ill-favoured smile. Then, furnished with truncheon and letter, he made ready to set out on his mission.

Ganelon and Blancandrin, followed by the Saracen body-guard, journeyed for three days side by side. The Pagan was not slow to perceive in a moment the hatred entertained by the Count of Mayence for Roland, and he rejoiced to see it. Let us hear what they are talking about.

"Whence comes it," said Blancandrin, "that your sovereign, instead of seeking an alliance with us, made war on us so fiercely?"

"It is Roland who is always egging him on. But for him, we should long since have returned to France."

They reached the camp of Marsillus. Fifty thousand Saracens surrounded the King of Saragossa, but they maintained perfect silence, for fear of losing a syllable of what was going to be said.

"May Allah and Mahomet preserve you, beloved sovereign! We have borne your message, and we bring back to you one of the noblest peers of the Court of France, to decide with you on peace or war."

"I am prepared to give him an immediate audience."

Marsillus and Ganelon remained shut up together for two hours—two hours, which laid the foundation of ages of regret. When the tent was re-opened the King of Saragossa came out, leaning on the arm of the French envoy. Had Roland come instead of Ganelon, that would never have happened.

Ganelon and Marsillus.

"Gentlemen," said Marsillus to his nobles, "welcome the preserver of Spain! This lord, although a Christian, is a true friend to us, and I desire that he be treated as such."

A Saracen advanced, drew his sword from its sheath, and presented it to Ganelon.

"This weapon is the best in the world," said he, "Its jewelled hilt alone is estimated at thirty thousand bezants, at the lowest, and yet the blade is even more valuable. Accept it, and may it serve you well against Roland."

"I will put it to the test," said the Count of Mayence, coolly; and the traitor and unbeliever kissed each other.

The queen passed by. Marsillus stopped her *cortège*, and bade her dismount, saying, "This is our best of friends. You owe it to him that we shall remain under that Spanish sky which you love so much. Embrace him for the love of us all."

"With all my heart," said the Sultana. "I wish you also, Sir Ganelon, to bear to your wife from me these bracelets, which are the finest in my possession. Neither the Pope at Rome nor the Emperor at Aix-la-Chapelle can boast anything to equal them among all their treasures."

All vied in paying the Count attention, and in loading him with the most precious gifts.

The same evening Ganelon returned to the French camp, accompanied by presents and hostages for the Emperor.

Three days later, at early dawn, Ganelon and his escort arrived at Charlemagne's quarters.

"So you have returned," said Charles. "Have you sped well with your mission?"

"Sire, you have nothing more to do here! The gallant King Marsillus is altogether your devoted liegeman. Behold the treasures he sends you, as a guarantee of others yet more valuable. See, too, the hostages whom I have chosen, thirty in number, all of them of the noblest rank. In a month the King of the Saracens will visit you at the French Court to receive baptism, together with all his nobles and knights."

"You could not bring me more welcome news, and I rejoice greatly that I chose you for the mission. Before long *you* will have reason to rejoice at it too!"

His audience concluded, Ganelon retired with his nephew Pinabel, to whom he wished to reveal the real state of the case. It happened that Mitaine preceded them into the stable, towards which the traitor took his way, and knowing the hate the count bore to Roland, her friend, she was curious to hear him speak openly. She therefore crept up in the manger, and hid herself among the hay in the rack.

This second Judas, going up to his horse, began to talk as follows:—

"Marsillus, who had treated me distantly enough in the morning, apologised at night for so doing, and, as a slight reparation, presented me with some valuable sables. I gave him to understand the dreadful

Ganelon tells all to Pinabel.

fate that awaited him, and assured him that Roland was the only obstacle in the way of our return to France. 'Hope for no mercy,' said I, 'while Roland lives.' 'How can we kill him?' said he. Whereupon I answered, I would undertake to do it with his assistance. 'What can I do?' he asked. 'I will tell you what I have planned,' said I. 'Before long we shall be on the march for France. The most dangerous post is the rear-guard, and that Roland will claim. When he reaches the pass of Roncesvalles, surrounded by the flower of our chivalry, twenty thousand Navarrese and Gascons, posted there by me, will hurl down a very shower of rocks. Take advantage of the surprise, and with two hundred thousand men fall on them in the rear. I won't guarantee your men's lives, but you must carry on the battle incessantly, and at last Roland must be slain.'

"'It is very well said,' answered the king; 'this counsel is worth ten mules, laden with gold pieces, and I will pay you that sum yearly as long as I live.'"

At this point Pinabel, observing that Ganelon's horse, although it had just come off a long journey, only smelt at the rack without touching its contents, took a pitchfork, and in order to find out what hindered the animal from eating, thrust it into the hay. One of the prongs pierced Mitaine's thigh, but she nevertheless remained silent, determined not to lose for a cry the advantage of the conversation she had overheard.

"There's nothing there," said Pinabel.

"What did you think there would be? Don't you know that a good horse never eats much in the morning?" And with that the worthy couple quitted the stable.

Mitaine had great difficulty in crawling back to Miton's tent. She dressed her wound with a celebrated ointment, which is still in great use—the "Balm of Miton-Mitaine"—and was able to present herself the same evening before Roland.

The Count of Mans listened to what his squire had to tell.

"This is good news you bring me, little one; and, with the aid of Heaven, I will find a way thereby to rid the world of this traitor Ganelon."

"What!" said Mitaine; "will you not alter your line of march?"

"Remember this: he who finds a snake in his path has two alternatives to choose between. He can either make a *détour*, and continue his route, by doing which he leaves an enemy in his rear; or he can go straight to the monster and kill it, which is the safer course. There is, by the way, a third solution of the matter—flight; but, of course, no one would dream of that. I shall take care not to neglect the opportunity which is offered me. In the meantime, swear to keep strict silence on this point!"

The trumpets resounded through the camp of Marsillus. The unbelievers placed themselves in ambush beside the French line of march, and waited for the next morning.

The clarions rang out through the camp of Charlemagne. The hour of departure had come. Charles rode proudly amid his gallant knights.

"Who will lead the rear-guard through the passes of Cisaire?" asked the Emperor of his nobles.

"Count Roland," suggested Ganelon, "since he is the bravest. Does not the place of danger belong to him?"

"Count of Mayence, some evil intention influences that speech."

"Why so, sire?" interposed Roland. "Sir Ganelon is right. The task is mine—I claim it."

"So be it," said the Emperor. "My peers shall accompany you with twenty-five thousand horsemen."

"The Saracens will have a hot day's work," said Ganelon to himself.

The Saracens were concealed in the forests at the entrance of the pass. The Navarrese and Gascons (everlasting shame upon them!) were lying in ambush on the heights, ready to hurl death upon their brother Christians.

The vanguard, consisting of twenty thousand men, led by Ogier the Dane, was first to present itself. But it was not they who were wanted—they were allowed to pass.

Charlemagne came next, with Ganelon in attendance upon him. For six hours the troops, the wagons, the booty, were slowly marching

Roland the Peerless.

through the defile. There was an abundance of wealth; but who dared touch it? They were suffered to pass. Finally came the rear-guard, led by Roland. Then the Pagans began to be on the move, the Gascons prepared for action. The great carnage was about to begin.

Marsillus was on horseback at the head of his troops. Buriabel, King of Alexandria, came swaggering up to him.

"Sire, I have brought you thirty thousand soldiers, fully armed. I have not hesitated to risk my life in your service. In return for this, I only ask one thing—the honour of despatching Roland. If I meet him, he dies!"

"You forget, it appears to me," said the King of Saragossa, in a severe tone, "that I am here. I am not in the habit of handing over difficult tasks to others; Roland belongs to me! You will have enough to do with the rest."

Then, armed to the teeth, they rode forward in serried ranks.

The Franks entered the pass. Roland halted them, and spoke: "Brothers in arms! We are going to have a tough day's work. But few of us will ever again behold fair France. Ganelon, the traitor, has brought us to this evil pass! He has sold us to the Saracens. In a few minutes these rocks will be hurled down upon us, and we shall hear the Saracen trumpets sounding. They do not know that we are fore-warned, and the sound of our bugles will be the signal. Let those who are in doubt about our safety, therefore, leave us to join the main body. But let those, who desire wounds more awful than death—those who are ready to sacrifice their lives, in order to be revenged on Ganelon— let those remain with me!"

Not a single knight quitted the ranks.

"If any one of us escapes, his life must be devoted to the extermination of Ganelon, and all his race. For my part, I swear to do this!"

All repeated the oath. Roland heard behind him a voice, shriller than any of the others, cry, "By the Shrine of St. Landri, death to the Count of Mayence!"

He turned, and saw Mitaine.

"Ah, unhappy child, what are you doing here? You know well what fate awaits us. Is this a place for babes-in-arms?"

"You do wrong to blame me, sir knight. You will, perhaps, have reason to be sorry for your words before sunset."

Mitaine was on the summit of a peak. She gazed around on all sides, and soon discovered the enemy. The sun was shining brightly, and glistened on corslet and casque, spear and pennon. At the same moment the neighing of horses reached her ear.

"The Saracens are coming from the Spanish side. They are so many in number, it is difficult to understand how any troops can be left to guard the cities. If we had to encounter so large a Christian army, the result would be doubtful. But these are Pagans, and Heaven will not fail us."

"If that be the case," said Oliver, "you had better sound your horn, friend Roland. Charlemagne has not gone far, and will return at once to our aid on hearing it."

"We must wield swords, not horns, here. The way is open, if you fear the adventure is too arduous."

"Trust me, comrade; in a few moments it will be too late. Wind your horn!"

"You give me base counsel! It shall never be told that Roland quitted his grasp of Durandal to wind his horn for aid against Pagans!"

"So be it," said Oliver. "We will not quarrel about it."

Roland turned to Gautier de Luz, and said to him—

"Dismount, Gautier, and let two thousand of our knights do the same. You will take the command of them, climb the mountain, and take these accursed Gascons in the rear before we enter the pass. Cut them up without mercy, like dogs as they are, and then, when you have accomplished the task, sound on your horn. We shall then draw on the Saracens in pursuit, and when I give the signal, do you roll down on them the rocks prepared for our destruction."

"Well conceived," said Hoel of Nantes. "An excellent jest. I would not exchange my place here for anything in the whole world!"

Two thousand knights dismounted, and with Gautier de Luz at their head, commenced the ascent. Mitaine, more active and lighter than the others, went first to reconnoitre. Roland followed them with his eyes until they disappeared behind the rocks.

In about a quarter of an hour, which, I can assure you, seemed long enough to those below, a great uproar broke out, and the Navarrese and Gascons appeared in disorder on the cliffs. They were close pressed, and those who were not put to the sword on the spot, were flung down into the ravine, in which there was soon an almost insurmountable heap of dead bodies. There was hardly a bush that was not adorned with some bleeding fragment or other.

Presently was heard the bugle note which announced that the heights were taken, and Roland, followed by some thousands of knights, rode out to meet the Saracens.

"What is the meaning of this?" said Marsillus, on beholding the Christians issuing from the pass. "It strikes me these brave warriors are afraid to attempt the pass. But we know how to compel them to do so. Their graves are dug there, and there they must sleep this night—and nowhere else!"

Thirty thousand Saracens spurred forward in haste, and grew doubly courageous on beholding the Christians turn to retreat.

"What have they been telling us about the courage of these people?" said Arroth, the nephew of Marsillus. "So far, there has been more of the chase than the combat. We need hardly have come in such numbers."

"Your words are wanting in sense," said Turgis of Toulouse. "Pray Heaven to allow your brains to grow old enough to perceive the folly."

The Saracens entered the defile in pursuit of the Franks, who had surmounted all the obstacles in the pass. Their pursuers, however, halted in wonder before the heap of dead bodies that barred their passage. Roland took advantage of their hesitation and gave the signal, on hearing which Gautier de Luz set to work. Huge blocks of stone crashed down from overhead, involving horses and men; living, dead, and wounded; Saracens, Gascons, and Navarrese, in one common destruction. The pass was completely blocked up.

The ambuscade.

"Truly," said Roland, "Ganelon contrived this trap very cleverly. But one cannot foresee everything in this world, and in this instance it is the hare that is hunting the hounds!"

The Pagans who returned to the King of Saragossa were barely eight thousand, including the wounded who had escaped destruction. They had flung away their banners and their arms in order to facilitate their flight.

"Is this what you promised us?" they cried, threateningly, to Marsillus. "We have just fallen into a snare laid for us by Ganelon. Ah, dastard of a Roland, treacherous Count of Mayence, coward of an Emperor, you shall hear more of us yet! By Mahomet, our vengeance shall be something to speak of, rascals!"

A hundred thousand Saracen knights pricked forward at full speed, taking a different road, which permitted them to cut off the retreat of the Franks. In the meantime Gautier de Luz and Mitaine had rejoined Roland.

Archbishop Turpin had ridden to a slight eminence. The twenty thousand knights were on their knees around him.

"Prepare to perish nobly, my brothers-in-arms," said he to them. "The heroes who do not shrink from the fight will sleep in Paradise by sunset. All your past sins shall be atoned for by cuts or thrusts of sword or lance. I absolve you all from this moment!"

He gave them his blessing, and they rose, comforted and encouraged.

Presently the sound of the enemies' horses was heard, and before long the two armies had encountered each other. Lances were shattered—the field was covered with fragments of arms and armour. Death had made a speedy harvest, and riderless horses were galloping hither and thither, amid the groans and cries of the wounded.

Everywhere destruction was being dealt out.

At the head of the Saracens rode Arroth, nephew of Marsillus.

"By Allah! Charlemagne must be childish to give the command of the rear-guard of his forces to Roland."

The Count of Mans heard him, but answered not. Lance in rest, he rode down on him. Good heavens! what a thrust!—nothing could resist it. It cave the shield of the nephew of the King of Saragossa, pierced his chest, broke his spine, and pinned him to the earth.

Fauseron, brother of King Marsillus, beheld Miton, and shouted to him— "Your Emperor, Charlemagne, must be sorely jealous of the fame of his knights, to send them to be slaughtered thus."

Miton dashed at him with uplifted blade, and dealt him three terrific wounds: a partridge might have flown through any one of them with ease.

"You lie, knave!" cried the father of Mitaine; "our Charles is the bravest of the brave, and whoever questions it shall die the death of a dog—as you die!"

Anseis charged at Turgis of Toulouse, and ran him through with his lance. The white pennon was stained crimson with the thrust.

But I should never finish if I told you all the wonderful blows they interchanged. At last the spear of Roland shivered. He drew Durandal and rushed into the thickest of the fight, slicing off heads with his sword as easily as a pigeon severs the heads of millet with its sharp beak.

The fury of the combat was redoubled. The Franks performed prodigies of valour, but the Saracens seemed never to tire of being slaughtered. No sooner were thirty thousand Pagans stretched on the earth than thirty thousand more offered themselves for slaughter. The swords were blunted with repeated blows, but the strength of the heroes wearied not. How many Christians had received the crown of martyrdom! Yonder they lay, trampled under the horses' hoofs, while their mothers, their wives, their daughters were, perchance, singing cheerily as they awaited their return.

At length came a time when there were no more Saracens left to kill. Of a hundred thousand Pagans but two survived.

"Mountjoy St. Denis!" resounded over the field. But lo! King Marsillus arrived with the main body.

They had only encountered the advanced guard!

"Brethren," said Turpin, pointing to the Saracens with his mace, "it comes our death-struggle. Let us be polite, and go meet it; we shall only be in Paradise the sooner!" and he rode off as swiftly as if he bestrode a swallow.

"Shame, false friend, to outstrip me!" cried Roland, spurring Veillantif. "Bishop, do not perish without me!"

Once more the contest raged furiously. Turpin perceived Abyme, the most unbelieving Pagan of them all.

"What deity do you serve?" cried the bishop.

"None," said the heretic; whereupon, with three mighty blows of his mace, Turpin scattered over the field the amethysts, topazes, and carbuncles that covered the Pagan's shield. At the third blow the soul of Abyme fled to the regions below.

Climborin smote down Angelier of Gascony, but he did not live more than ten seconds to enjoy his conquest. Miton had seen the deed, lowered his lance, and pierced the Pagan's throat.

"There, dog! you may go boast of your victory!" said he, as he rode off.

Oliver had rested but little all this while; he drove right and left at the ranks of the enemy, brandishing Hauteclaire, mowing the Saracens down like stubble.

His shield was of gold, charged with a red cross.

"That is a foul blazon," said Valdabron, striking the shield with his lance.

"Nevertheless, you shall bow to it," answered the brother of Aude, and with one back-stroke he beheaded the paynim.

The Duke Sanche was slain: it was Maucuidant who struck the fatal blow; by his hand, too, perished Gerin and Anseis, Beranger and Guy de St. Antoine.

But Roland rode right at the Pagan, and with the hilt of Durandal crushed his face in, and flung him, an unrecognisable corpse under his horse's hoofs.

"It is truly sad that we can only kill once a hound who has done so much mischief."

Then the knight stood up in his stirrups, and gazed around him. Merciful heavens, what a sight! Out of the twenty thousand Franks who had come there, but sixty remained alive.

"By my hopes of Heaven!" said Roland, "I should die the happier if I could but bear Marsillus with me to the grave. But how can I find him amid such a *mêlée*."

Mitaine heard him.

"I will show him to you, if you will follow me;" and she began to strip off her armour piecemeal. Roland caught her by the arm to stop her—

"What proof of madness are you going to give us now?"

"You take wisdom for folly, my lord. Do you think I should be suffered to pass, wearing your colours? My mother used to scold me for spoiling my clothes; they might get damaged now."

"And you think I am going to let you perish like this?"

"Is it not absurd to make all this difficulty about it? Have we not come here to die?"

And Mitaine freed herself from his grasp, and sprang on a Saracen horse that she caught as it went riderless by. She was naked to the waist, and her golden hair floated around her shoulders. She seemed like the spirit of youth. Death fled from the presence of such lofty courage.

"Come and seek me, dastard of a Croquemitaine!" she cried. "Here I am well protected from thee."

Roland followed her; his eyes were blinded with tears.

"Merciful heaven! what will they say of me for all these deaths? I shall scarce dare to show myself to-night in Paradise."

Mitaine had caught sight of the King of Saragossa, and made direct for him, without looking right or left. Miton, whose headlong courage had carried him into the ranks of the foe, was beside her, surrounded by the Saracens. He was striking out right and left at random, thinking only to hack and hew the bodies of Pagans. Alas for the double misfortune! Mitaine drew near him, and her father's sword traced a gory slash across her shoulder. She turned, and father and child recognised each other.

"Is it you, my father? It was a good stroke, but 'tis wasted!" Horrified at the sight, Miton for a second forgot to defend himself. In another moment poor Mita was a widow!

Meanwhile Mitaine had ridden close up to Marsillus, and rising up in her stirrups, to make sure Roland should see her, smote him on the face, crying, as loud as she was able— "Behold the King of Saragossa! Mountjoy for Charlemagne!"

She could say no more. Marganice, King of Carthage, and uncle of Marsillus, dealt her a blow on the chest that was far heavier than was needed. The poor girl sank, insensible, and rolled under the horse's hoofs, with blood gushing from her lips and nostrils.

When Roland saw this, his rage overpowered him. He drew near Oliver, and said, "Brother, shall we go slay that boastful Marsillus yonder?"

"It shall be done," said the other.

They dashed forward, followed by a few of the Franks still remaining on the field—Beuve, Lord of Beaune and Dijon, whose death was a sore loss to Charles—Yve, and Yvoire, and Gerard of Roussillon. Roland and Oliver penetrated farthest into the infidel ranks; at last they came within a few paces of Marsillus.

"Is it you, then, whom they call the King Marsillus?" said Roland.

"It is a name the Franks will not forget."

"I am called Roland. If you never knew me before you shall know me to-day;" and with that he smote off the King's right hand as he raised it to strike.

The Saracens shouted in alarm, "Mahomet preserve us!" and fled like doves before an eagle. If they had found legs to bring them thither, they had found wings to take them away.

There remained on the field only a thousand Ethiopians, the forces of Marganice. They were drawn up at a distance, and seemed undecided whether to advance. Roland put his horn to his lips, and blew a blast so powerful that it echoed and re-echoed for twenty leagues around.

"What are you doing?" said Oliver. "Have you lost all shame, and do you no longer fear to sound for help against Pagans?"

"These are cruel words, comrade!"

"Why disturb Charlemagne for such a trifle? We are three yet. If you had been less brave we should not have bequeathed this defeat to our country. If you sound the bugle on my behalf, do not trouble yourself—henceforth I do not desire to live. If for Turpin, our friend only survives by a miracle, and will be dead before any one can come to his aid. If you sound, it is for yourself; and, by Heaven's truth! you will be a brave man to face Charlemagne."

"Truly," said Turpin, "you might do better than quarrel now. Wind your horn, Roland, not for our sakes, but for the honour of France. We shall be avenged, and our bones will be laid in consecrated soil. Wind your horn, Roland!"

The Count of Mans lifted his bugle to his lips, and blew so loud and long, that the veins in his temples stood up like ropes, and the blood flowed from his mouth.

The Emperor reined up his steed.

"Did you hear, as I did, the bugle of Roland?"

The Count of Mayence trembled, but he answered, "'Tis some goatherd calling together his flock."

"Do you think I've grown childish, that I should mistake a horn for a pipe? It was Roland's horn, past a doubt."

"Well, sire, he sounds his bugle for nothing often; perchance he is chasing some wild animal."

"By your leave, sire, the horn has a mournful sound," said Naymes of Bavaria, "and it is but due to your peers to go and see what has befallen them."

"You are right, friend. Ganelon, you will remain here;" and Charles called for Besgue, his head cook, and entrusted to him the custody of the Count of Mayence.

"It is the duty of your scullions to guard this criminal. Have you any stout rope to put him to the question with?"

"I have, sire, the rope, saving your presence, with which I tie up the pigs when I stick them."

"That will do well! And now, my comrades, let us hasten to Roland."

"There is no need to hurry," said Ganelon, with a grin; "Roland does not ring the bell until mass is over."

"Even so, renegade," said the Emperor, "we may arrive in time for vespers, and so much the worse for the Pagans."

Roland was the only one left alive on the plains of Roncesvalles. To the shouts and yells of conflict had succeeded a silence infinitely more terrible.

Dismayed at their success, the Saracens had fled. The work was accomplished; the vultures would fitly succeed them. Insatiable parasites of the King of Saragossa, these new comers seldom had time to wipe their beaks between the banquets.

Roland dismounted for the first time in the four-and-twenty hours. The brave knight could scarcely stand. Leaning his brow on his horse's saddle, he cried like a child—he had poured out all his blood, and he had nothing left to shed but tears!

His wounds seemed nothing to him. It was despair that was killing him. In his grief he knelt beside the body of Oliver, and clasped it in his arms. He laid it on the turf, unlaced the helmet, kissed the cold brow, stripped off the armour, and examined it all over, unable to believe that he had really lost such a friend and companion in arms.

He did the same for Turpin, Miton, and Gautier de Luz. But of what avail was it to lavish cares upon the lifeless clay? Their spirits were in heaven.

Roland raised his head. He fancied he heard a faint but sweet voice pronounce his name. What happiness if there yet survived some one!

"Do you not know me, my dear lord? Come hither and bid me farewell!"

Pale, stretched on the field among the slain, lay the godchild of Charlemagne.

"Heaven be praised, my pretty one! To see you still alive makes me almost fancy Heaven smiles upon me. You will not die—I would not be the cause of your death! Charles will be here soon, and will bear you back to our own beloved France."

"You deceive yourself, Roland. I shall never again behold the great Emperor—never again my native land! Before long I shall meet my father once more. But tell me, have the Saracens retreated?"

The grief of Roland.

The death of Mitaine.

"They have retreated into Spain."

"Then the victory belongs to us two! By the shrine of St. Landri! I am happier than I ever dreamed of being."

Roland knelt down, took off one of his great gold spurs, and fixed it on Mitaine's heel. "There, brave little hero, none ever better merited the rank of knight!" and he buckled it on. The two little feet of the squire would have both fitted easily into the single spur.

In an ecstacy of joy, Mitaine raised herself, and flung her arms round Roland's neck.

"Quick, quick, my beloved lord! give me the accolade, for I feel I am dying!"

And Mitaine sank back on the turf, plucked with a last effort two blades of grass, which she fashioned into a cross, and expired while kissing it with fervour.

Roland felt very solitary now. Feeling the shades of death gathering round him, he stole up to Veillantif.

"My brave charger, your mouth is not meant for the bit of the Saracen, nor your sides for the Pagan spur."

And Roland, having kissed its soft muzzle, killed his favourite steed with one blow of Durandal.

"Now, my treasured Durandal, what shall I do with thee? Thy hilt encloses one of the teeth of St. Peter, and a hair from the beard of St. Denis. Neither must thou fall into the hands of unbelievers!"

He called up all his strength, and struck his sword upon the granite. It cave the rock, without denting its blade. Three times he essayed again, but with no better success.

His sight was failing him. A cold chill seized him. He sank down beside a granite peak, stretched upon his invincible sword, that people might know well that he died a conqueror.

Roland had just ceased to breathe when Charlemagne arrived on the field.

You will imagine, my young friends, that the Emperor made the Saracens pay dearly for the loss of his knights. It was not until he had utterly destroyed the infidel army that Charles would consent to dismount from his horse on the plains of Roncesvalles. Alas! the butchery of Saracens could not restore life to Roland or his companions.

Poor Charlemagne! he tore his grey hair and long beard, and having ordered the bodies of the Count of Mans, Turpin, Oliver, Miton, and Mitaine to be placed in coffins of black marble, he had them borne back to France with every mark of honour.

As he approached Aix-la-Chapelle the Emperor saw a long, long line of weeping women, all attired in black, coming out to meet him. It was the fair Aude, supported by her widowed sister Mita, and followed by a suite of three hundred ladies.

Charlemagne, deeply affected by the sight of such affliction, dismounted, and pressed the fair Aude to his heart.

"My poor child!" said he, "you are a widow or ever you were a bride."

The fair Aude opened her lips to reply, but she had not the strength to speak.

The Emperor felt her sink back in his arms, and, turning to the attendants, he asked—

"Is there a place for her in the coffin by the side of Roland?"

A few days later were celebrated with great pomp the obsequies of the betrothed of the Count of Mans. At the same hour, dragged on a hurdle, between two of the executioner's assistants, the disfigured corpse of the traitor Ganelon was carried to the charnel.

"And Croquemitaine, won't you tell us something about it?" you would ask me.

Croquemitaine does not exist, my dears.

The death of Aude.

The last struggle of chivalry.

Coachwhip Publications

CoachwhipBooks.com

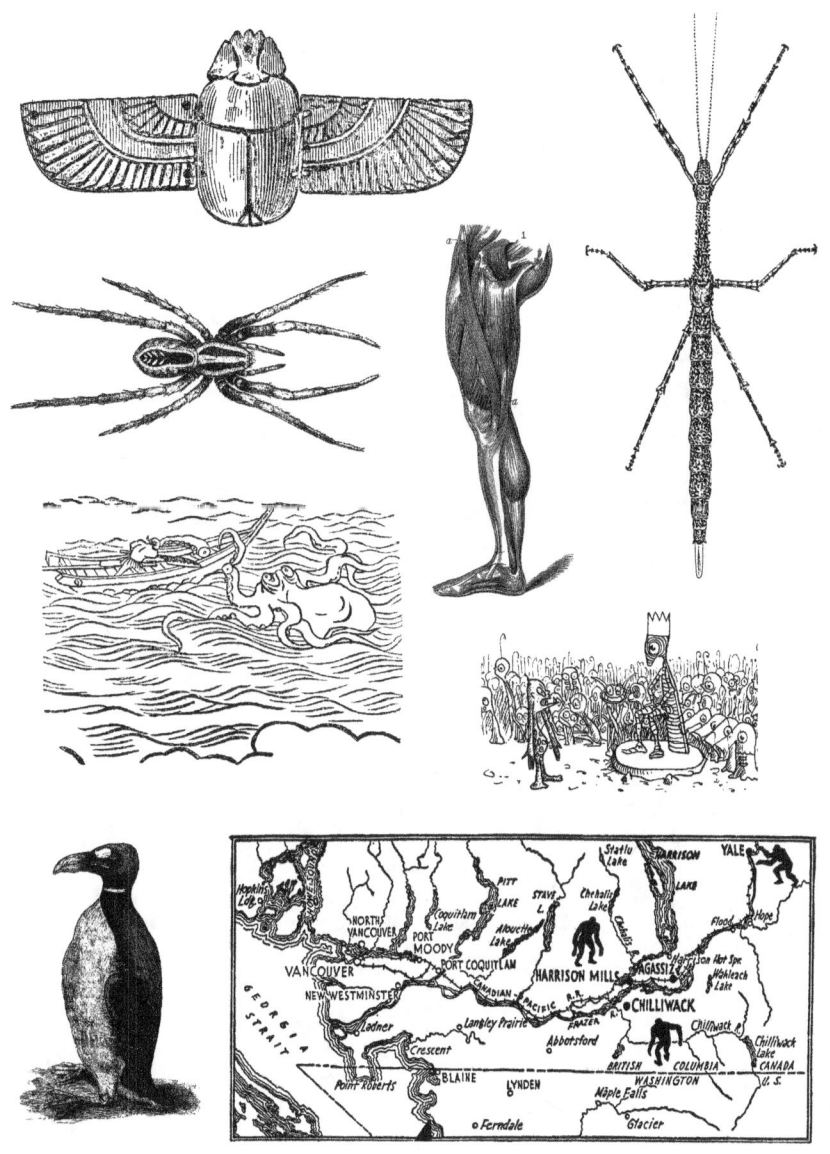

www.ingramcontent.com/pod-product-compliance
Lightning Source LLC
Chambersburg PA
CBHW080900020726

47502CB00008B/2292